THIRD TIME'S THE HARM

A Deco Desk Mystery

LORAN HOLT

FROM THE TINY ACORN…
GROWS THE MIGHTY OAK

Third Time's the Harm, A Deco Desk Mystery

For information, address Acorn Publishing, LLC,
3943 Irvine Blvd. Ste. 218, Irvine, CA 92602
www.acornpublishingllc.com

Edited by Laura Perkins
Cover design by ebooklaunch.com
Interior design and digital formatting by Debra Cranfield Kennedy

ISBN-13: 978-1-952112-58-4 (hardcover)
ISBN-13: 978-1-952112-57-7 (paperback)
Library of Congress Control Number: 2021906975

DEDICATION

To my grandfather, who always thought I was a writer.

Who typed all the "stories" I told him.

I'm still telling them, Grandfather.

ACKNOWLEDGMENTS

My many thanks go first of all to my husband, who stands behind me, brags about me, and reads my work faithfully.

Then to my wonderful publishers, Holly Kammier and Jessica Therrien, who have made publishing *almost* easy. My very helpful project manager, Evelyn Lawhorn, who is ever patient. Laura Perkins, who edited and reedited *Third Times the Harm* until it was ready for publication. My cover designer, who has produced a cover that could not be more expressive of *Harm's* storyline.

Lastly, to my beta readers, who read *Harm* with enjoyment and urged me to publish.

Thank you all.

THIRD TIME'S THE HARM

A Deco Desk Mystery

CHAPTER ONE

I gripped the letter, staring at the glowing red letters standing out starkly in contrast to the creamy bond paper with its embossed "O." I felt panic rising like the spring tides . . . .

All right, I guess I had better begin at the beginning . . . it's all about inheritance.

Yeah, yeah, I can hear the exasperated sighs right now. I know; you think you've read this story before. Favorite niece, or granddaughter, or *something*—young, single, and *lots* of cleavage—inherits her uncle's or grandfather's, or *someone's*, entire estate, including old house and business. Things happen—this is known as the plot. It never happens in real life. Right?

Well, it *does* happen; and I did—or rather, it did and I did. Okay, that wasn't quite clear. In other words, my father's oldest brother, James Whitehall Olivian, III, someone I had never seen, or even heard of, died and left me all he had *because* he was "pissed off" at my father. I am quoting *directly* from the will.

There is a slight difference between those other stories and mine, however. Firstly, I'm not all that young, forty-five—in fact I'll be forty-six in July. I look pretty darned good for forty-five, but it's that doggoned *for* part that makes me grit my teeth. Besides that, I'm not single—well, I *am* single at the moment, but I've been married twice. As for cleavage . . .

Strangely, I appear to be named for said unknown uncle, being Jamie Whitehall Olivian. *That's* obviously an old story I have *yet* to hear from my Dad. How *did* I hear about it? And why not before? I'm getting right to that.

The first I knew of my seeming namesake, James Whitehall Olivian, III, was when I received a frightfully formal letter from Ackbury and Ackbury, attorneys-at-law, summoning me to their office for an unexplained meeting. When I called the office to see if there had been some mistake, a frightfully formal secretary assured me that if I were the daughter of Harold Whittaker Olivian, there was no error and I should arrive promptly at 10 AM this coming Friday. When I bluntly and succinctly inquired, "Why?" she informed me she was not at liberty to discuss it. My curiosity was piqued, a phrase I've always wanted to use, so I agreed and hung up.

My budget, that is, the one I allow myself, doesn't run to Manolo Blahnik or Jimmy Choo firsthand, but I do dress pretty well for a librarian. Yes, I confess, that's my career. Why? What can I tell you? I *like* books; so, after my second divorce, I hied myself back to school and got a master's in Library Science. I know what people think of librarians, but not all of us wear thick glasses and sensible oxfords. Resale shops and vintage shows are my Mecca, clothes are *important*.

Therefore, I dressed for the role, attired in a 1947 light-weight tweed suit from Bullocks Wilshire children's department, which consisted of short bolero jacket, three-quarter sleeves, and matching swingy skirt boasting two box pleats fore and aft. I paired this with a russet silk blouse that perfectly matched the slubs in the tweed. My shoes were real alligator, also vintage but never worn (I have the box to prove it), sling backs. These had the tiniest of platforms and "open-toes," because nobody said "peep" in those days. Appropriate, and I thought, hip, for the occasion. Thus, garbed in the tasty uniform of propriety, I did the "promptly at 10 AM." bit and stepped into Ackbury and Ackbury. Why do I tell you this? Well, remember the librarian bit?

I don't know what I was expecting, but it was fabulous—sleek, impeccable taste, and expensive—totally Deco and the genuine article. I felt like I'd entered a time tunnel straight to the Jazz Age, which just happens to be my favorite era. When I die, I'm hoping to own an Erté original design to be buried in. I may not be able to take it with me; but I'll take it as far as it'll go.

When I announced myself to the frightfully formal receptionist, who sat at a desk I would have killed for, she looked me up and down and gave a sniff intended to put a lesser female in her place. But you can't tell a book by its inches, so I returned the look and the sniff in spades.

Did I mention that my parents are well to do? Potentially, I'm worth more than Ms. Sniff will earn in a lifetime. Of course, I like to make my own way and not call too much attention to that fact. That's the reason for the self-imposed budget, which amuses the heck out of my parents. Nevertheless, every garment I put on my person is either a designer label or from the *very* best stores, resale notwithstanding. Of course, knowing your potential (money) helps, too. Reluctantly, Ms. Sniff acknowledged that Mr. Ackbury, Jr. wished to see me right away. Her attitude conveyed that I obviously wasn't up to Mr. Ackbury, Sr.

A door behind her swung open and another frightfully formal female inquired, "Ms. Olivian?"

"Whitehall," I corrected. In case you're confused, after my second divorce, I decided to just use my middle name, and get rid of all the other baggage. My mother understood perfectly, "She just wants to start fresh, Hal, she's not rejecting you." Dad was not convinced, but only said, "Whatever makes you happy, Squirt." I'm 4' 11", and never outgrew "Squirt," as far as he was concerned.

In the meantime, Frightfully Formal II was waiting. "This way, Ms. Olivian."

I shrugged, rolled my eyes and followed her through the door. After all, I *was* perishing of curiosity.

She led me to an office bigger than my apartment, where I got another surprise. Mr. Ackbury, Jr. was every bit as gorgeous as his surroundings. Tall, handsome, but not dark, prematurely gray in fact, which sat well on him, eyes almost the color of a Tiffany's box and just a hint of five o'clock shadow. I must have been gawking like a teenager, because those incredible eyes twinkled and a hint of dimple appeared in one cheek.

"Ms. Olivian?"

"Whitehall," I automatically responded, still taking him in.

He looked somewhat bemused for a moment; then his brow cleared. "Ah."

He motioned me to a chair, but rather than retreating behind his desk, he took the chair next to mine. He smiled, flashing expertly whitened teeth, and said, "You've probably been wondering why we asked you here, but the mystery will be solved very shortly."

Eek! Please, please, do not let him talk like a made-for-TV movie!

Some of that must have shown on my face, because he laughed and added, "I know that sounded a little scripted, but what with all the hush-hush, as well as formality, you *must* have wondered."

This sounded reasonable, and I agreed.

"We were obliged to adhere strictly to our client's wishes—our *deceased* client's wishes. It was, or I should say, will be certainly to your advantage."

I raised my eyebrows, indicating interest.

"You're an heiress," he proclaimed, and grinned.

I almost fell into the grin, but managed a weak, "Yes, I know."

His face fell at my obviously underwhelmed response, "You know?"

"Well, yes, I'm my parents' only child and they've discussed it with me many times. Outside of a few small bequests to charity, I will receive the bulk of their combined estates."

Again, "Ah."

We sat in silence for a moment or two.

He grinned again. This time, the dimple was deep enough to wade in.

"I didn't think you had the proper picture. You are the sole heir of your Uncle James, since he had no children."

The utter blankness on my face must have been a second disappointment, because once again the grin faltered a bit, and the dimple shrank to a puddle.

My brilliant contribution to the dialogue with Gorgeous was, "Huh?" My second was, "Who?"

"Your Uncle James—James Whitehall Olivian, III."

"I see there's been a mistake." I gathered up my Dooney & Bourke bag, and started to rise, just then the name hit me. I plopped ungracefully back in the chair, and made my third brilliant contribution. "That's *my* name."

Gorgeous surveyed me quizzically and observed, "We know that." The grin returned, all 250 watts.

"I don't understand . . ." I stammered.

He transformed from gorgeous lawyer into just gorgeous guy. He slouched back in the chair, "I'd never have guessed if you hadn't told me," he commented dryly. "I take it you were not exactly acquainted with Uncle James."

"Never heard of him."

"Your father's eldest brother."

"Never heard of him."

"Five years older than your father, two years older than your Uncle Richard."

"Never heard of him."

I stared at him silently while my thoughts whirled. Uncle Richard, the only sibling of my father I was aware of, had been killed in Vietnam when I was an embryo. Obviously, I had never known him, and just as obviously, there was a whole lot of other stuff I hadn't known. Why not? My parents were always wide open, weren't they?

Guess not, Jamie.

The stunned silence must have gotten to Gorgeous, because he abruptly reached out and took my hand. "Are you free for dinner?"

More brilliance on my part. "Huh?" One more of those and I qualified for hearing aids.

"Dinner, the evening meal, you've probably heard of that."

"Mr. Ackbury, I really must apologize, I'm usually able to hold up my end of the conversation, at least. I'm just . . ."

"Surprised?" he ventured, "and you can make it Dennis."

"Mr. Ack . . . Dennis, surprised is not the word. First of all, I just acquired a relative, not to mention an estate, from someone I have never heard mentioned in any context. Secondly, I usually know someone more than twenty minutes before we're dating."

His laughter was genuine, "Ms. Olivian . . ."

"Whitehall," I corrected.

"Whitehall . . . ," he looked briefly distracted, "Jamie . . . , I'm now *your* lawyer, and I'd like to take my new client to dinner, and give her the whole story over a stiff drink, and a good meal. You look like you could use it. You would like to hear the whole story, I presume."

"I'm not altogether sure," I said honestly.

He laughed again, and patted the hand he was still holding. "How about seven? I have the address."

Naturally, I accepted; I may be an idiot, but I'm not *that* big an idiot. He helped me to my feet (I was sure I had knees when I came in) and released my hand. "Seven."

I tottered away, out the door, down the hall, and past Ms. Sniff, who repeated her earlier comment. I ignored her with what I hoped was dignity, but probably looked more like shell-shock, descended to the garage, and reclaimed my car from the valet. I don't remember getting to the library, nor much of the day after that.

◆

IT WAS ONLY after I was home, showered, and trying to decide what to wear, that I suddenly felt a little chill. His offhand remark, "I have the address," reminded me that Gorgeous was a complete stranger, and a big office (okay, Gargantuan) didn't make him any less so.

I was uncomfortable, when I remembered my rather smug recital of heiress status, as well as my rather advanced age. Dennis Ackbury could easily have his pick of starlets twenty years younger than I am, and bursting with curves, at that. Even in my best days, men didn't fall face forward when I entered the room, so just what was his angle?

I started to reach for the phone to call Mom and demand an explanation, but something arrested me in midmotion. Why hadn't I ever heard of the man I was named for? How did he know *anything* about me? There was more, lots more, here than met several eyes.

I gave speculation up as a bad job and concentrated on what to wear. Tonight, I expected to have a great meal and a great time with a knock-out guy, and. decided to emulate Scarlett O'Hara and "think about that (the angle) tomorrow." Besides, I was *still* perishing of curiosity about mysterious Uncle James and his out-of-the-blue bequest, therefore looking forward to having all revealed.

I settled on a genuine fifties periwinkle-blue linen sheath that made the most of the curves I do possess—that, and my Victoria's Secret bra, strappy red sandals, and a Kate Spade bag that was an absolute steal.

I don't wear my heels too high, since it throws off my proportions, and I'm very sensitive about proportion. Absolutely no modern platforms, of course. Vintage platforms are okay, since they don't make you look as though you ought to be pulling a milk cart. I prefer not to stump along like Long John Silver, only on both legs. My preference is to glide as gracefully as I can. When you're even shorter than Lady Gaga without shoes, attention to detail is paramount.

I can proudly proclaim, however, that I do retain a head of

heavy auburn hair, which I left loose to swing around my shoulders. I tell myself that it's a little bit like camouflage, and manages to distract from the *slight* hint of crow's feet in the eye area. Discreet eye shadow and mascara, with a light touch of lipstick, completes my toilette. At forty-five a female needs a bit of enhancement, *au naturel* doesn't quite cut it. Surveying myself in the mirror, I wasn't too displeased with the overall result.

At the last minute, some impulse caused me to trade the miniature-sized Kate Spade for a roomier tote. Roomy, but not too; I didn't want to look like I planned to spend the night anywhere but home alone. No sense giving Dennis any wrong ideas . . . yet. Besides, I wanted to be able to conveniently stash whatever papers I was sure he would have for me to peruse and, just in case he turned out to be Jack the Ripper in lawyer's clothing, it weighed more.

CHAPTER TWO

Promptly at seven, the buzzer for my apartment did what buzzers do, announcing Dennis's arrival. When I let him in, I was delighted to see what looked like appreciation in his eyes; it might have been wishful thinking, but I'll take what I can get. I was also delighted to see that memory had served me well, and he was just as gorgeous as I remembered. Again, he was perfectly tailored in a subtle Glen plaid sports coat and gray slacks, no tie this time, just a tee shirt in a slightly lighter gray than the slacks.

"French food okay with you?" For a lawyer, so far, he wasn't coming across as a great talker, either.

I swallowed the urge to say hot dogs were okay with me, and settled for "Lovely."

"I think you'll like this place; nice ambiance, and fabulous food. You do eat, don't you? I mean, you're not on a diet, or anything like that?"

Remembering his comment that I looked like I could use a good meal, I felt a tad annoyed at his assumption that I was on a deliberate starvation regimen, but I bit my tongue and smiled.

Fortunately, I can still eat like a stevedore and not gain an ounce, so I hastened to assure him that I was capable of ingestion without indigestion.

Although I wasn't expecting a coach and four, in the back of my mind I had sort of pictured a Ferrari, maybe a vintage Corvette, or a cherried-up '38 Packard waiting for us at the curb, but his car was an eminently serviceable gray Lexus SUV.

Married, with children, flashed through my mind.

Seeing my look, he chuckled, "Carry over from my divorce; haven't gotten around to replacing it yet."

This was the second time he seemed to read my mind, or at least my face. But then, he was a lawyer, so a facility for reading people would be invaluable. Although, it simply might be that I had little or no practice in hiding my feelings, since the library environment seldom called for much work on that score. Shushing rambunctious youngsters was generally the most emotional arousal I encountered in a day.

"Ah," I responded. It's obvious I'm also a sparkling conversationalist.

Once again, a perfectly reasonable explanation, but something kept niggling at the back of my mind. I felt uneasy, without being able to put my mental finger on a good reason why. Our attempts at conversation sputtered in fits and starts on the way to the restaurant, suggesting that he felt just as uncomfortable with me. A dampening cloud of depression started to descend on me; I had hoped for at least one good evening with Gorgeous, but it looked like I was already doomed to disappointment.

He left the car with the valet, helped me out, but then continued to hold my hand tightly on the way in. He didn't relinquish it even after giving his name to the maître d', only letting go while we made our way to the table. We were shown to a booth, where he promptly joined me on my side, and took my hand again. Instead of lightening my spirits, this made me even more depressed and ill-at-ease than before. I'm not overly self-deprecating, my personal *angst* is fairly well-controlled, but since I'm neither feeble and in need of assistance, nor do I stop men dead in their tracks as a rule, all this unnecessary gripping made me want to scream, "Unhand me, Masher."

As was swiftly becoming a habit, he read me for the third time, saying, "I don't make a career of holding my clients' hands—you're an exception. For two reasons," he added.

My eyebrows jiggled a question at him, so he enlarged. "First of all, you're the cutest client I've had in years."

My eyebrows practically waved like Old Glory.

"I mean it. I'm going to be blunt, so be prepared. I'm not exactly an innocent abroad, and yes, they've, uh, occasionally, been younger than you, and some have been, well, let's call it starlet material. I'm not proud of this, but they, uh, happened, not only before and after my marriage, but during, as well." He dropped my hand at this, and stared into space for a long minute. "My wife was long-suffering, but . . ."

He took a gulp of his water, and went on. "I like to think I learned a lesson. She's happily remarried, and I'm, well, I'm single—really single."

I gave the Great Eyebrow Wave, again.

"And," he grinned, "you're just adorable." The grin widened, "Mute, but adorable."

I couldn't help it; I broke down and laughed heartily. He laughed with me, and the ice seemed to be broken.

"I don't believe you for a minute," I demurred playfully (all right, that sounded icky) but I really enjoyed hearing it."

"I meant every word. Maybe it's because your feet didn't

touch the floor when you sat down. Or maybe it's because you've got all that hair. Or maybe," he put in wickedly, "it's your eyebrows."

I had to laugh again, and decided to relax and enjoy the rest of the night, ahem, I mean the evening. And, lest you think I'm a total pushover, I *didn't* believe him for a minute.

The waiter came with menus; thus, forcing my new lawyer, or suitor, or whatever he thought he was, to release my hand for the time being. I felt a surprising sense of relief. As undeniably attractive as he was, he was coming on far too strong and too fast for my just-a-little-bit-old-fashioned taste. Not that I don't like to be pursued, but even counting the meeting at his office, we had known each other less than an hour and a half.

At least he didn't insult my intelligence by ordering my meal for me. He praised my decisions then made completely different choices for himself, earning a brownie point for not looking like a control freak. After we had ordered, he surprised me once again by moving to the far side of the booth.

"I noticed you were a lefty," he said in explanation, "I'm reluctant, but I figure you need that hand to eat." The 250-watt grin lit his face again. "Besides, I have some paperwork for you to look over, and you'll need a little space."

Honestly, with that dimple facing me, it was hard to feel I needed any space at all. My emotions seemed to bounce back and forth like a Djokovic and Nadal match. When the soup came, it was a relief to have an excuse to look down rather than at him. I knew he was aware of the effect he was having and he knew that I knew, and I knew that he knew that I knew. Aargh! I was reverting to my adolescence, or at least to the period of my first husband.

Get it together, Jamie, it hasn't been that long since you had a date.

We made small talk through the remainder of the meal—you know the kind. Where did you go to school? How did you get into law? Where did you grow up? Etc., etc. I learned a little more about his wife, who actually sounded like a pretty nice person. It was refreshing to hear a man discuss his broken marriage with regret, but with no desire to go back, having learned something and moved on. He had nothing but good things to say about her; and generously, about her new husband as well.

He listened attentively to the tales of my two exes, about whom I was a tad less generous, although after his recital, I did my best. He shook his head as I related the departure of the writer after only three years. "Too immature," he interposed. He looked properly indignant, when I rolled out the story of ex-number-two, the independent film maker. Whom I had caught filming his blonde leading lady between the sheets of our own bed, coincidentally after a similar three years. But he only commented with a painful sigh, "I've been down that road. The so-and-so (that's not what he said) just didn't know when he was well off. I'd like to kick his ass around the block, but I'd have to kick myself at the same time."

He laughed heartily when I added, "Well, *he* was ready for *his* close-up, but *I* fixed his zoom lens." And, he nodded with understanding when I explained why I chose to use Whitehall instead of Olivian for my surname.

All of it perfect, well-rehearsed (why did I think that?), well-chosen phrases that should have been as reassuring as a cuddly blankie. When I looked at him, they were. Every time I stared into those ocean-deep eyes, I felt like a melting gummy bear; but when I looked away, the little niggle popped up again.

Gathering myself together, I prompted firmly, "About Uncle James . . ."

He sighed once more, and acknowledged that it was time to get that business out of the way. Opening the briefcase he had discreetly stashed in the corner of the booth, he took out a sheaf of papers, on the topmost of which I could make out the word Will. He glared somewhat hostilely at the file for a moment, as though it had given offense; then proceeded to read in nearly a whisper, so that I had to lean forward and strain to hear him. I straightened up when I noticed that his eyes had a tendency to stray from the page. He gave me a slightly sheepish grin, but his eyes twinkled with mischief.

"Ahem," he cleared his throat, and started over in a louder voice. "I, James Whitehall Olivian . . ." The pucker between my eyebrows got his attention. As was becoming the rule, he guessed the reason, "I don't know why you're named for him, Jamie; he didn't choose to tell me you had never met him."

I looked down at my hands, and felt an unaccountable lump rise in my throat. "Nobody told me anything."

He looked distressed, but went back to his recital.

I won't bore you with the details, but the substance of the will was that I had inherited all that Uncle James had managed to amass—money, house, and . . . "You also get the consulting *cum* dealership business. Your uncle specialized in medieval manuscripts."

At that last revelation I shrieked "What?" a couple of octaves higher than my usual dulcet tones. Several heads turned in our direction.

"What?" I repeated, *sotto voce*, "I don't know the first thing about manuscripts, medieval or otherwise."

"You're a librarian," Dennis pointed out.

"Yes?" I bristled a bit, defensively.

Dennis only responded "Good."

"Good! What does that have to do with it? So I can contribute my profound expertise in *Good Night, Moon?*"

"Your Uncle James seemed to think so. Not only do you get the business, but the rest of the inheritance is contingent on your assuming his position."

I fell back in the booth. "Contingent," I whimpered. Then I sat up, squared my shoulders, and told Dennis just what I thought Uncle James could do—well, yes, he couldn't really do anything—with his contingency and his inheritance. After all, since I had never known Uncle James, never expected to be his heir, and most of all didn't need his bequest (heh, heh, heh), I was in a good position to do so.

Dennis eyed me quizzically during my outburst; pulled out a sealed envelope which I could tell even upside down had my name on it; and said, with just a touch of malice, "Uncle James seems to have anticipated you."

"Do you know what this says," I demanded.

He shook his head. "Absolutely not, it's been sealed since he gave it to us." He looked thoughtful, "which was just a couple of days before he died, come to think of it. Look on the back."

To my amazement, the envelope, which was heavy and opaque, was sealed with three old-fashioned lumps of sealing wax, each displaying a prominent initial "O" in the center. I tore open the envelope, careless of the seals, and read:

CHAPTER THREE

———•———

My dearest niece, *if you don't mind my addressing you that way. Even though you don't know me, I feel I know you, and always think of you that way. You are so like your mother, my dear.* Hmm, strikes me there's a clue there, somewhere.

Forgive an old man for dropping a bombshell in your lap, but since you are reading this letter, I am obviously no longer able to speak to you in person. I want—no, I need you to assume the burden of being my successor. And, yes, I know you are unprepared. However, you are uncommonly intelligent, have a love of the printed page, and most of all, you never give up.

I'll admit tears came to my eyes when I read that last bit. I felt unworthy of his praise, especially the intelligent part. Smart, yes; intelligent, well, consider my exes. Nevertheless, it was like a loving hug from the beyond, and warmed me to Uncle James in spite of myself. I stared, unseeing, for a brief instant before continuing.

As I said, my dear, since you are reading this, I am in no position—'boxed in', you might say, if you'll forgive a bad pun—

to do what I am about to ask you to do. Find out who was responsible for my death.

My shocked gasp brought Dennis's head up in a snap, and he immediately requested that I tell him the contents of the letter. My first thought was to comply, but caution overcame impulsiveness, and I stammered lamely that it had to do with my parents, and their "falling out." Dennis looked suspicious, but let it ride.

I continued . . . *You find that shocking, don't you, my dear? As though we were together, having a conversation . . . Yes, murder is always a shock, but rest assured that I am not a foolish old man who is having delusions. Someone wishes me ill, and I do not know how much time I have left. I have, in my possession, an object of great value which would rock the world of Academia—no, it isn't a first folio by Shakespeare—but it would have a profound effect, nevertheless. It would seem, word has leaked out, and another, or more than one other, seeks to possess it for himself, or themselves. I am taking a chance even writing of this object, since I do not know whom to trust, and I do not want to put you in danger, but I can think of no positively secure way to pass my message on to you, and so must chance it. I have, nevertheless, devised more than one other way to insure that this message comes to you unaltered. You may, if you wish, simply throw this missive away and go on with your life as before. However, I don't think you will—I've been watching you.*

Your very loving uncle,
James Whitehall Olivian, III

I looked up blankly at Dennis, and then gave him what I hoped was a casual smile, but probably looked more like I was having an attack of severe heartburn.

"He sort-of explained what went on with him and Dad," I forced out, as unnaturally as possible.

Dennis obviously thought so too, since he observed dryly, "Must have been some falling out."

I mustered my wits, and gave it another shot. "It was rather a shock. Dad, Mom, Uncle James..." I broke it off without really saying anything very definite, and actually, Uncle James phrasing did sort of give him away. *You are so like your mother, my dear.*

"One thing I don't understand," I went on to cover my shock. "His letter is so, well, old-fashioned, I guess. He doesn't sound anything like the same man who would use 'pissed off' in a legal document."

Dennis snorted. "I think he was quoting your father, if I understood him correctly. You're right, though, he was old-fashioned in a way, gentlemanly, like he'd stepped out of the 1910s. I was surprised when he insisted on inserting that phrase, that's when I got the idea he was quoting someone else."

I thought of my father, who rarely but occasionally used four-letter words. "Maybe," I said, doubtfully. "Yes, probably," I added more confidently, more for Dennis's benefit than my own.

There was a lot here that had me rattled and confused. Nevertheless, I felt that it was best to conceal much of that confusion. I wasn't sure why, but I knew it in my bones.

Mustering another one of those teeth-barings that I hoped were passing for smiles, I asked Dennis to tell me about the house. I had never owned a home, even during my marriages, and the thought of being a real landowner gave me both thrills and chills.

He perked up immediately and became animated. "It's a Craftsman in Pasadena," he enthused, "but instead of Stickley, which you'd expect, your uncle filled it with Deco. When you walk in it kind of takes your breath away. It's not that big, but it isn't too small, either—1800 square feet, I'd estimate."

I knew exactly how maidens in the nineteenth century felt when they dropped into a swoon, my eyes practically crossed with lust. If there was anything that could take my mind completely off Dennis, or even a movie star for that matter, it was a house full of Deco furniture.

Figuratively licking the drool off my chin, I inquired, subtly casual, "When can I see it?" My voice came out in a squeak that would have assured me a voiceover job as Minnie Mouse.

Dennis gave another snort. "Tomorrow's Saturday. I'm good if you are."

A sudden thought wiped out my anticipation—Uncle James had claimed that he was murdered. How could I have forgotten?

"How old was Uncle James?" I asked Dennis.

He blinked a little at the abrupt switch in topics, but answered, "Just turned eighty. Why?"

Oh yes, five years older than my father. "Was he in poor health?"

Another blink, "No, he was actually in pretty good shape for eighty, but you never know."

"Did he have a sudden stroke, or something?"

"His doctor thought it was heart failure. It caused him to fall and hit his head on a corner of his desk; he never regained consciousness evidently, and died before they found him."

"They?"

"He had a housekeeper who came in once a week, and a gardener who did the same. They were both there and called 911."

I thought that over. "I see," I remarked finally.

"What's this about?"

I dissembled. "I was just curious. It seems awfully sad that he died without any family or even friends with him, and he and Dad never got back together."

I heaved a big and, to tell the truth, overly dramatic sigh. It *was* sad, but I had never known him, so I couldn't feel *that* much grief—at least not right away.

Dennis seemed to accept my explanation. "Are you feeling a little edgy about taking over a house where somebody died?"

I seized on that excuse. "Yes, I have to confess, it bothers me a bit."

"You're not eighty, and you don't look like a heart attack waiting to happen."

"Thank you, I think."

The dimple returned, "You can't say I don't know how to charm the ladies."

I laughed and fluttered my eyelashes at him, which earned me even more dimple.

"Back to tomorrow," he recaptured my hand. "Are you up to seeing the house?"

I pretended reluctance. "I think so. I just hope I don't picture him lying beside his desk. I thought I wanted to know, but now, I'm sorry I asked."

He patted my hand in that infuriating way men have; I really expected him to tell me not to worry "my pretty little head." Well, it was my own fault, for the last half hour I had lapsed into my very best imitation of itty-bitty dolly, rather than adult woman of competence. As a matter of fact, with the exception of the biographical interval of the evening, my conversation had barely risen above the level of "me Jane, you lawyer." From his "mute" comment, Dennis seemed to agree.

He was evidently getting the idea that Librarians were a branch of the Trappist monks.

Knowing it was too late to alter that perception, I smiled and gently eased my hand out of his under the pretext of taking a swallow of water from my glass. The constant contact, instead of giving me a thrill, was striking me as just creepy. Too lounge lizard, if you know what I mean.

"Would eleven be okay with you," I asked. "I'd like to run a couple of errands in the morning—cleaning, etc.—but I'd be free by then."

"Eleven suits me just fine. I don't like to get going too early on Saturday, since I have to punch the time-clock during the week. Metaphorically, that is."

"I don't have to work on weekends at the library so I feel the same way, although I'm a tad guilty about it, since the reason I don't have to work is that the library is closed due to budget cuts."

Dennis managed to look properly distressed by my statement, and murmured something noncommittal, then added a coherent, "Pick you up at eleven."

"Good." I looked at my watch. "I guess I should go home and sleep on my news, since I'm feeling a little overwhelmed at the moment. I just don't know how I'm going to handle the manuscript expert business. Flying under false colors isn't the half of it."

That wasn't the only half of it. Manuscripts, schmanuscripts, murder was the other half.

If Dennis was disappointed or expecting something more, he covered it well. "Yes, you try to get a good night's sleep, and . . ." he gave a pretend leer, "I'll do the same."

I giggled, as he was expecting, and gathered up my purse,

the will, and the letter, stuffing all securely in my purse for further perusal.

He saw me safely to my apartment door, gave me a chaste peck on the cheek, but squeezed my hand meaningfully, saying, "Eleven," then he was gone.

CHAPTER FOUR

hank God, was my ungrateful reaction. After all, the man had done nothing more than buy me an excellent meal, give me the scoop on my inheritance, and slightly overdo the hand-holding bit. He had been a good listener, said all the right things, and never suggested anything out of line. On top of it, he was the best-looking man who had ever crossed my path. Shaking my head, I wondered if middle-age was assailing me. Putting *that* thought firmly out of my mind, I tried to tell myself Uncle James's letter was to blame, but knew the discomfort had begun immediately with our meeting in his office. He'd started the come-on bit practically from the beginning—very suspicious, at my age.

Yes, I know; I'm constantly harping on the forty-five number. All right, I'll come right out and admit it: I'm very sensitive about it (there, are you happy?). Forty didn't bother me a bit, well . . . maybe a bit . . . but forty-five really got to me. I may not be fat, jowly, wrinkled, or gray, but let's face it, half the world is younger than I am. Why would someone as gorgeous as he is—okay, I keep harping on that, too, it's a sort of reverse ego thing—latch onto me as though I were the next best thing to Angelina? After approximately fifteen minutes? It's not as though I spent my life clinging to the wall, as I said. Guys liked me well enough, but I never had to wade over a pile of fainting bodies, either. Was that it? Just a case of lowly-librarian-lack-of-self-esteem? I sent that thought to join the previous one.

No, there was more to it than that. A whole lot more, if Uncle James's letter was anything to go by. However, I still couldn't put my finger on why the whole setup seemed strange from the get-go. I had felt it even before I entered the hallowed halls of Ackbury and Ackbury.

I needed to reread Uncle James's letter. Boy, did I need to! I wandered back into the bedroom where I had left my purse. It still lay on the bed, just where I had tossed it, but something made me pause, goosebumps rising on my arms. My purse was open, and the letter was sticking straight up out of it.

Fighting the urge to run screaming from the apartment, I tried to calm my racing heart and think rationally. My apartment door was locked; no one could get in the building without being buzzed up. I had only been in the bathroom a matter of minutes, and I would have heard anyone in the room through the open door. The closet! Was someone lurking there? Had been lurking there since before I returned? Logic told me there was no way they could have broken in, but logic didn't seem to be covering the situation at the moment.

I stared at the closed closet door for a heartbeat, and then looked around me as casually as possible for a weapon. *Come on Jamie, get real! This isn't Inspector Barnaby, you don't have a weapon.* Of course, neither did he, but that's beside the point.

Grabbing my purse from the bed, the letter dropping to the

floor in my haste, I brandished it like a club—well, I told you it was heavy—rushed around the bed and wrenched the closet door open. An exquisitely tasteful wardrobe, but no intruder, unless he was disguised as a vintage Valentino. Breathing deeply, I thought things out more calmly. Obviously, I had failed to close my purse after I had put my keys back inside. When I tossed it carelessly on the bed, it had popped open and the letter had popped up. Satisfied with my clever analysis, I went to retrieve the letter from where it lay mournfully on the floor.

Armed with the purse into which I had restuffed the letter, I meandered into the kitchen to make a cup of what I call "beige." Just enough cocoa powder to tint the milk, and not even a touch of sugar, I like my chocolate on the bitter side. It's really pretty much warm milk, but I like the pale ecru shade. I carried it back into the living room, purse under my arm. If I happened to meet an intruder on the way, I'd have to cocoa him to death.

Settling into my favorite chair, I turned the TV on with the sound off, somehow it made me feel more secure to be accompanied by even a two-dimensional crowd. The letter episode had definitely unnerved me, even if I had come up with what I thought was a sensible explanation. Leaning back, I opened the envelope, and with the letter in one hand and the cup in the other, I started to reread Uncle James's message.

One sentence into the missive, I set the cup as carefully as possible back on the saucer. Even then it wobbled almost uncontrollably and threatened to dump its contents into the lap of my periwinkle-blue sheath.

Should have taken this off, I chided myself, trying not to have hysterics.

Why? Well, you should ask. The letter started out the way

it had in the restaurant. *My dearest niece,* after that, things got more than a little crazy. For starters, some of the words were now glowing a bright red. As distracting as Dennis's blue eyes might have been, I knew I couldn't have missed *that* on the first run-through.

I dropped the letter as though it had metamorphosed into Cleopatra's asp. Backing away I grabbed my cell phone and hit a number. I carry an up-to-date smart phone if you're interested. If I could have carried a vintage candlestick-style from the Deco era, I would have, but that doesn't quite cut it these days. Did I call my parents? No, I was still held back by that odd reluctance. The police? "I've got a red letter." "Yeah, lady and I've got a brass badge." Dennis? Don't be ridiculous. I called Margo, my BFF, who else?

She's a practicing Wiccan by the way, and prefers to be known as Margaux, including at her job. That's really kind of hilarious, since she's an accountant for a title company. Because we've been best friends since middle school, however, she's just Margo to me—old habits die hard.

Was it late? Would she be in bed asleep? Yes, and yes. Did I care? Not on your tintype.

When a foggy voice said "H'lo," I all but screamed, "It's me. Get over here."

The phone went dead, and in exactly seventeen minutes the buzzer began sounding furiously. I acknowledged, and let her in to the apartment scant seconds later. She had thrown her ceremonial cape over her Fred Flintstone pajamas (ghastly but efficient). Her hair, waist-length and black as ebon, to coin a phrase, looked like she'd been standing on her head all night. Margo's small, like I am, but no one could ever accuse her of being a *fashionista,* since most of her wardrobe comes from the boy's department at Macy's. On her curvy little figure, it looks fabulous, on me it would look like I was auditioning for a remake of *The Kid*.

"Well," she demanded, through clenched teeth and crossed arms.

"Come over here." I picked up the letter by one corner and held it out.

Seeing my caution, she accepted it the same way.

"Read it."

She complied, and then cocked her head at me with no comment.

"Are some of the words red?"

"Yes." The head remained cocked.

I took the letter from her gently and motioned for her to sit. She plopped on the couch without changing the cock of her head.

"Let me bring you up to speed."

"A good idea," was the terse rejoinder.

I gave her the whole story, including Dennis. At the end of my recital, she retrieved the letter and gave it considerably more close attention.

Raising her head, she gave me a troubled stare, and inquired, "Have you gone over the will again?"

I confessed that I had dropped the letter like the proverbial hot potato, and hadn't even touched the will.

"I called you the first thing."

"Thanks, I think."

"You're entirely welcome, and I mean that sincerely."

She snorted, and then sobered. "I suspect Uncle James wants you to give them both a closer look. He sure knows how to get your attention."

"He's dead," I protested.

"Uh huh," was the laconic reply. "Gone but definitely not forgotten. Not even all that gone, I'd say."

"No! No! He isn't here! I refuse to even consider it. He used some kind of trick ink, turns red when you expose it to air."

"Mmmm, it's a possibility. Let's see the will."

I lifted it out of my purse as though I expected it to explode in my hand, which wasn't far from the truth. Joining Margo, on the couch, I spread it out on my lap. All was unchanged, with the *slight* exception of the phrase "pissed off" which now glowed that eerie neon red.

"Mmmm," murmured Margo, alliteratively.

She didn't need to point out that the will had been typed by Dennis's frightfully formal secretary. Uncle James's imaginary trick ink would have had a hard time operating in the computer, and the chances that the computer could have been altered in some way to produce a sea change, or an air change actually, were between slim and none.

I sank back on the couch and, to the utter astonishment of both of us, burst into tears. "I don't want this," I wailed.

Usually the most compassionate of humans, which is why she's my BFF, Margo regarded me unsympathetically, and observed, unnecessarily it seemed to me, "Well, you got it."

She marched to the bathroom, returned with a wad of Kleenex which she thrust into my hands and ordered, "Dry up." I never realized she was so cranky when she was awakened suddenly.

I mopped up my eyes, blew my nose and whined, "You want a cup of beige?"

Her unrestrained gale of laughter rattled the windows—another reason she's my BFF.

"Sounds good, only let's actually put some chocolate into it this time. You need the caffeine."

I went whole hog and threw in a teaspoon for each of us.

"Oh, thank you, Your Meagerness," Margo rhapsodized. I stuck my tongue out at her.

Resettled on the couch, we read and reread the creepy documents.

"Okay, 'pissed off' and 'boxed in,': P.O. Box, obviously," was her interpretation.

"I agree, but which one, where?"

"It looks like Uncle James intends for you to find out, little by little. He says in the letter that he's found a way to get the message across, starting with the rubrics." Margo was silent for a minute, then took hold of my wrist. "Uncle James sounds like a nice old guy, but he must have known he was making you a target just by writing this letter. I'd stake my Wiccan butt on the fact that *somebody* has already seen it, seals or no seals."

"Dennis?"

"Can't rule him out, he certainly had plenty of opportunity, but he's probably not the only one . . . No, I can't guess who, or how," she answered my unspoken question.

I chewed reflectively on my lower lip, when a sudden thought struck me.

"The Witnesses!"

"The Dates!" Margo chimed in simultaneously. "Let's take another look at that will," she went on.

We pulled out the will again, and looked it over. With the exception of the redly-glowing words we had noted before, it was unchanged. The signing date had not taken on an unearthly sheen, nor did the witnesses' names light up like a restaurant sign. Disappointed, we both sank back as one man—or as one woman, actually.

"Do the witnesses' names mean anything to you?" she asked hopefully.

"Are you kidding? Uncle James's name didn't mean anything to me."

She gave a disgusted snort. "I don't suppose you thought to ask if Uncle James had any business partners."

"I told you, I got as far as murder and just shut down."

She again acknowledged that that might do it.

"I'll pump Dennis for info tomorrow." I took another look at the witnesses' signatures. "Gleason Marden and Quincy McNair. Did they make those up, do you suppose?"

"They do sound like nineteenth-century stage players, 'Gleason Marden *is* Iago.'"

I gave a little shudder, "I hope not. Try a different role."

"Okay, Gleason Marden *is* the Scarlet Pimpernel."

"Was the Pimpernel ever a stage character, or just a book, and a movie?"

"I don't know, I just liked the sound of it."

"It always made me think of an adolescent with zits."

"Or a street-walker with very few clients."

I gave her a modest punch, and suggested we go to bed.

"I'm for it, you woke me from my beauty sleep, and my eyes are starting to resume that position. Your recent history may be exciting, but Morpheus calls, and he's my favorite date."

Laughing, I remembered that fact all too well. In our high school days, I could barely drag her out before noon on weekends. We retired.

CHAPTER FIVE

———•———

In spite of her usual habit, Margo was up and dressed by ten, showing every sign of impatience to get going. I was the one experiencing an odd reluctance. One would think that just the idea of owning a home chockfull of Deco goodies would have me perched on the edge of my chair (where I was having a cup of beige at the kitchen table), quivering like a bird dog. Just the opposite, I was all in favor of going back to bed and throwing the covers over my head.

"What's up?" Margo glanced at me and frowned. "Never mind," she answered herself. "You don't really want to meet Uncle James face to face."

"Other than the point that I can't, you're right on the money. I kept dreaming that I was staring down at a giant pool of blood, with Uncle James's body floating face down in it."

"Face down, because you don't know what he looked like," she commented sagely.

"That's probably it, but I do know what blood looks like, and I don't want to spend another night dreaming it up."

"That's all it was, a dream. Even if there was any blood,

that housekeeper of his will have cleaned it all up by now."

"I don't think I can do the desk."

"So, sell it as soon as you can. It's entirely your prerogative, now."

Something about that gave me a *frisson* of discomfort. "You know, I haven't told my parents, yet."

She goggled at me in disbelief. "You haven't *told* them?"

"I'm not sure how. It looks like there was bad blood (I shuddered over that word) between my Dad and Uncle James that dates back a long way. I don't know how they'll feel when I do tell them, especially since Unc's been keeping an eye on me all these years."

"Yeaaah." She drew the word out thoughtfully. "*You're so like your mother, my dear,*" she quoted from the letter.

"There you have it. I don't want to open any old wounds."

"What's your other choice? Claiming you won the lottery and decided to spend all of it on old houses?"

"You're no help." Sighing, I attempted to drown my difficulties in beige. The raucous zzzzt of the buzzer made us both jump.

"There's Dennis, right on time, as usual." The clock over the sink had just registered eleven.

"I rather imagine he's going to find me Madame de Trop," Margo voice was so dry, the African violets almost withered.

"Tough, I know, but he'll get over it."

When I let him in, Dennis glanced at Margo in surprise, but recovered quickly, saying, "Two beautiful ladies, I'm a lucky man."

When he turned to me to ask, "Ready?" Margo made a gagging gesture behind his back. Keeping my face straight with an effort, I nodded to indicate readiness, not sure I could trust my voice.

Quelle surprise! The previously utilitarian SUV had become an up-to-the-minute *and* bright red Cadillac crossover. Fortunately, it hadn't turned into anything two-seater, or Margo was going to have to follow on roller skates. She glanced at me with an arched eyebrow, and prepared to take the back seat.

Dennis favored us with the blinding grin-plus-dimple, "I didn't think you were all that fond of the last pumpkin, Cindy, so I traded it in."

"Overnight," I gasped.

"Well, no," he admitted, "actually I ordered this a couple of months ago, before I met you. It's just fortuitous that I was able to pick it up today, before I picked you up, so to speak."

Just when he had me thinking he was the King of Smarm again, he made me laugh and the pendulum swung back into the "isn't he adorable" range. As though once more reading my mind, I got another flash of dimple while he bowed me into the front seat.

CHAPTER SIX

The house was modest from the outside, but a little jewel of the Airplane Bungalow genre. I was starting to get a feel for my Uncle James, and it seemed to suit the impressions that were vaguely forming in my imagination. I was somewhat surprised at the neutrality the house projected, I guess I expected it to shout MURDER as soon as we pulled up to the curb. Instead, it was just a charming old home.

"I expected bigger," observed Margo.

"Uncle James evidently had a restrained exterior," I rejoined.

"Wait until you get inside," cautioned Dennis, "this is that proverbial book you can't judge."

He opened the door with a flourish and motioned us both inside.

"Aaah," was my involuntary response.

"Woo hoo," came from Margo.

The interior was a gorgeously (yeah, I know I also bandy *that* word around a lot, but what can I tell you, if it's gorgeous, it's gorgeous) restored, right-out-of-a-Stickley's-magazine, backdrop for a nearly breath-taking Deco stage set. The juxtaposition, which could have been jarring, absolutely sang in harmony, something like Fred and Ginger as Vernon and Irene Castle. I kept my mouth firmly closed, after the first gasp, for fear I would simply babble like a demented woman, also because unsightly drool is so off-putting socially.

For a few moments, I totally forgot Uncle James and his suspicious demise, and just basked in a Deco glow. However, that lovely warm feeling vanished instantly when Dennis asked, "Ready for the rest of the house?"

The nasty world of probable murder snapped back into focus, and I swallowed hard, before nodding. We followed Dennis through the dining room with its lovely built-ins, into the kitchen, which boasted state-of-the-art appliances, cleverly and unobtrusively installed behind oak cabinets to direct attention away from themselves. Above the sink, two stained-glass-topped windows looked out on a lovely little garden, and—I was getting breathless—there was even a breakfast nook.

Then, back the way we came to the "parlor," believe me that was the word, which was separated from the dining room by pocket doors (my favorite). The furniture—what can I say—looked like a zillion-dollars-worth of glorious Deco, each piece chosen to harmonize perfectly with its Craftsman setting. Something like Charles Rennie Mackintosh meets the Queen Mary.

Margo and I made admiring noises, but I could feel my palms starting to grow clammy, and I was finding it harder to breathe naturally.

"Where's the office?" I suddenly blurted out, my voice rising.

Margo shot me a frowning look which suggested "Get a

grip," while Dennis tossed the keys thoughtfully up and down in his hands. "Are you sure you're ready for this," he inquired, with a dubious look, evidently expecting a fit of adolescent Valley-girl hysterics.

"I'm sorry," I apologized, "I just thought if I got the place where he died out of the way, then I could just enjoy the rest of the house. I guess I need to sort of, er, make my peace with the idea," I added lamely.

"Yes," he agreed, "it's tough when it's someone you know that dies, especially a relative."

"Well, I didn't really know him, but it looks like he knew me fairly well, so I feel like I knew him too. Does that make sense?"

"Of course," Dennis patted my arm reassuringly, "even if you didn't know him personally, he was still your uncle."

I smiled tentatively, as though I was only suffering a loss, and not expecting signs of a violent struggle. All right, that's a little dramatic since I knew there wouldn't be any, but I couldn't keep my imagination from going into overdrive.

"This way," directed Dennis, and we left that fabulous living room and dining room behind, stepped across the hall, and into the room Uncle James used as a combo office/den.

I paused, puzzled, just inside the door. Rather than the icy chill up my spine I anticipated, the room seemed to enclose me in warm, loving arms, and a sense of welcome that nearly over-whelmed me. I was brought back to earth by the sound of a pair of "oofs" behind me as Dennis and Margo collided with each other, not expecting my sudden stop.

"Oh, sorry," I temporized as I moved farther into the room, "it's just a really pretty room, and I was taking it all in."

I made a circuit of the room, the warm feeling following

me throughout. Summoning up my courage, I pointed to the beautiful macassar ebony-veneered desk which dominated the chamber, "Is that where he fell?"

"I've been told that, yes," Dennis agreed uncomfortably. "I didn't actually see, but that was my assumption. As I said, the medical examiner felt that your uncle might have had a small stroke or heart attack, which caused him to lose consciousness and fall against the desk, striking his head. There was a quantity of blood beneath him"

Firmly putting that thought out of my mind, I looked at the rounded corners of the Deco desk (which by the way, almost made me forget murder, since I was sure it was Ruhlmann). I repeated, "Might have had? He didn't know?"

Dennis looked increasingly uncomfortable. "He thought it looked that way."

"He didn't do an autopsy to make sure?"

Even more uncomfortable, Dennis answered, "He didn't feel it was necessary." Seeing my face he added, "As I understand it."

I made a noncommittal noise, and dropped it for the moment. *It was someone you knew well, wasn't it, Uncle James?*

Yes, heart's dearest, said a pleasant baritone voice in my head, *it had to be, but unfortunately, I didn't see who.*

I made a strangled sound, and grabbed at a small occasional table for support, knocking the lamp on it galley-west. The others stared at me opened-mouthed as the lamp crashed to the floor and shattered. Tears came to my eyes as I surveyed the damage, hoping that it wasn't an irreplaceable object—not for its intrinsic value but for Uncle James's sake.

I looked at the others, who were still standing agape, and tried for an offhand air.

"Oh, darn, I tripped over the foot of the table. It's just like me, I'm always tripping over something if I don't watch myself. I guess I was paying more attention to the desk than to my feet."

Margo, who had never known me to trip over anything, cocked her head quizzically. I gave her the smallest of headshakes, and directed a rueful smile at Dennis.

"I hope that doesn't come out of my inheritance."

Dennis gave a small snort and said dryly, "You know where to send the bill."

"I think I'm just a bit over my head, delayed shock, or something like that. I get an uncle, lose him, get a house, get a business, all this getting is starting to get *me*."

They both chuckled dutifully, although Margo continued to regard me with a thoughtful gaze that guaranteed an Inquisition as soon as we were alone.

Dennis interrupted, "The other room on this floor is your uncle's bedroom; he didn't feel he needed more than that."

"Wait a minute," I countered. "Isn't there another story?"

Dennis's grin grew sly, "Why, yes, it just so happens, there is."

"Show us," I demanded.

"Right this way, Madam," he produced another flourishing bow, and led us to the stairs.

THE WARM FEELING diminished when we left the den, but still clung like a remembered shawl around my shoulders as we made our way upwards, Dennis leading the charge. He threw me one of those grins when we reached the landing, and made a big production out of finding the right key, inserting it in the lock, etc., until I almost let him have it with the resale Dooney I was carrying today.

When he finally threw open the door, I don't think I can even begin to explain the magnitude of the impression made by the room beyond. Margo and I both fell back a step simultaneously, sucking with identical indrawn breaths. As a matter of fact, I drew mine in so far, I was in danger of levitating like a Macy's balloon. The entire upper story appeared to be one room—one room that just happened to be filled, floor to ceiling, with books. Not just any old bunch of books, as I discovered when I got up close and personal, but first editions of contemporary authors, manuscripts that were old when the Renaissance was young, and a nice smattering of the eighteenth and nineteenth centuries.

Letting my breath out with a whoosh, I managed to whisper, "These are mine?"

Rather than laughing at me as I would have expected, Dennis put a surprisingly gentle arm around my shoulders, gave me a short, nonsexy squeeze, and acknowledged that that was the case.

"Almost too much to take in, isn't it?" He nodded with complete understanding.

To my horror, and I confess everlasting embarrassment, I sank to the floor and burst into tears. I didn't even cry like that over my ex-and-unlamented husbands. With that unexpected understanding again, Dennis sat on the floor beside me patting my back and mopping my face with his handkerchief (the man even *had* one, and clean, at that!). Not to be outdone, Margo sat on my other side and held my hand tightly. After I subsided into hiccups, the flood having slowed to a trickle, Dennis pulled me to my feet and announced, "Lunch."

I started to protest that I hadn't really looked at everything, but Dennis stopped me. "Uh-uh, that's it for today. We'll come back and do this in easy stages. You need food and a really stiff latte."

I let him pull me down the stairs, out the front door, and into the gleaming red chariot.

He earned more brownie points in my mental ledger by going back a second time to make sure the front door was firmly locked. In the car, he deposited the house keys in my hand, saying soberly, "I want you to call me to go with you before you go back again. Promise?"

When I made a weak demurral, he lifted my chin and stared intently into my eyes. "I mean it, I want you to promise."

"Uh, well, okay, I guess."

Margo made a small noise in the back seat.

"I think Margo should be with you, too," he went on, "you need some emotional support for a while."

I started to bridle at the idea that I was an emotional cripple, but he added, "Yes, I know you can, and have been, taking care of yourself. This is different, that library upstairs is worth millions—no, I'm not kidding—and I just want you to have someone around to . . ." His voice trailed off. Minutes of silence ticked by before he added, "Someone might want to take advantage."

My mind whirled as I tried to extract the meaning of "advantage." Did Dennis suspect foul play, too, or did he have personal knowledge?

CHAPTER SEVEN

———•———

"All right, let's have it," demanded Margo when we got back to my apartment.

We had had lunch, where I didn't have that "stiff latte" Dennis had suggested; I had a burger, fries, and chocolate malt, which seemed to amuse him no end. He dropped us off with a jaunty wave, as though he hadn't just been warning me about going to the house alone, and furthermore, with no mention of a next time.

Margo pulled me into the foyer impatiently, and tapped her foot all the way up in the elevator to my floor. Fortunately, I'm only on the second.

I heaved another of those dramatic sighs which were becoming a habit, along with several other tics I seemed to have picked up lately, and motioned for her to sit down. "This is going to take something stronger than hot chocolate," I said firmly, went to the pantry and brought out my one and only bottle of wine—A Christmas gift—and two Baccarat glasses which had come with them.

These had been presented to me via UPS, with a card

reading "Thanks for the memory." That's it, not even a good-bye, not even a signature, so much for that grand, three-month affair. I had kept it, unopened, with the hope that I would want to share it with someone new. That hadn't happened so far and I felt this was definitely the time, even if Margo wasn't exactly someone new, or male, for that matter.

I poured, thrust a wineglass into her waiting hand, and then just stared.

"Earth to Jamie, out with the story. What was with the 'silly, little, old, clutzy me' bit? If there was anyone who knew where her feet were going, you're the one."

I took a preliminary taste of my wine, then managed to choke violently. Between gasping whoops, I wheezed out, "Uncle James."

When my breathing returned to normal, I elaborated, "I heard him."

I thought for a minute Margo was going to choke me herself, however she managed a semirestrained, "Would you like to fill in a few more details?"

"It was when I looked at the desk, I was thinking that it had to be someone he knew well; as a matter of fact, I think I phrased it as a question." I took another small sip of wine and neatly avoided drawing it into my lungs before I continued, "It was like . . . like he answered me."

"AND?"

"He said it was . . . no, he said it had to have been, but he *didn't see who.*

Without batting an eye at the means of transmission, she demanded, "How could he not see who it was? They had to get close enough to hit him over the head!"

"I know that," I answered crossly, "you know that, but

Uncle James didn't tell me, we really didn't have time for a conversation."

I pictured myself, staring into space communing with the unseen, while Margo and Dennis hung on the shade's every word. Shaking my head at the absurdity of my fantasy, I returned to the present. "What can I tell you? You know I've never believed in anything supernatural, especially the 'dearly departed,' but I heard *something*."

"Not to mention *saw*," Margo reminded me, "what about your red-letter day?"

Taking another small sip of my wine (I'm a cheap drunk, because of my size, so I'm cautious), I acknowledged the truth of her remark.

"Let's take another look at the will and letter," was Margo's suggestion.

"We've looked at them until I'm cross-eyed," I retorted, "what more can we squeeze out of them?"

"I dunno," Margo admitted, "but they're all we've got at the moment, unless you can scare up—no pun intended—Uncle James."

I stared at her without speaking for several heartbeats; then ventured, "He was in the office, he *wasn't* in the *library* . . . or maybe he *was*. What do I know?" I drooped with indecision.

She grabbed my hand, "Let's go," she demanded peremptorily and pulled me from the chair.

"Wait, wait," I hung back, *very* unwilling, "Dennis said I shouldn't go alone."

"Do I look like alone?" she countered.

"But, but," I sputtered, nevertheless letting myself be dragged to the front door. Grabbing my purse from the hall table, I followed Margo out the door.

I LET MYSELF be pulled into the elevator and down to the garage—whining all the way. Margo finally snapped, "Stuff a sock in it. I get the message; you don't like this idea."

"You're darn tootin'," I affirmed.

"Darn tootin'?"

"For want of slightly less lady-like phrases."

Margo faced me squarely and seriously. "You need to do this, Jamie. You need to know whether you *did* actually hear your Uncle James, or . . ."

"Or?"

"You just have a very sensitive feel for your surroundings."

"In other words, a crazy imagination."

"No! Absolutely not! Being sensitive to ambience is not a sign of an overwrought psyche. It just means you pick up on things that others don't."

"Have you *ever* known me to display this talent before? Consider my exes."

"Well . . . no," was her reluctant admission. "But that could mean you just haven't been in the right place, with the right atmosphere. Or, you've been repressing it, or . . ."

"Or it's nonexistent," I finished for her.

"How would you prefer to explain the voice in your head?"

I subsided. *How did I explain it? I didn't, at least not yet. Margo was right, I had to find out.*

BY THE TIME I reached the point of agreement, we had pulled up in front of Uncle James's, no *my*, house. I didn't even remember actually starting the car, or following the route we had taken previously. That worried me more than a little, as I was feeling a bit fuzzy, but I clamped down on pursuing that line of thought.

I had to admit a thrill of pleasure washed over me as I walked up to the front door. In spite of some rather (okay, definitely) unpleasant associations, Uncle James had wanted me to have the absolute answer to my dreams, and I felt a glow from that knowledge.

Once inside, however, the glow evaporated with a shiver. Uncle James had been killed for what he possessed; now *I* possessed it even though I had no idea what it was.

"Come on," urged Margo impatiently. "Let's get it over with before you lose your nerve."

"Lose it? I never found it to begin with." Nevertheless, I headed for the office.

Pushing open the door, I could feel my pulse speed up until I felt my whole body was throbbing along. Taking a few deep breaths, which only made me feel dizzy rather than calm, I teetered at the doorway until Margo gave me a sharp push through into the room.

"Ow!" I futilely tried to rub the spot between my shoulder blades where she had poked me with a sharp fingernail.

"Well, you were going to stand there all evening."

"Okay, O Brilliant Wizard, what do I do now?"

"You talk to Uncle James."

"Hi there? How's it going on the other side?"

"Don't insult me, *or* him." Margo bit out with asperity. "Take this seriously."

I sagged. "I know, I just . . ."

She gave my arm an understanding squeeze. "Why don't you just do what you did before."

I considered it. I wandered over to the desk and, hard as it was to do, I put my hand on the top. *Was it here, Uncle James?*

Oh, no, my dear, not in this room. A pause, and then in a reconsidering tone, *at least, I don't think so. Maybe, it was . . . I'm not sure . . . maybe I . . . I know I . . .* his entirely in-my-head voice trailed off. Then he continued, *as a matter of fact, I really can't remember.*

I dropped to my knees beside the desk and shrieked, somehow the very human indecision he displayed made it all the more real.

Margo was down beside me in an instant, her arms around me like a fierce mother hen guarding her chick. All right, they have wings and no arms, but you know what I mean.

"He wasn't here," I finally choked out.

"Huh? Who? The killer? Then why . . . ?

"Uncle James."

She rocked back on her heels and regarded me for a long moment.

"You heard *him.* "

"Uh, well . . . maybe."

"He was found here."

"But he wasn't killed here . . . I guess . . . maybe. He doesn't seem to know," I quavered, as I realized what I was saying.

"You heard him again," she stated firmly, "and you *really* heard him. I know what you're thinking."

"No, you don't," I surprised myself by contradicting her. "I'm not thinking I'm crazy. I'm thinking . . ."

I trailed off. What was I thinking? Even if the first time had been my imagination, it would never have occurred to me to imagine he was killed anywhere but here where he was found. Putting that all together with the weird changes in the will and letter, I was thinking I was going to have to revise everything I had believed up to now.

What's the answer, Uncle James?

I can't tell you any more now, my dear, than I could when I was still there. Death does not immediately confer omnipotence, I'm sorry to say, a hint of wry humor.

"Hey! Where are you?"

I came back to myself to see Margo peering at me with concern.

"We were having a chat," I said calmly, and then fell backward on the floor.

I opened my eyes to find Margo slapping me, hard, on both cheeks.

"Why do I have to keep saying OW! around you?" I inquired crossly, pushing her hands away.

"Because you keep spacing out on me. Duh! You're going to have to work out a better arrangement with Uncle James. You can't continue screaming or passing out."

I sat up. "You're right. It's inconvenient."

Margo started to giggle and in seconds we were both hysterical (I use that word advisedly). I heard a slight chuckle in my head.

Wiping my eyes, I started to get to my feet, when a noise froze us both in our places. The noise came from the front door which was opening cautiously, just making the faintest of squeaks.

Behind the desk, my dear, said my head, and I grabbed Margo, making a shushing gesture and pointing. Together, we scrabbled behind the desk as quickly and quietly as possible.

Footsteps echoed in the hall, a man judging from the weight of the sound. The footsteps continued up the stairs to the second floor where we heard muttered curses and then a splintering sound. The splintering was followed by an exclamation as the intruder presumably took in the splendor, as well as the extent, of the library.

Who is it, Uncle James?

I don't know, my dear, I can't see any better than you can.

Can't you just look?

No, my dear, I wish I could, I've tried with no success.

You mean you're just stuck here?

It would seem so.

That sucks.

There are worse places—or so I've heard. More wry humor.

Another noise assailed our ears. This time it sounded like things being thrown around. Thrown around! My books!

Heedless of danger—as well as bereft of good sense, I leaped to my feet, ran out the door and up the stairs, screaming, "What are you doing to my things?"

The noise stopped, followed by running feet and a ski-masked, dark-clad figure brushed past me nearly flinging me down the stairs. I clung to the banister, fighting to keep my balance, as the figure ran out the door and disappeared.

"What in the Goddess's name did you think you were doing?" demanded Margo. "Uncle James nearly died a second time; and I almost joined him."

I sat down on the stairs, trying to catch my breath. "I didn't think."

"Oh, we'd never have guessed," she dripped sarcasm.

I thought a minute, "How do you know what Uncle James was feeling?" I asked jealously.

"I couldn't hear him, of course, but if an icy-cold whirlwind is any indication I'd say he was a little upset."

"Oh dear," I felt remorse, and on reflection more than a little scared.

Reentering the office, I did my best to calm the whirlwind Margo had described. Papers flew everywhere and the curtains did their best imitation of Marley's ghost.

"I'm sorry, I'm sorry! Uncle James! It's all right, I won't do anything like that again! I promise."

I realized I was screaming this out loud, but gradually the tumult died and Uncle James addressed me sternly in a mental dressing-down. In view of his manifest distress, I found myself practically promising seven years of servitude chained to the desk to calm him down.

I called the police to report the break-in, and was surprised to see that, along with two uniformed members of the constabulary, a dejected-appearing homicide detective, whose name I didn't catch, showed up as well.

While the two officers looked everything over, dusted for fingerprints, etc., the detective questioned me.

"That's all the description you can give me, Ms, uh . . . ?"

"Whitehall."

He shook his head and tried again, "Didn't you get any other impression?"

"I have told you everything I can, Detective. He nearly threw me down the stairs and all I saw was his ski mask. He had on black everything—clothes, gloves, I couldn't even see his hands."

"That's why no fingerprints," he observed, unnecessarily.

He turned to Margo, asking, "What did you see?"

She shrugged, "I caught only a glimpse of his back as he went out the door."

The detective closed his eyes for a minute; then gave it another shot.

"Tall? Short? Heavy? *Anything?*"

"It was too fast, Detective, and I was too busy trying not to go into free fall."

He nodded, "Yeah, I guess I appreciate that." He left, looking dejected. Well, since he had arrived looking that way, I mean even more so.

I made Uncle James more promises concerning my safety, and Margo and I left, as well.

CHAPTER EIGHT

O n our return, I suggested we finish off the bottle of wine which we had left behind.

"Now that it's open, let's not waste it." I poured a generous slug out of the bottle for both of us, and handed a glass to Margo.

My only possible excuse is that I was still unnerved by our visit to Uncle James's, no, *my* place, but I found myself swigging the wine like an accomplished tippler. Rather than my cautious sips, the glass went down like 7 Up. I needed Dutch courage to discuss our expedition and I hadn't gotten it yet, so I sat silent mulling over my mulled wine. Well, no, it wasn't mulled, it was straight from the bottle; that just sounded romantic. The several more swigs I'd taken hit me with a sudden jackhammer punch, and I turned into Maud Maudlin. Sniffling, I murmured, "Poor Uncle James, alone and murdered."

Margo gave me a disgusted look, "Did you expect him to be murdered in a crowd? Put down that glass, you're starting to sound like you should haunt bathrooms." Margo hadn't touched hers, just sat twirling the liquid in the glass.

"You're right." I tried to dispel the fogginess from my brain, but was finding it a losing battle. "Need something to eat," I muttered, trying to raise myself from the couch. Margo's image wavered in front of me; I heard her say something, but the words made no sense. I staggered up, knocking over the wineglass . . .

◆

"SHE'S COMING around now," announced a deep, but mellow male voice. "We weren't sure for a bit, she got a fair amount of that combo, but she's tougher than she looks."

My eyelids made feeble, fluttering movements. Who knew eyelids weighed so much? After a few false starts, I actually managed to get them up half-way. A much too bright light told me that was a horrible mistake and I let them slam shut again.

Margo's voice, sounding much too high, ordered, "We know you're in there. Wake up!"

Intelligent speculation was beyond me, so I resorted to cliché, "Wha' hap'?"

"The wine was an unusual vintage, woody, slight fruity suggestion, touch of vanilla, and a pleasant dose of chloral hydrate."

My blood gelled. "Gghhg," I responded.

"Yeah, I thought so too," was the dry rejoinder. "I'm leaving now, you're safe with your parents." I had thought I heard their voices, but had assumed it was some sort of hallucination.

Margo's voice sounded like the Last Trump. Everything seemed exaggerated—every rustle, every squeak—like the volume of my inner iPod was set *way* too high. Did I have a headache, or had I simply been decapitated and they'd set it on the loudspeaker?

"Dah . . . gah," I wheezed.

Margo gave a little chuckle, which came out sounding a tad on the grim side. "I have to, uh, spread the news. Your attorney and some, uh, associates (slight emphasis) need to know."

"Ta . . . ta . . . sumah . . . wih . . ."

"I'll see."

The door closed behind her like the Gates of Paradise swinging shut.

No one left with me but my parents, who not only did not know what was going on, but *could* not know. Besides, until my tongue had shrunk to fit my mouth again, I couldn't tell them a blasted thing.

I didn't have to open my eyes to guess that my mother was clenching and unclenching her hands compulsively, or that Dad was pulling out his wallet to look inside and putting it back in the same compulsive repetition.

"Wah wah," I grunted. Reversion to childhood is *sooo* demeaning.

"What's that, honey?" My father dropped his wallet in his haste to service my every wish.

"Wah wah;" I tried again.

"She's thirsty, dear."

Dad sprang into action, fumbling desperately with the straw and managing to nearly drown me in the process.

"Oh, for Heaven's sake," my mother took charge, evidently wrenching the glass from Dad's hands and pouring the entire contents on me.

"I meh . . . ing, I meh . . . ing," I managed to croak, and broke into hysterical giggles.

Panic ensued, as my father flew out the door hollering like a madman, all the way to the Nurses' station.

Mom mopped frantically with paper towels—I felt like I was being sanded to a fine point—all the while murmuring, "Oh, Jamie, Baby!"

I futilely tried to ward off the sanding, but my hands might as well have been lasagna noodles. I was saved only by the duty nurse inquiring, "Well, what have we here?"

Moving to the bedside, she gently removed my mother, as well as my soaked gown. After substituting a dry one and, oh blessed woman, covering me with a blanket straight from the warmer, she withdrew. I had opened my eyes just long enough to catch the wink she threw my way.

Surprisingly enough, the dowsing had improved not only my alertness, but my mood.

"Mom," wonder of wonders, a complete word. "Can you get me some more water?" A whole sentence!

Mom was taken aback, as well. "Jamie, you're talking."

"Needed time to wake up." Not entirely there, but much better.

Voices sounded in the hall, Dad's and someone else. Male, but I couldn't quite pin it down. Sounded somewhat like an argument.

"The door opened, shut, opened and shut again, finally opened to admit two furious seeming men, obviously arguing in *sotto voce.*

"Jamie!" histrionically.

It was Gorgeous. He rushed to my bedside, grabbing both hands dramatically. I could feel Dad's collar getting tight. Despite the drama, I thought I could read real concern in Dennis's baby blues.

"And you are?" My mother's voice put Jell-O to shame.

"This is my attorney, Mom." I struggled to get more out, but one sentence at a time seemed to be the limit.

"Your attorney?" Dad was going to break a tooth if he kept gritting them like that.

Gorgeous introduced himself, and began an explanation. My father cut him off furiously, "A little familiar, aren't you?"

"Dad!" "Dear!" Mom and I remonstrated simultaneously.

"I apologize, Sir," Dennis said smoothly, "I've never had something like this happen to a client of mine before. It came as a great shock. Our firm is, well, rather conservative, since we deal mainly with wills and estate planning."

"Wills?" Dad's ears pricked up.

I shot Dennis a look of warning; he made a quick reversal. "Jamie is very wise, in considering her estate and its disposal, well before she has need. If only more of my clients were as intelligent and mature."

I decided to kick his shins as soon as I had shoes on.

Dad seemed a bit mollified but continued to throw suspicious glances Dennis's way.

"Who would do this to you, Squirt?" he kept asking in agonized tones.

Since I didn't have the lay of the land yet, caution seemed the better part of valor where Dad was concerned. Phrases from the letter kept coming back to me, and I decided the less Dad knew at the moment, the better.

"Haven't a clue, Dad." This was the literal truth, if not exactly everything.

"Your husbands . . . ?"

"Haven't seen them in donkey's years, Dad."

I knew Mom was just as curious and agonized, as Dad, but

she was willing to wait until I had recovered a bit before the grilling began.

To my consummate relief, that lovely bearer of warm blankets returned and announced it was time for the patient to get some rest. Mom and Dad made demurring noises but acquiesced. Dennis shot me a look that said he wasn't going anywhere—at least not far. I didn't know whether to feel pleased or pissed. I blinked my eyes twice to indicate awareness, or something—that was the last I remember.

CHAPTER NINE

awoke finally, to see Dennis stretched uncomfortably on the one visiting chair.

"How . . . how long . . . ?"

"Four hours," was the tight-lipped reply.

"You've been here *all* that time?" I was aghast.

"Yes."

"Why did they let you stay?"

"I told them we had just become engaged."

"What?"

"Well, I had to give them some reason."

"What *is* the reason?"

"There's nobody guarding you, Jamie. Someone just tried to murder my client; I'm not going to let them try again."

Up until then the reality of my situation hadn't hit me. Dennis's matter-of-fact pronouncement chilled me like Mom's ice-water dowsing. My teeth began to chatter, and my entire body became a shivering jelly, as big tears slid down my face.

Dennis, alarmed, leapt to his feet. "Oh, no, I didn't think . . . . Oh, Jamie, I'm so sorry . . ."

The next thing I knew, I was wrapped tightly in his embrace. Wow! Who needs blankets? He was kissing my hair, my eyes, my neck—okay, you get the idea—and murmuring in my ear. To tell you the truth, I didn't know what he was saying, because I couldn't hear him over my teeth. Once I could get my jaws to keep quiet, it was too late; he'd stopped talking. I wasn't sorry however, because he had progressed from ear to mouth. If this is resuscitation I'm going for lessons.

The nurse made an untimely arrival at just that moment. "Oh, I see you're awake." Snide, that woman.

Dennis sat up, cleared his throat, and straightened his tie. "I think she could use another blanket, she seemed cold."

"Mmmm," she turned and walked out.

Dennis retreated to the chair; the nurse returned armed with another toasty blanket. Somehow, it didn't look as good as the first one.

"You should be warm enough now," she observed with what was nearly a smirk.

After she left, Dennis cleared his throat again breaking what was fast becoming an awkward silence.

"I'm having a bed brought in."

"Huh!"

"You didn't think I was going to leave you alone the rest of the night?"

"My parents," I gasped.

I got one of those high wattage grins, this one with an evil edge.

"I'll just tell them we're living in sin—at the hospital."

As before, I had to laugh.

"I'm serious, though, how can I explain my so-called attorney camping out in my room?"

"So-called?" Dennis looked affronted.

"Ah, you know what I mean."

I expected another grin, instead he looked serious. "Jamie, I *am* your attorney. I'm a real one and you're a real client with a *real* estate, and I have a fiduciary duty to you. I don't take that lightly. I don't take *you,* lightly.

His emphasis almost convinced me, but again, even in the midst of the thrill of pleasure I was getting there was that tiny, little niggle of unease. Too much, too soon? I'd asked myself that question before.

Dennis was looking at me with an air of consideration.

"You haven't yet met, or heard from, your Uncle James's partner, have you?"

"No."

"That's more than a little peculiar."

I thought about it. Obviously, he *must* know of Uncle James's death. Equally obviously . . . wait a minute, maybe not so obvious.

"Has he contacted *you*?" I asked. "Does he know the terms of the will?"

"Yes, and yes. He was informed immediately of the death, and I spoke to him not only in my office but at the funeral."

"How did he react?"

"He . . . well . . . he seemed a bit put out. Not that you were inheriting I don't think, but maybe the fact that he was sharing the business with a complete newbie. Or maybe . . . well, I just don't know."

"I can certainly relate. Even though I'm the newbie, I'm just as put out."

Dennis chuckled but said, "Your uncle was sure you could do it, Jamie."

"I wish I had his confidence."

"Don't knock it until you've tried it."

"You said that before." Thinking about the business made me grumpy.

"Think you could handle a little food?" the nurse again, accompanied by a tray-carrier.

"Uh . . ." I thought about hospital food.

"I'll see if I can give her some." Dennis, smooth and giving them the grin.

Both ladies were sucked completely into the grin, of course, and relinquished the tray to him with identical sighs.

"Shame on you," I said after they left.

He looked at me with genuine puzzlement. "Was I rude? I didn't mean to usurp their places."

I slapped my forehead. "Never mind."

Realization of a sort dawned. "Oh, was I too, uh . . . I mean, did I look uh, too . . ."

"Like a lounge lizard?" I prompted, helpfully.

He actually blushed.

Rolling the table under my chin, he started looking under the metal covers. "Ugh," was his encouraging comment.

"You really know how to stimulate a girl's appetite."

"I hope so." Grin with evil edge, again.

"Back off," I said but with a smile.

"Take a look for yourself."

"Ugh! It's the yellow food."

"Told ya."

He started reaching under the table, just as the rollaway bed arrived. Hastily grabbing a spoon, he scooped up some nasty-looking pudding and thrust it into my mouth.

"Aargh," I gurgled.

Once the bed people departed, Dennis retreated to the chair once more.

"Thank God they're only keeping you overnight."

My eyebrows waved enigmatically but forcefully.

Dennis laughed.

CHAPTER TEN

'll skip over the night.

We chatted desultorily for a bit; Dennis talked a little about his childhood. Saying he loved to ride horses on their "ranch." My mind filled in the details of an upper-middle vacation home with a pony for the only child. I knew a little about that myself, coming from a similar affluent upbringing. I, too, had had a pony when I was going through my "horsey" period. We kept Lola—yes, that's the name—at a stable, but I rode every chance I could get. As with most girls I outgrew Lola, who was getting a little long in the tooth, when I switched to boys. I still ride occasionally, however.

When my eyelids drooped again (which wasn't long) Dennis cut it short.

SOMEWHAT TO MY chagrin, he was a perfect gentleman and wore almost as much to bed as he wore during the day. He was also either very clever or very sneaky, because by the time my parents had arrived to spring me from the Big House he was dressed in a different suit, fresh shirt, and was following my parents in the door like a recent arrival.

The trailing nurse with the wheelchair gave me a twinkling grin accompanied by a glance toward Dennis.

"Well, you're certainly getting a complete sendoff," she remarked breezily, "everyone arrived together."

Dennis cleared his throat and said, "Yes, they were just entering the building as I drove up. I had to hustle to catch up to them."

My mother looked from me to Dennis, and her face took on a thoughtful expression but then she nodded brightly and said, "Yes, it was perfect timing."

It was Dennis's turn to look thoughtful.

The door opened, and Margo bounced in. "Good," she wheezed. "I was afraid I was I late. I ran from the parking lot, and took the stairs."

We goggled at her simultaneously.

"Five floors?" my Dad managed.

"Yes . . . well," she stopped to gasp. "I'm kind of a fitness freak."

This patent untruth raised my eyebrows past my hairline.

"Some friends," she emphasized, "wished you well."

I nodded to show I understood. "How did they hear?" I inquired mildly.

"I, er, just *mentioned* you were under the weather. *You know,* we were supposed to get together with them today."

"Oh, right, I kinda forgot."

"You'll have to give *them* a call, so they know you're okay."

The thoughtful look returned to my mother's face. Before she could comment, however, I had another visitor.

It turned out to be the same homicide detective who had shown up at the break-in. This time he introduced himself to everyone as Detective Sergeant Randon from Homicide, whom I instantly dubbed Sergeant "Rundown" since the poor man looked like he was in desperate need of a new battery.

Just as dejected as he had appeared previously, he wore a rumpled brown suit along with a generally world-weary demeanor, his tie was flung over his shoulder like a noose and he even flaunted a fedora pushed back on his head. He looked like Edmond O'Brien had been dragged through a time-slip backwards.

"We meet again, Ms, uh, Whitehall," he said dryly.

Dennis and my parents reacted to that with identical expressions of both puzzlement and shock.

All three started to say something but the Sergeant, as out of it as he might look, picked up instantly that at least some of the group knew nothing of the break-in and covered swiftly.

"She doesn't remember, of course, she was still unconscious."

Dennis immediately became lawyerly, "I'd like to know, Sergeant, why my client was left unprotected last . . . ?" he began officiously.

The sergeant cut him off. "There was a plain-clothes man in the hall all night. Me, as a matter of fact, since we had two guys out sick. My date is still pissed off."

Ah, serious rumple explained.

Dennis turned red and gargled out an apology.

Sergeant Randon grinned, which transformed his whole face, and added, "I noticed she had plenty of protection anyway."

I managed to knock over my water pitcher before he got any further. In the ensuing confusion, I was able to make a cutting-my-throat gesture to the detective who again picked it up without missing a beat.

"The nurses were in and out all night checking on her."

He followed it up smoothly with the suggestion that my parents and Margo wait outside for a short bit while he asked me a few questions. *Naturally,* my lawyer could stay. My father grumbled but let my mother drag him out into the hall.

Before he could ask me anything, I had a few questions for him. For example, "Just what the he . . . heck happened to me?"

"It seems you got a slight case of chloral hydrate poisoning, a 'Mickey Finn' in other words." There was just the slightest of quirks to the corner of his mouth.

I remembered what Margo had said, "Chloral hydrate? Isn't that awfully old-fashioned?"

"It's still around."

"How did I get it?"

"You were drinking a bit of wine, according to your friend."

I gave a little squeak of protest.

Rundown looked a bit abashed. "Sorry, I didn't mean to sound disapproving. She actually did say it was actually only a glass. The combination of the wine and the chloral hydrate on one your size . . ." he shook his head and tsked.

"Lucky you weren't alone when you collapsed."

I stared at him in speechless horror.

Fortunately, I'm not a solitary drinker of anything other than cups of beige, but it could have been *that*. The thought . . . my mind blanked. Wait a minute! The wine was sent to me!

The note that came with it had been unsigned, so I had simply assumed it was the guy I'd been seeing. He hadn't called again, so it sure seemed like a dumping gift. However, I had wondered about the Baccarat glasses—not his style, or bank account, but I imagined it was just guilt.

Uncomfortable at my continuing silence, Randon looked at the file folder he held in his hand. "Jamie Whitehall Olivian," he read from the folder he was holding, "although that's not the name you're giving me. Sounds familiar . . . very familiar." There was sardonic emphasis on the last.

"I go by Whitehall. I don't use my parents' surname, I prefer to use my middle name."

His interest sharpened and I saw suspicion dawn although I had no idea why, he then requested that I tell him what else I knew.

It took very little time, since I couldn't admit to knowing anything other than that James Olivian was my uncle; a connection that had already been made by the sergeant. He looked frustrated when I finished, "You can't think of anyone who has it in for you?"

"No."

"But somebody had it in for your uncle."

I was startled. "It looked that way to me but I thought I was the only one."

"You were but there've been some, well let's call them inconsistencies, that made Homicide, me that is, take another look. The break-in was just one more of them and now this."

"What 'break-in,'" demanded Dennis.

Shamefacedly, I had to explain the whole thing. Both men looked exasperated.

"So why *were* you there, Ms. Whatever," inquired Rundown.

Dennis broke in, "Mr. Olivian left my client his entire estate."

That seemed something of a *non sequitur* right then, then I realized it was intended to explain why I was at the house at the time of the purported break-in (I use the word, because I was horribly afraid the Sergeant regarded it as 'purported').

"Ah," the Sergeant sat back in the chair and regarded me intently. "I'll see you again when you're feeling better, and ask some more questions. If you think of anything you've left out," again that intent gaze, "let me know. I don't have to point out it might be good for your health."

I suppressed an urge to whimper.

CHAPTER ELEVEN

Once we were at my apartment both my Dad, and Dennis, who had followed us from the hospital, insisted on going through each room, examining everything at close range and throwing out virtually all my food.

At my objection, my Dad remonstrated gently, "Honey, we think fresh food would be better for your health. We'll take you to the store tomorrow and buy new."

Deflated, I apologized.

Dad patted my arm. "Now, Squirt, you go pack a few things, and we'll," a sidelong glance at my mother, "take you to Margo's," he finished hastily.

ONCE AT MARGO'S my parents bid goodbye reluctantly, leaving Dennis and Margo staring at me expectantly.

"What," I demanded. (I stared at them just as expectantly, resulting in exasperated sighs from both of them. They frowned at each other, obviously suggesting that I was still more than a bit slow.)

"Your *friends,* remember?" Margo said.

At the exact same time, Dennis said, "Give."

I looked from one to the other. "How?" I said to one. "What?" to the other. Tonto couldn't have put it better.

They each motioned for the other to go first but Margo insisted, "You go first—I want to hear what she's supposed to 'give.'"

Dennis's smile lit the room, and caused me to wobble a bit. After all I'd just been a patient—well a victim, at least, if not at all patient.

Regarding me with a bright blue but unnerving stare, Dennis chewed out slowly like one speaking to the slightly deficient, "What's. Going. On?"

As I drew in a breath to fabricate a story, he added, "Can it. I want the truth."

"The, uh, the truth?"

Silence. Just the gimlet-eye.

I scrubbed my face with both hands.

"You'll just put me right back in the hospital. Besides," I whined, "why do you think there's anything besides what you already know?"

"A few too many *friends.*"

I sighed, "We need to go to the house."

Dennis looked startled. "You can't tell me here?"

"No." Definite, and in unison from Margo and myself.

Dennis checked his watch. "I told my secretary I had a last-minute meeting that wasn't on her calendar, seems as though it ran on longer than expected."

PULLING UP IN front of my house (ooh! that gave me a thrill), I clutched Dennis's arm as my throat clutched at the same time.

"Promise me you won't say *anything* until I'm done."

The urgency in my voice must have impressed Dennis, because he nodded wordlessly, and covered my hand with his.

Inside, I led the way to Uncle James's office, to be met by a cyclone. The entire office looked like an Oz movie with the desk standing in for Dorothy's house.

Dennis jumped back with the first swear words I had heard him utter, whacking Margo as he did so.

"Ow!"

"Uncle James, Uncle James," I cried into the whirlwind, "I'm okay, I'm okay, you can see . . . ."

The wind died down, the curtains resuming their downward flow rather than emulating sails from the Flying Dutchman, and the papers on the desk assumed neat piles.

Dennis sank to his knees then proceeded to perform a face plant on the rug.

"Oh, dear," I rushed to turn him over and rub his cheeks.

His eyes opened, stared vacantly for a beat, and then focused on me. "Ah," he remarked.

Margo and I pulled him to his feet—Margo doing most of the pulling since I wasn't too steady yet, myself.

On his feet, Dennis politely inquired, "And, how is Uncle James?"

"Well, he *was* worried."

"Yes, *of course* he was," calm, with an edge of Screaming Meemies.

A peculiar noise in my ear told me Uncle James was actually snickering.

He followed up, however, with what for him was an almost painful roar. *You will move in here today, young lady, and you won't go anywhere unless you have me as a guard.*

I grabbed my ears and thought back, *Uncle James, you can't leave the office, remember?*

Uncle James muttered to himself in frustration, then asked, *What about that tomfool lawyer?*

I gave a snort, Dennis and Margo cocked their heads.

Let me tell him the whole thing in some other room, Uncle James, I pleaded. I didn't think the story was going to go down well with Uncle James spectrally hanging over Dennis—if it went down at all.

More muttering, another question, *By the way, where's that partner of mine?*

A good question. Where was he indeed? I shrugged.

Uncle James let it go and directed me, most grudgingly, to tell Dennis the entire (crazy) story.

"Let's go to the living room." I plastered another one of those teeth-baring expressions on my face, which in my case seemed to be passing more and more often for smiles, and led the way.

Dennis allowed himself to be herded out of the office and into the living room without a word of protest. He was far too quiet and outwardly composed for my liking. I found myself wishing he'd shriek like a girl, tear his hair, rend his perfectly tailored suit—something—not just look the way he looked.

"Sit Dennis," I had to remind him. He sat.

"I know how this . . . surprises you . . ." I began feebly.

"Um," he responded.

"Dennis, *listen.*" I let a touch of exasperation creep into my voice, for some reason feeling that if I sounded annoyed, I could somehow make a dead uncle haunting the office desk seem normal.

Well, *that* wasn't going to work. If it didn't seem even slightly normal to *me,* it sure wasn't going to seem normal to Dennis. Of course, he had seen or at least experienced, Uncle James first hand … I sucked in a breath so deep; my stomach nearly met my spine.

I started over, "I know, I thought I was crazy too, but I'm not and neither are you. Hear me out."

I began at the beginning and went on to the end; Dennis made no comment throughout my recital. Once I was done, Margo and I stared at him. Dennis stared back impassively for a beat, and then wilted.

"Okay, I saw it. Something happened. If it wasn't Uncle James, it was the scariest thing I've ever seen. You know we can't tell anyone and we've got to keep Uncle James calm. You said he can't leave the desk, right?"

I nodded. "That's what upsets him the most, when he can't help me and can't do anything about it."

No sooner had I finished saying what sounded like an apology, than a bubble of resentment rose in my throat. Why did I need to apologize for *anything,* much less Uncle James, and why did Dennis sound like *he* was taking charge?

"Hey, wait a minute—this is my Uncle James. What is this *we* business?"

Dennis got a startled, but somewhat abashed, expression on his face and Margo giggled.

"She gets a little jealous," was Margo's dry comment.

"Seems to me you recovered pretty fast," I went on grumpily.

Dennis turned the full force of his baby blues on me, "I

have to either believe you, Jamie, or believe we just had an indoor tornado—confined to your uncle's office by the way. I didn't mean to sound like a lawyer, however."

What could I do? I assembled my "good grace" manner and accepted Dennis's apology.

"We've got to go back in and talk to Uncle James," I insisted.

Dennis waved a "wait a minute" hand. "You said he can't leave the office . . . ?"

"Yes, and he seems to be stuck to the desk."

"I wonder . . . Yeah, let's talk to him—uh, that is, you talk to him."

Another giggle from Margo.

With dignity, I led them back to the office.

A short conference with Uncle James confirmed that it did seem to be the immediate area of the desk that held his, um, essence.

Dennis opened a drawer, and carefully removed it.

"Can you latch on to this, Mr. Olivian?" he asked the air.

The contents of the drawer fluttered, startling Dennis who nevertheless maintained a tight grip on the drawer. Slowly, he began to back away from the desk. The papers continued to rustle and flutter. Margo and I held our breaths. Dennis reached the door and paused. I actually saw his Adam's apple bounce, as he gulped.

"Okay," he muttered through a tightly clenched jaw.

Oh, so slowly, one step at a time, he backed into the hall. The papers flew into the air with a loud "whoosh" that even elicited an *"eek"* from Dennis.

They settled back into the drawer and I ventured a cautious, "Uncle James?"

Right here, my dear, was the smug reply.

I sagged against the doorjamb. "It worked! Gorgeous, you're a genius."

Uncle James's bellow of laughter in my ear, more than Margo's and Dennis's astonished gapes, alerted me to what I had just said.

Uncle James stopped guffawing. The least gentlemanly I had known him to be so far, but then I hadn't known him long.

Well, yes, he certainly is good-looking, although not my type. Uncle James can evidently be snarky, too.

Don't let looks be too persuasive, my dear, he finished on a more sober note.

Bless his heart, Dennis decided to ignore my rash outburst and just said, "Now he can go most places with you, Jamie, and maybe we can figure out how to make him even more portable." He even managed a straight face as he passed me the drawer.

I got an odd feeling. No, not Dennis. I remembered something from the first day I had met Dennis. An image of the letter he had given me, standing up straight out of my bag, rose in front of my mind's-eye. If Uncle James couldn't leave the office (and why couldn't he leave the office if he wasn't killed there?), who, or what, had directed my attention to the letter? And, how about the will? How to explain the glowing red letters?

"Uncle James?" I began out loud.

Yes, my dear, I know just what you are going to ask, and, no, I'm not reading your mind. You want to know how I managed to alter the letter and the will, of course, I can certainly guess that without a crystal ball. Remember, I'm not entirely alone, where I am.

I got a picture of a sort of ectoplasmic Internet, or perhaps in Uncle James's case, Western Union.

"You mean you can, uh . . . there are others who can . . . ?"

My mind stuttered to a halt, and goosebumps stood out on my arms. Uncle James was one thing; an entire spectral nation was something else.

It takes a fair amount of effort, heart's dearest, but yes, there are others who are more mobile than I.

Dennis and Margo waited, with heads cocked in identical poses.

Slipping into her Mentalist act, a look of comprehension spread over Margo's face, "The Will," she exclaimed, "and the Letter!"

"Uh huh," I agreed.

Dennis continued to look blank. For more than one reason I figured.

I made it short. "Uncle James can post messages on 'Face-spook.'"

I swear, Dennis's hair actually stood on end.

To my surprise, he addressed Uncle James directly. "Mr. Olivian, if you have a posse, er, that is, if you have acquaintances, uh, around, did any of them witness your demise?"

I could feel Uncle James considering his answer. *Hmmph! Inform my erstwhile lawyer, that if that were the case, we wouldn't all be standing in the hall. And I wouldn't be perched on a pile of letters*, he added.

I translated, "He says no."

Margo shot me a look. However, Dennis got an expression I couldn't read. I started hoping it wasn't relief.

CHAPTER TWELVE

———•———

The doorbell rang. All of us, including Uncle James if the letters were any clue, jumped as if shot. While we stared at each other it rang again. If a doorbell could sound impatient, this one did.

"Okay," I gathered my wits, "I'm going to answer the door."

The doorbell rang a third time before I could even get there. A little annoyed now, I flung the door open rashly, oblivious to the fact that it might not have been a friend.

I found myself staring eye to eye, at a frizzy-haired, slightly paunchy, garden gnome (male, if I didn't say so), who was just reaching for the doorbell again. He was nearly as short as I am, which went a long way to explaining the, unusual for me, eye-to-eye bit.

"Jamie," the stranger said crossly, "why do you not answer door?"

A muffled snort came from behind me, and I might add, from the pile of letters in the drawer.

"Jamie," said Dennis, "may I present your new partner."

"Jamie," said the gnome even more crossly, "I am coming in!"

Obeying an impulse that came from I knew not where, I embraced the gnome enthusiastically with one arm, and exclaimed, "I'm so glad you're here!"

The gnome seemed nonplussed but somewhat gingerly returned the embrace.

"I am also glad. I did not think I would be," he retorted, a little enigmatically.

Didn't think he would be glad? Didn't think he would be here? I didn't know whether to be insulted or worried.

"You go through the papers?" He pointed to the desk drawer, still clutched in my hand.

Reverting to attorney mode, Dennis inquired a little sternly, "Mr. Percheff, where have you been?"

"Hospital," was the succinct answer.

"Hospital?," three of us gasped in unison.

The gnome turned an inquiring eye on Margo.

"Forgive me," Dennis apologized, "I should have introduced everyone more formally, although you seemed to know Jamie well enough without an introduction. Mr. Percheff, this is Jamie's long-time friend Margo."

The gnome (Okay, I've got to stop that. Enough with the nicknames, I was already in hot water.) took Margo's hand, bent over it and kissed the air just above it.

"Twins of the soul," was his gnomic (I've *got to* stop that, but I can't resist a pun) comment.

"Jamie," Dennis repeated, "may I introduce Zalman Percheff, your Uncle James's partner, and now yours."

Rather than acknowledging the introduction, Percheff rounded on me with more cranky accusations. "Jamie, why do I not see at funeral?"

Taken aback for a moment, I took a couple of deep breaths before answering as evenly as possible, "I didn't know there was one."

It was Percheff's turn to look taken aback. He swiveled to glare accusatorily at Dennis.

"Mr. Percheff, at my client's request (slight emphasis), Jamie was kept entirely in the dark until well after the funeral. She didn't get the news of Mr. Olivian's demise for nearly a week."

Dennis spoke as evenly as I did, but more authoritatively. Evidently Zalman Percheff was going to take some getting used to.

"I am fool. You are grieving now you are knowing. Is too soon." Percheff's face softened, and his eyes moistened.

The papers in the drawer actually giggled. I began helplessly, "Uh . . ."

Grieving? I was holding Uncle James (well, sort of) in my left hand. I glanced first at Margo, then at Dennis, eyebrows awave. Margo shrugged. Dennis shifted from foot to foot in obvious discomfort.

Uncle James?

Your secret is fast becoming a YouTube performance, my dear—and going viral, I might add.

I gave a little squeak at Uncle James's evident familiarity with technology, and then was ashamed of myself. He wasn't some old coot in the backwoods. He was, or had been, an up-to-date businessman.

What should I do? I asked Uncle James.

My darling, (I have to say his use of endearments reminded me of my mother, to whom I was always "my baby," "my darling," or "my precious") *use your own judgment. I have always trusted Zalman implicitly, but perhaps that was a failure on my part.* The last contained a hint of bitterness.

"Mr. Percheff," I ventured.

"Uncle Zalman," he corrected, "we are old friends."

"We are?" My eyebrows met my hair.

"I am watching you grow up. Always beautiful, from baby. Always so smart, so capable, not always wise."

Snorts all around this time, including Dennis.

I was confused, "How . . . ?"

"Your uncle, he show me every picture he take. I take some myself at your graduation—high school, then college."

"You were *there?*"

"Of course," was the complacent reply, "both of us, *natürlich.*"

My thoughts whirled. However, afraid Uncle James could read at least some of them, I struggled to keep them as neutral as possible.

Uncle James?

Yes, my dear?

Do you, that is, can you read my mind?

No, my dear, only when you direct your thoughts at me.

Forgive me, but that's a relief.

Especially where certain lawyers are concerned? His amusement let me know that while he might be other-worldly he obviously wasn't unworldly.

Just in general, I blushed, *no girl likes to be an open book.*

Uncle James chuckled. At that I realized everyone was staring at me, "Uncle" Zalman, in particular.

I took a deep breath (how had I gotten oxygen before this?) and nodded at Dennis and Margo. "Mis . . . uh, 'Uncle' Zalman, can we go into the office?"

He looked an inquiry but followed me without comment.

Once in the office, I carefully replaced the desk drawer. Going to "Uncle" Zalman I took both of his hands.

"Promise me, you won't collapse when I show you something."

"This is something which will make me collapse, yes? How then can I promise?"

"It's a good thing... I think," I added, suddenly unsure. This small, not young, old friend of my uncle's might respond with horror, or disgust—I couldn't predict.

"Please Uncle Zalman," I begged, "for my sake, promise me."

"Jamie, if for you, anything."

I let out my breath with a whoosh. *"Uncle James?"*

I will be as careful as possible, my dear. I don't know how Zalman will react, either.

The curtains began a gentle billow, then the objects on the desk started to rearrange themselves very slowly, but picking up speed. After that the desk drawers opened and shut quietly several times in a row, in what seemed to be a pattern. "Shave and a haircut," I swear.

"Uncle" Zalman stared with goggling eyes. Then to the astonishment of the three of us, rushed to embrace the desk with both arms, all the while exclaiming, "James, James," on his knees.

CHAPTER THIRTEEN

I dropped beside Uncle Zalman and put my arms around him, the tears rolling down both our faces. I heard sniffs from the watchers, so I knew I wasn't the only one affected by Uncle Zalman's very plain delight.

"Jamie, this is so wonderful. We have not lost him."

"You're okay with this?" I wanted to be sure.

"*Okay?* This is so beautiful, like wonderful dream."

I hugged him again. "I seem to be the only one who can hear him, however."

I wasn't sure whether that would be a difficulty.

"Of course," "Uncle" Zalman agreed, "you are favorite niece, that is how it should be."

That went well, my dear, Zalman was more a believer than I when I was alive. Uncle James made a rather rueful noise. *Naturally, I'm now a believer as well. Tell him he is to take care of you.*

"You are listening, I see. He is speaking to you now, of course, he wants me to take care of you."

"How did you know? Did you hear him?"

Uncle Zalman found that very amusing, "I don't need to. I am knowing already that is what he wants, James is saying always."

I began to think I could write "Uncle" Zalman off the list of suspects—of which there were exactly two, Uncle Zalman and Dennis. But that same little niggle I felt every time I got comfortable with Dennis, tickled the back of my mind. After all, Uncle James had made it clear he hadn't seen who hit him.

I shook my head. The picture of Zalman Percheff whacking my Uncle in some unknown location, dragging his body to a car, and then depositing him in the office, was almost laughable. I didn't think 'Uncle' Zalman could even manage that with me as the victim.

Belatedly, I remembered what my putative Uncle had said when he came in. "Uncle Zalman," I began, "you said . . ."

He cut me off. "I was in hospital, yes?"

"Do you read minds as a general rule, Mr. Percheff?" Margo regarded him with smiling interest.

"Only Jamie's." He gave a gnomish twinkle. "I know for long time. I know thinking. Of course, she need to know about hospital. Is easy to see. But *natürlich*, Uncle James more important. She hear, we do not. She is much loved family person. Uncle Zalman is second in line."

I sat back on my heels and laughed. Uncle James might not be able to read me from the other world, but in the here and now it looked like "Uncle" Zalman was more than up to it.

I turned sober immediately. He looked very frail, and I worried that his hospital visit boded something serious.

"What was the problem, Uncle Zalman?

"I think I am murder victim."

This matter-of-fact announcement left us all speechless.

Dennis recovered first, so like a lawyer. "I think you should explain, Mr. Percheff."

"I am having glass of wine . . ." gasps all around. Telephone ring, I answer, is wrong number. I come back, pick up book, pick up glass . . . then I am in hospital. Is chloral hydrate."

"How did you get to the hospital? Weren't you alone?" I was horror-struck.

"Housekeeper find. She come two times a week. Lucky, was one of those two times, was still there." He gave a wheezy chortle.

Since Uncle Zalman and I were still sitting on the floor, I rose to my feet and suggested we go back to the living room and discuss the "murder" further. Dennis helped Uncle Zalman up, raising his eyebrows as he did so. He managed to whisper to me as we filed back through the hall, "He doesn't weigh any more than you do."

Great. One more thing to worry about.

Once in the living room, I explained what I knew (not much) and what I had heard from Uncle James. I finished with the statement that Uncle James couldn't leave the desk but that we had managed to move him in a drawer.

Uncle Zalman clapped his hands in glee at this revelation, exclaiming, "Now we can take him with us, everywhere," in a seeming transport of delight.

Did that definitively rule out Uncle Zalman, or was it just a blind? I chewed that one over in my mind as Uncle Zalman gave us more details on the purported murder attempt.

When he finished—I have to admit, my mind was elsewhere—he wheeled on me, demanding, "Jamie, have you gone to safety deposit box?"

With one of my brilliant "Huhs?" I managed to convey the

fact that I had not and how did he know about it anyway? Uncle Zalman "humphed" in return.

Leaping up he ran back to the office and grabbed Uncle James's drawer, banging the door behind him. Thrusting it into my lap, he ordered, "James, tell her to hurry."

The papers chortled. *Zalman could never sit still for a moment.*

Uncle James, I thought the box was a secret.

No, my dear, only the contents.

Uncle Zalman doesn't know about the You-Know-What? Since I didn't know either, I couldn't give it a name.

I thought, at first, no one did. Obviously, I was mistaken. I never told Zalman the exact nature of my discovery, but it's only too apparent that someone knows something. If it is not Zalman, then we face a very clever opponent who has managed to discover the "discovery," so to speak.

What made you feel you were in real danger, Uncle James?

It was subtle at first, he admitted, *just a sense that things had been moved around in my office, and elsewhere. Someone was entering the house in my absence. Then it grew more obvious. For one, I had a "brake failure" much too soon after I had had my car serviced. Then my car was nearly forced off the road, in what I thought at the time was simply a case of road rage. However, put together with the other incidents, I decided was actually an attempt on my life.*

Why didn't you tell the police? I asked, appalled.

Foolishly, I felt I needed more proof. A whuff of breath (breath?!), *I certainly got it.*

Did you even guess who it was?

I confess I was hard pressed to put a name to my unseen stalker. It could have been any one of a number of people.

Who else is there, Uncle James? Dennis is the only other person I know of.

And you'd rather it were just about anyone else. Not a question.

I ignored the implication. *Well, I wouldn't like it to be your long-term partner either.*

Uncle James's tone was sad as he replied, *Neither would I.*

Well, then, who does that leave?

Only a few hundred book experts, my dear.

I choked. I hadn't given a thought to the book community at large.

Oh, my God!

It's a slightly bigger problem than you thought, my dear.

I am ashamed to say I got a little cross with my dearly-departed. *What did you get me into, Uncle James?* I asked with more than a little temper.

Uncle James sounded chastened. *I didn't mean to sound either facetious or condescending, darling.* He added with dismay, *but I can see I was stupidly naïve to think you would not be put in danger. I should have foreseen.*

I stirred impatiently. *Too late now,* then felt ashamed of myself. *You couldn't have foreseen everything, Uncle James. The murderer wouldn't necessarily expect me to know anything.*

That sounded thin even to me, so I hastily went on, *What about all those book people?*

Actually, there are only four or five whom I consider high on the suspicion list. You will meet them very soon at the conference.

What conference?

Zalman will fill you in.

I turned to Uncle Gnomish (all right, I'm a bad person) who had been waiting patiently with a slight smile, and stated on a rising note, "Uncle James says there's a conference."

"Yes, yes, at Kalamazoo. You can see BOOKS. Is big."

"Big?" I pondered the idea of something "big" in Kalamazoo. Well, it's a funny name. All right?

"Many, many scholars, dealers, many rare books, manuscripts, new ones, too. Is for Middle Ages group."

For a minute I thought he was referring to people around fifty; then realized he was talking about the medieval period. "Just for book sellers, or appraisers?" I asked.

"No, no, is for speaking, dealers try to sell."

I was getting used to Uncle Zalman's shorthand—or shortspeak, I should say.

"It's a conference for medieval scholars, and it attracts dealers, as well."

"Yes, yes, is so."

"In Kalamazoo."

"Yes, yes, is almost biggest."

"Biggest!"

I groaned inwardly. I don't think I ever felt so helpless, hopeless, and insecure. How I was going to measure up to the overwhelming mass of experts was beyond me.

"Some are librarians," put in Uncle Zalman, "they do not sell or give talk. They come to see books, hear speech."

"Wait a minute, I'm a librarian."

"Of course," Uncle Zalman agreed, placidly.

I considered it. *Hey! I have a degree! Maybe I'm not just a weak reed—I just might know something.* I grinned at Uncle Zalman. "When do we go?"

"Will be May 5."

One week away.

CHAPTER FOURTEEN

Back in my apartment, after assuring *everyone* that I would not make a move without them, and of course accompanied by Margo, I lay on my bed staring at a faint water stain that reminded me of Leonardo da Vinci—you know, beard, lots of hair, baggy eyes—and contemplated the upcoming conference. Kalamazoo? How in Heaven's name was I going to drag my entourage there? Even though Uncle Zalman would be with me, I knew Margo wouldn't let me go without her, Uncle James wouldn't let me go without him, and it looked like I had to include Dennis, as well. I set that one aside for the moment.

Uncle James had given me a short list of names which he felt might contain the one of his killer. All were respected members of various bookish fields, i.e., bookbinders, appraisers, rare book dealers, and librarians like myself—ten, in all. My mind staggered at the enormity of the task Uncle James had set for me. Of course, I would get a little help from him, and supernatural is not to be sneezed at, if I could only figure out a way to unobtrusively carry him with me. Hauling around an unexplained desk drawer was going to become more problematic than not, and didn't seem practical, besides. We were just going to have to test various objects from the desk to see what worked. A pen would be nice, I could carry that without looking unusual, although talking to it might be a different story. I blushed at the thought of Uncle James residing in my breast pocket. Uh-uh!

My lease on the apartment was coincidentally up at the end of the week, and I had notified the manager I was not renewing. I paid an extra month's rent to mollify him for the lack of notice. I—O frabjous day!—was moving into *my* house. Yeah, yeah, I know I'm overdoing it, and strictly speaking it was still Uncle James's house, but you can't rain on my parade. It was going to make consultations with Uncle James a lot easier.

Somehow, I had felt uneasy about bringing his drawer to the apartment with me, and over his objections had restored him to the desk. Not uneasy for myself, I hasten to add, but for him. Anyone, as I now knew, could gain entry to what I thought was my impregnable abode, and if they got their hands on the drawer, we could lose him forever. Just the thought of someone burning the drawer, or dropping it into the ocean, gave me chills. In the desk, where he could move around, he had a fighting chance. Or so I reasoned, never mind that it wasn't exactly intuitively obvious to intruders what the drawer contained. He agreed with me reluctantly but maintained a disapproving silence when I said goodbye.

I had asked, and been given, the next few days off from the library, so I could pack what I needed to before the movers arrived. *My* stuff was going into storage, for the time being, until I knew what to do with it. But I had agreed with the gang that Margo and I would spend the nights in the house—sleeping under the desk, if Uncle James had had his way. Margo and I had opted for bedrooms, however, or I should say bedroom since there was only one that we knew of so far and we had agreed to share. If we hadn't, the tornado in the office would have permanently damaged the furniture. Dennis and "Uncle" Zalman had been just as adamant, so it was easier to acquiesce.

Still going over all of it in my mind, I fell asleep, to dream uncomfortably about being chased by a Deco desk brandishing an illustrated manuscript.

THE NEXT THING I knew it was light and the phone was ringing. After fumbling dazedly in my purse, I squinted one eye at my phone and saw that it was my mother. I held it to my ear, and said, "Yeah, Mom," while still trying to get both eyes into the "open" position.

"Jamie, we were driving down the street on our way to the Dalton's and saw you letting a weird-looking man into a strange house! Your father seemed a little disturbed."

"Yeah, Mom," I repeated and fell back on the bed with a muffled wail. I knew I had to face the music, sooner or later, but later was my favorite word.

"I'm off from the library, today, Mom. I'll be by in a little while and give you the story. I'm . . . uh . . . looking at a new house. 'Bye."

I hoped that would hold her for at least long enough to let me get dressed. Mom doesn't get agitated too often but when she does, she's like a remora; you can't pry her off. And, let's face it, a few weird things have been happening. She doesn't know how weird, but she's maternal, not stupid, and she was still waiting for some explanation for the attack on me.

I reeled into the shower where a few minutes of cozy, warm, downpour gave me a new lease on life. Tenuous but new, and I padded into the other bedroom to shake Margo awake. She moaned, resisting, until I said, "It's Mom!" Both eyes flew open—she's known my mother a long time—and she sat bolt upright, grasping the cause instantly (I told you she was a witch).

"She knows!" she announced in a sepulchral voice.

"Not exactly, but something like that."

"Should we stop and get Uncle James?" was her unexpected query.

"Oh, my God!" I sat on the bed and contemplated one more revelation. "No, just the least amount of facts we can get away with."

She grinned, "The truth, nothing but the truth, but not quite whole?"

"You got it."

We got ready, grabbed a fortifying bite at IHOP, and drove to my folks. I had rehearsed exactly what I was going to say, but I knew my mother, too. She winkles the whole story out of you no matter what *you* want. I suspected her of witchy genes, as well.

AT THE HOUSE, I gave Margo a despairing look, inflated my lungs, and prepared for the interrogation—take that, KGB. Mom had seen us drive up and was standing at the door. She gave Margo a hug and kiss, and said to me, "Brought your back-up, I see."

Margo said, "Hi, Mrs. Olivian," (no first names for Mom) and rolled her eyes at me.

"Is Dad home?" I devoutly hoped not.

My mother actually twinkled, "No, I sent him on some errands."

She didn't need ESP to know what I was thinking. If anybody was going to be hysterical, it was going to be Dad. Mom may be a tsunami, but my father is Mount St. Helens.

Mom marched us to the living room, and ordered, "Talk."

She looked shrewdly from Margo to me. "And, no carefully rehearsed scripts. That's for your father."

I looked at Margo, who shrugged and rolled her eyes, again. It was just like junior high. Yes, I'm aware it's middle school, now.

I debated several approaches and at last, gave up. "Get your purse, Mom," I finally said. "We're going to look at a house."

She got that thoughtful expression again and complied.

CHAPTER FIFTEEN

"Mmmn," nice," Mom murmured as we pulled up. "Is this the house you're thinking of buying?"

"Hold on, Mom. Wait until you see the inside." For some reason I couldn't pinpoint, I had a hunch that would go a long way toward explanation.

I opened the door and motioned her in; she stepped across the threshold and halted as though she'd run into a wall. Taking in the surroundings slowly, she wandered from table, to chairs, to sofa; touching each piece as though greeting old friends. In particular, she stopped before a painting of a bucolic scene that evoked an earlier time, a gentler place. With shock, I realized it was one of Mom's—no mistaking her style. Margo made a faint sound, and I knew she had made the same realization.

"James," was Mom's only word, fat tears rolled down her face. Instant understanding.

"He left it to you, Jamie. That's why you had a lawyer. He always said..." she stopped abruptly and clamped her lips together. After a minute she continued," and, of course, that was Zalman, I just didn't recognize him immediately from the back—it's been a while since I've actually seen him."

"It looks like I'm not the only one with a story, Mom," I observed, taken a little (well, a lot) aback.

"I'll show you mine, if you show me yours," Mom twinkled again.

Margo and I both waved our eyebrows.

"Mom!" I exclaimed, shocked. She never says things like that.

Mom gave me an exasperated glance and rolled her own eyes.

"It's obvious that James has passed on," she observed briskly, all evidence of tears gone. "And, I suspect, it wasn't heart failure," she followed up with, to my surprise.

"Come in the living room and sit down, Mom." I led her in and waited until she sat.

"He was murdered, Mom. Someone hit him on the head." It's always best not to beat around the bush with my mother.

Her face lost its color, but she said with an astonishing steadiness, "I was afraid of that."

"Oh my God, Mom! Why?'

"The book business is not as benign as you think, Jamie, and James was involved in transactions that meant a lot of money to some people. And, there were other . . ." she broke off.

I realized I didn't know Mom nearly as well as I thought. Again, it was best not to beat around the bush, "He also left the business to me, Mom."

Her face got even paler but she surprised me once more by saying calmly, "He must have had confidence in you, Jamie."

"Yes, Mom, that's what *he* keeps saying," I spoke totally without thinking.

My mother's gasp, and Margo's alarmed squeak, told me just what I'd done wrong.

I flopped back in my chair and put both hands over my eyes just as I did when I was little and Mom caught me misbehaving.

"Jamie Whitehall Olivian!," she used the same voice, too.

Margo slapped her forehead two or three times and dissolved into "I-knew-it" laughter.

"I don't think your father needs to know this, just yet." Not a question. The speculative gleam in her eye turned into a searchlight probe, pinning me in its glare.

I bowed to what I had known all along was inevitable, I could never keep anything from Mom if she wanted to know. To give my mother more than credit, there were a lot of things she just didn't ask.

"Let's go into the office Mom." I felt like that was the most popular phrase of the moment. It felt like I'd said it more often than "hello" and "goodbye."

One more time my mother stepped over a threshold and froze in place. Without any prompting from me, she repeated just that single word, "James."

The curtains began their gentle sway and my mother gave the most brilliant smile I have ever seen on her face. Whatever she heard, or saw, or felt, produced a radiance I had never seen when she looked at my Dad. Both Margo and I were spellbound and then Mom whirled abruptly and almost ran from the room. I started to follow, but Margo grabbed my arm and shook her head furiously.

There wasn't a peep from Uncle James for a *really* long minute, before a tremulous voice in my head commanded softly, *Talk to your mother, my dear.*

I glanced at Margo who nodded doubtfully, and we absolutely tip-toed back to the living room. I peeked around the door to see Mom staring at nothing, but instead of the violent emotion I expected, she was just smiling slightly and completely relaxed. She turned her head and beckoned us in.

"Sit down, you two . . . yes, you as well, Margo. You might as well hear the whole thing, under the circumstances."

We settled ourselves on the couch like two *very* well-behaved children and stared raptly at Mom.

CHAPTER SIXTEEN

"I'll make this short," she stated firmly.

"Before your father and I were married, James and I, well . . . we were engaged. I loved him deeply, and he loved me. However, circumstances arose which made it necessary to call off our wedding plans. Your father had always cared for me, and after the broken engagement, I learned to care for him as much . . . Just in a different way," she added after a moment.

From the look on her face, Margo was seeing something I wasn't.

Mom went on. "When your father asked me to marry him, I said yes. James should have been the best man, but . . ." she hesitated, then resumed with conviction, "I was the only *woman,* James ever loved."

My breath came out in a loud whoosh, when I realized what she was saying. I didn't know I was holding it until then.

Mom looked at me soberly. "Your father is a good man, Jamie, but he just couldn't adjust to the idea that *his* elder brother . . ." she sighed, "it was very different in those days."

Thinking of some recent events, I wondered if "those days" were actually behind us. I was torn by a welter of emotions, sympathy for my Dad, along with contempt, understanding, and uppermost, shock.

"And . . . Uncle Zalman?"

Mom raised an eyebrow at the "Uncle," but merely said, "Zalman always loved James, but they weren't . . ." she trailed off. "There was someone, of course, or maybe more than one," she added wryly, "but I never knew who, James was very discreet. However, your father and I never," her eyes were mournful, remembering, "had any contact with James again."

Margo cocked her head at my mother's careful wording. *Someone* had kept Uncle James up to date on my milestones, and I doubted it was the *Los Angeles Times*.

"We *must* keep this . . . some of this . . . from your father, Jamie."

"Ye Gods, Mom, that's a job for Obvious Man! At the rate we're going, we'll be having an Uncle James block party before long. You, me, Margo, Zalman, and, um, my lawyer—Uncle James is getting practically as many groupies as Beyoncé."

Mom's infectious laughter pealed out, then she frowned and said primly, "About your lawyer . . ."

I cut her off at the pass, "Yeah, Mom, I know, he's out-of-this-world, but I'm not throwing myself at him, yet."

Margo's face assumed a bland, utterly unconvincing, neutrality.

Pursing her lips, Mom declaimed sententiously, "Handsome is a handsome does."

A gurgle from Margo made her grin.

"I know you're a big girl, Jamie, but your prior experiences have been . . ."

"Unfortunate," I finished for her. "I know that, Mom, and I'm being *fairly* careful. Especially under these circumstances—murder by a person, or persons, unknown, that is. However, it was Dennis who discovered a way to get Uncle James out of the office."

"Out of the office?" my mother looked bewildered.

"Sorry, Mom, I forgot to explain. Uncle James can't leave his desk for some reason."

"He was murdered in the office?"

"Actually, and this is the strange part (oh, right, the *strange* part). He thinks he might have been killed somewhere else and brought back to his office to make it look like he died there. Maybe," I added doubtfully.

"He doesn't know?" Mom's eyes widened.

"He can't quite remember."

Mom looked puzzled, "But wouldn't the lack of blood have been a . . . ahem . . . a giveaway of the, um, unusual death?"

I started to laugh at Mom's avoidance of the "M" word, but broke it off as something struck me.

"It seems there *was* a lot of it, Mom. That's really weird. Uncle James thinks he was killed somewhere else and shouldn't he know best? Of course," I added, again doubtfully, "he can't be sure, which is even weirder."

"I've read," Mom began. I gave her a look and she continued, "well you know I like to read everything." She grinned, "Anyway, I've read that it may be, that when we first arrive on the other side, it takes a while to recover all of our memories. Of course, it's possible he was just unconscious," she finished.

"Mom, he said he was dead! Besides, he's in the drawer!" Then, I wondered. Do the dead always know? Is there a period of confusion, or doubt? And where do those authors get their information, anyway?

My mother pondered the blood question, "Did they analyze the blood? Do they know it was his?"

"I don't know," I acknowledged. "I got the information from Dennis, and he didn't seem to know all that much about anything."

After a moment's thought I added, "What's also weird, they didn't even do an autopsy, just 'assumed' that Uncle James had a heart attack or stroke. I really don't understand that part; you'd think any self-respecting medical examiner would want to be sure."

Mom agreed. We shelved that for the time being.

I flashed on Sergeant Rundown, oops, Randon. How could I find out about the blood without giving away the fact that I knew what I couldn't possibly know? Unless, that is, I was the perp.

I mulled that for a few minutes, until inspiration struck. "I think I have a plan to find out, Mom," I offered.

"The Sergeant?" Mom asked doubtfully. Mom's no dope.

"Yes, he told me to call if I remembered anything new. I think I just 'remembered' something."

"You're not going to lie to him, are you, Jamie?"

"No, Mom." No reason to tell my mother that I wasn't going to give a completely straightforward story, either.

I whipped out my phone, dialed (Tapped? Thumbed? Fingered? We need some new vocabulary) the Sergeant, and made an appointment for later.

Meanwhile, my mother, who had been doing some heavy thinking, said, "We do have to tell your father that his brother is dead, and that you are the only heir."

I quailed at the thought. "What will Dad say?"

"I don't know, Jamie, but he has to know; we cannot keep that much of the news from him." She averted her eyes, and continued, "We just won't tell him about the murder, yet. Although..." she trailed off, obviously thinking of the attack on me. Squaring her shoulders, she decided, "We'll just say you've bought a house, for the time being, and... ," she hesitated, "maybe we'll leave Zalman and the business out of it."

I stared at my mother with the weird feeling that I didn't know either of them at all.

I decided I had to go back to the apartment and change; I was getting so caught up in this whole mess that I was giving scarcely any thought to my wardrobe. Well, I *was* dressed in Holly Golightly Capris, with a wrap shirt tied at the waist, and ballerina flats. Very Audreyish, I felt, but I needed to look business-like, and eminently sane, to meet Randon.

"We should say goodbye to Uncle James, Mom, I have to do some things before I see the Sergeant."

Mom turned a surprisingly fetching rose-color, tittered nervously, and suggested I do the honors. Just *what* had transpired with Uncle James?

CHAPTER SEVENTEEN

Skewering me with his disturbingly intense gaze, Detective Sergeant Randon rose politely, and waved vaguely at an uncomfortable-looking chair. The feeling, that he was a little too much like my mother for comfort, swept over me. Before I'd even gotten started on my slightly expurgated story, I wanted to confess all—even if I wasn't sure what *all* was.

He prompted me, "You remembered something, Ms. Olivian?"

"Whitehall."

He blinked, but made no comment.

He prompted again, "It was?"

"I forgot about the letter."

He looked expectant, but again made no comment. I *knew* this was a tactic guaranteed to make the suspect talk, but it worked fine with me.

"I got a letter from Uncle James after he died," I babbled, "uh, that is the letter came to me after, that is, I received it after his death." So much for preparation.

"Written before, I assume." Rundown was enjoying this.

"Of . . . of course."

"Ms. Ol . . . er, Whitehall, everyone who talks to the police acts as though they've got something dastardly to hide. Take it easy and just give me the facts."

Just the facts, Ma'am. I would have loved to see the look on Randon's face if I "gave him the facts."

I sucked in and started again. "When I met with my uncle's attorney, who is now acting in my behalf . . ."

Quizzical grin. I ignored it with dignity and went on, "He gave me a copy of the will, and there were some other papers, as well. One of them was a sealed letter from my uncle, stating that he had some misgivings about his safety. He didn't name any names, but he sounded, that is, the letter sounded very worried."

"You say the letter was sealed?"

"Yes, with what I was told was Uncle James's personal seal."

"You hadn't seen it before."

I hesitated, feeling my face redden, "I hadn't even seen Uncle James."

Randon made an inarticulate sound.

"You're telling me again you didn't know the man?"

"I'm afraid that's true."

"He left you everything," flatly.

"It's complicated."

Surely, I was too young for hot flashes, but I felt like I was sweating under the third degree. Remind me not to go in for a life of crime.

There was silence; then I finally said, "He loved my mother, but she married my father." It wasn't the whole story, but it was true in the essentials.

"And you look like her." Could the Sergeant be a romantic?

The Sergeant reverted to all business. "So, the envelope was sealed and didn't look as though it had been tampered with?"

"Yes."

"But he was concerned for his safety?"

"It sounded like he was very sure."

"Do you have the letter, Ms. Whitehall?"

A literal chill ran down my spine—*flaw in reasoning, Jamie*—I couldn't let him actually *read* it. I grasped at a ridiculous straw. "I, uh, burned it."

"Umph?"

"I know you'll think this is crazy, but my best friend thinks she's a witch, and she said I should burn it to get rid of the bad luck." Silently, I asked Margo to forgive me.

Randon passed a hand over his forehead, as I plummeted in his estimation. Okay, we just threw out business-like and eminently sane; how about flighty and dim-bulb, instead?

"Didn't you think, just for a minute even, that you were destroying possible evidence?"

I didn't have to be an actress to look really uncomfortable.

"It looked like an accident . . . I didn't think . . . I didn't know him then."

Rundown cocked his head. "And now you do?"

"Yes . . . no . . . er, that is, I've talked to his friends. That is, his partner, and, er, others." I was losing credibility with every "er." "Everyone says he was not one to go off half-cocked, or imagine things. My mother . . ." I broke off, feeling a fresh burst of sweat trickle down my sides.

"Mmmn?"

"She hasn't seen him in years, of course."

"Of course."

"Well, she said, *when* she knew him; that he was always reasonable and very successful at his business. Not one to have flights of fancy."

"Mmmn."

I wondered if Detective Randon could see through my handbag to my crossed fingers.

CHAPTER EIGHTEEN

I gritted my teeth and started over, "At the time I read the letter, Sergeant, I was hearing about my uncle for the first time. I'm sorry, but I jumped to conclusions and dismissed his concerns as fanciful, but there was no hint of foul play, then."

I was getting in deeper and deeper with my completely made-up story; I was even starting to believe it, myself. "And, since he was not a young man, it was perfectly possible that he had a dizzy spell, or a slight stroke and fell against his office desk."

"He didn't, of course."

My eyebrows did their usual, and I was gripped with excitement. Now was my chance! Well . . . maybe.

Trying to look as stupid as possible—*not too hard*—I ventured confusion. "I don't understand."

"Didn't hit the desk. As a matter of fact, we, that is to say I, think he may not have been killed there at all."

I repeated the confusion act. "But I understood there was . . ." I added a moue of distaste for verisimilitude (okay, I like words, too), "a great deal of blood."

"Not his," was the succinct reply.

I couldn't believe my luck. He told me! And I didn't even have to manufacture a reason for asking. My confusion was real, this time, however.

"But, if it wasn't his, whose was it?'

"Beef."

"Huh?" My voice hit the stratosphere.

"From a cow."

"But that's crazy! Beef blood!" I reiterated, unbelieving. "That just screams Murder! And if he wasn't killed there, why would the murderer want to call attention to the fact? Why would someone use cow blood? Wouldn't they know you might analyze it? Since there wasn't an autopsy, he might have gotten completely away with it." I ran out of breath.

"That was one of those 'inconsistencies' I mentioned," the Sergeant drawled out, sardonically. "Murderers don't always think straight, but I suspect it was just a red herring—to buy time."

"That meant the murderer had it planned in advance. You don't just go around with cow blood. Why were you called, in the first place?'

"Ordinary police procedure, in deaths of this kind."

"I still don't understand why there was no autopsy," I complained.

"The medical examiner asked your uncle's doc for his medical file. Turns out he hadn't met your uncle either, just taken over the practice from your uncle's long-time doc. Found some papers indicating your uncle had a heart condition. Medical examiner just gave them back with no comment and signed off."

I blinked and swallowed two or three times. It took every

bit of willpower I had not to blurt out that I knew, for a fact, Uncle James had nothing of the kind.

"Then what made you decide to analyze the blood anyway?"

"Neat body."

"Huh?"

Randon's mouth quirked a bit, "The body was too neat. Didn't look like a fall, looked more like he was laid out—an 'arrangement,' if you will. Sometimes I have to go with my gut, because sometimes what *looks* isn't what *is*. I get the same feeling about you, Ms. Whitehall, what *looks* isn't necessarily what *is*. You're holding back, in spite of the 'I'm just a tiny idiot' pose. Where, for instance, did you get the idea that he 'wasn't killed there,' and there was 'a great deal of blood?'"

I ran my hands through my hair; both annoyed ('tiny' really pushed my buttons, funny that 'idiot' didn't bother me a bit) and panicked. Then had a flash of inspiration. I ignored the implications of his last question, beyond a curt "Assumption," and responded to his earlier appraisal.

"I didn't want to bring my mother into this," I knew Mom would have been absolutely upfront, so I didn't feel guilty (almost) about throwing her under the bus. "She's been in contact with Uncle James from time to time. That's how he knew so much about me."

"Ah."

"No, Sergeant, it's *definitely* not what you think. Uncle James was not . . . that is . . . he was . . ."

"Gay."

I jumped in surprise.

A slight smile quirked the corners of Randon's mouth, "It seems you *didn't* know what I was thinking, Ms. Whitehall."

I blushed to the roots of my hair.

"I am a detective, Ms. Whitehall, and I do, occasionally, detect. For one thing, your uncle's partner—very uncomfortably, I might add—told us. Evidently, he didn't want to bring your mother into it, either," again a sardonic note sounded in his otherwise neutral statement.

"Uncle Zalman?" I squealed. *Why hadn't he told me?* "When?"

"When we interviewed him regarding *his* episode with chloral hydrate."

I sank back in my chair, chewing my lip. *Buy time! Beef blood! Everybody knew about Uncle James, except me.* I pouted mentally with that last thought.

Out loud I said, "Uncle Zalman didn't say anything about it."

"And that makes you cranky," Randon observed shrewdly.

I affected a dignified silence, which was hard to do under Randon's penetrating stare.

He made another observation which surprised me. "You're a thinker, Ms. Whitehall, and you want to have all the pieces of a puzzle in your little hands. That's why you do what you do— it puts you close to a lot of answers."

I goggled at him. This was what? Our second meeting? Third? Furthermore, one was under what one might call "difficult circumstances." Where had he come up with that totally right-on assessment of my personality?

He continued, "That's also why I don't believe for a New York minute, that you burned your uncle's letter." He started shuffling through the papers on his desk. "When you decide to tell me the truth, let me know."

I was dismissed.

CHAPTER NINETEEN

stood outside the Station feeling stunned *and* chastened. I had learned a great deal about Sergeant Randon (I couldn't think of him as "Rundown" ever again—ell, maybe), police procedure, and myself in the bargain. I had also learned some things I wanted to know, and some that really pissed me off.

Uncle Zalman must have known that Uncle James wasn't killed in the office, I paused in that thought. *No, the police would never have told him about the beef blood. Right? They asked him about Uncle James's relationships, and he wanted to protect Mom. Right? Aaaaand, he wanted to protect me, in case Uncle James hadn't told me anything. Right? Aaaaand, Uncle James wanted to protect me, in case I was more like my Dad than my Mom. Right?* Somehow, that last thought *really* pissed me off, although I wasn't sure at whom.

Okay, let's go over it again. The cops suspected that Uncle James might have been killed somewhere else. The beef blood only added to the complexity of the puzzle. "Buy time," Randon had said—*to establish a foolproof alibi, of course, and presuming our killer isn't a vampire* (something that it would not have occurred to me to consider in the past, but now—who knew?) *cow's blood would probably be easier to get than human.*

I pondered that one, realizing that I had absolutely no clue how to get *my* hands on a fifth of Old Bossy. Was the killer a butcher on the side? Somehow that didn't jibe with my picture of rare book dealers.

How was I going to satisfy Randon regarding Uncle James's letter? *Why was I even asking myself?* I already knew I was going to forge a second one. I wondered if Uncle James had enough ectoplasm to sign it; if so, technically, it wasn't forgery.

I was suddenly aware I was now standing beside my car, keys in hand, with no memory of getting there. *Earth to Jamie! A little more alertness, if you please.*

I felt a little tingle at the base of my skull—something wasn't right. I couldn't put my finger on it until my eyes focused on the slightly open door to the gas cap, which was more than just slightly askew. Being a trifle OCD, I knew I had replaced both precisely when I filled up. On the other hand, did I know? I could have been distracted for a moment . . .

The tingle grew. Feeling rather foolish, I turned on my heel and marched back to the police station.

"So soon, Ms. Whitehall?" was Randon's sardonic query, as I was once more admitted to his presence.

Tongue-tied, I just stood, not knowing whether to say anything, in case he just laughed. On the other hand . . .

His gaze sharpened, if that was possible, "What happened?"

"It's my car . . ." I began.

He was on his feet instantly, "Show me," he ordered.

Back at my car, I tried to make light of the whole thing.

Randon, however, was like a California condor spotting a ground squirrel.

"When did you last fill-up?

"This morning."

"You replaced the cap carefully?"

"I'm *almost* positive I did. I'm a tad obsessive that way—jars, bottle caps—you know," I finished lamely.

"I'll bet," was the amused response, "and closets just so, and pencils just so, just not crucially important letters."

I felt like a stand-in for a Target commercial. Jamie White-hall, big, red-faced, bullseye, that's me.

"It may be nothing, but we're going to have your car checked out, just in case. I can call you a cab, or send you home in a squad car, or . . ." He shifted his feet, looking suddenly unsure, "you can wait half an hour, until I get off, and I'll take you home. Just to make sure you're safe, of course."

I almost laughed out loud. Unbeknownst to me, had I morphed into a somewhat mature *femme fatale*? Randon couldn't hold a candle to Gorgeous for looks, but there was a Robert Mitchumy sort of aura (I'm a TCM fan) about him that had its appeal.

"That would be very kind, Sergeant Randon," I said formally.

He smiled, becoming a whole new person. Again, it didn't have the wattage of Gorgeous, but there was a kindness in it that Dennis's lacked.

Back in his office, he astonished me again, by offering me a cup of tea.

"I have Earl Grey, or Blackberry-Sage."

My head spun—real tea! Whoda' thunk it.

"I'll have Earl Grey, please."

He left the room and returned with a small kettle, which he

perched on an equally small hot plate. Reaching into his desk, he pulled out a tea pot, an infuser, two cups and a pair of spoons.

"What, no rabbit?"

He gave a short bark of laughter. "Regardless of what you've heard, Ms. Whitehall, cops come from homes, too."

"No, no," I protested, "it was just … It was like one of those circus acts, where all the clowns get out of a tiny car. I didn't see how you could get all that in your desk."

He smiled a little shamefacedly, "It's supposed to be a file drawer."

This time I did laugh.

◆

MOM, WAITING at the apartment, gave the Sergeant a questioning look as he dropped me off, but simply bestowed a gracious smile on him and thanked him for his thoughtfulness.

The Sergeant looked a bit deflated at not being able to do the Supercop bit and search the premises, but left it at, "Nice to see you again, Mrs. Olivian. I'll be on my way," and promptly went on that way.

I'm not sure what I expected. The ride home had consisted mainly of small talk; only veering once or twice toward the crime, and then just going over already covered ground. No further mention of the letter. No "how about dinner?" No nothing. I decided I was mistaken and his only interest was that I was safe. I "humphed" mentally.

Mom, of course, wanted to hear the whole story, so I filled her in on our conversation—leaving out the gas cap scare, naturally. I turned it into a dead battery and a tow job.

When I finished, Mom sat and stared for a bit, before

stating the obvious, "Beef blood! That doesn't make any sense at all, Jamie; not only does it say murder right out loud, but it immediately calls attention to the fact that he was killed elsewhere."

"That's what I thought at first, too, Mom, but then I realized the killer didn't want an alibi to be somewhere else, but one to be at Uncle James's."

Mom gave that convoluted logic some thought, "In other words, you mean the murderer might have wanted to be seen at James's home, so that he couldn't have been killing James somewhere else? But that still begs the question of why he wanted it to be known as murder, no matter where he was."

"Yeah, I guess that's what I mean. Really over-complicated, don't you feel?"

"Yes, but it's working so far as a confusion herring. The papers in James's file, that's another herring, how could they have been there? I know from Zalman," she reddened slightly, "that James was in excellent health, and had nothing wrong with his heart." She waved her hand in exasperation.

Changing the subject suddenly, Mom inquired, "Isn't the conference next week?"

"Yes, Mom, and yes, I know you want to come—I'm going to have more groupies than Lady Gaga."

"You just won't have the shoes," observed Mom, dryly. No fleas on Mom, as my Grandma used to say. "Who-all are you expecting?"

"Well, Margo, Dennis, you, Uncle James if we can figure it out, and Uncle Zalman, of course."

For some reason, the list struck Mom as unreasonably funny, "Which one of us has to carry the amps?" she sputtered, followed by another gale.

"Yeah, yeah, Mom, hilarious."

She attempted a straight face, "How did you say your lawyer was managing the time off?"

"He's supposed to be handling some necessary legal work."

"And Margo?"

"She's taking some unused vacation days. Why will Dad think *you're* going, Mom?"

"I've already explained to your father that you were going to your first professional conference since you got your degree. I told him I wanted to see what that would be like, since it would be nothing but medievalists, and how you were going to handle yourself among them. He just said 'Mother Hen' and clucked. I thought it went rather well," she said smugly.

It was my turn to be amused.

IN BED LATER, I considered our rather over-the-top group outing to the conference. Not being the independent, do-it-all-yourself star of a suspense novel, I had no objection to traveling with a posse. Nevertheless, I gave that matter some serious consideration, since my posse consisted of a desk drawer, my seventy-year-old Mom, a would-be witch, and two possible murder suspects. I fell asleep, picturing the desk drawer assuming a Kung Fu pose.

CHAPTER TWENTY

I took no part in the preparations for the conference—obviously, because I knew absolutely nothing about anything. Zalman and Uncle James had extended confabs, however, chewing out every last detail at what seemed to me excruciating length. How? Well, Uncle Zalman threw questions at me, and I channeled Uncle James, who threw questions back at Uncle Zalman. I felt the way Wall must have felt with Pyramus on one side and Thisbe on the other.

I fell into bed at night, exhausted, with my head reeling. How was I ever going to catch on before I was retirement age? The realization that my uncles were considerably older just depressed me. I consoled myself with the thought that this was my first week on the job, and that they'd been doing it for a lifetime. Didn't help.

THE TRAVEL-TO-the-conference day finally dawned after one of the longest weeks of my life. Mom, Margo and I had all spent the night at Uncle James's (mine, mine, mine), and Uncle Zalman arrived promptly on the dot of three hours before our flight. Dennis surprised us by showing up with a stranger.

The "stranger" turned out to be Dennis's father, Ackbury, Sr.—not at all like Dennis. Short, a bit thick-set, although not fat, just squarishly-built; dark-eyed, silver-haired, rather bouncy. He radiated the sort of mechanical charm that seems to come with a prosperous business, along with an affluent life-style.

Dennis introduced Margo and me, and Dad made appropriate remarks, all the while eying me with an avidity I found rather off-putting, along with a less well-defined expression. Hostility? Surely not. Unless Dennis had expressed an interest in me and Dad disapproved; not something I imagined Dennis doing.

Dennis's father already knew Zalman and my mother, so no introductions were necessary. However, I noticed a coolness in their responses, not only from Mom, but from Uncle Zalman, as well. I couldn't quite put my finger on why Ackbury, Sr. left me cold, too; maybe I was picking up Mom and Uncle Zalman's vibes.

"Off to the conference, my dear?" Ackbury, Sr. made one of those unnecessary social inquiries.

Since no answer was necessary, I made none.

Undaunted, and oozing charm, he continued, "Dennis will see to all your legalities, my dear, so you won't have any worries on that score. As pretty as you are; you can just have fun, and leave the all the business folderol to him."

If he had patted me on the head, I would have bitten him.

Dennis, sensing that steam was about to come from more

than one pair of ears, hastily suggested that we gather up our belongings and get into the waiting limo. "Goodbye, Dad," he said forcefully.

Still radiating oblivious goodwill, Dennis's father bade us all elaborate goodbyes and departed. I let out my breath, unaware that I had been holding it.

"I apologize," said Dennis, "he comes from another generation."

"Another world," muttered Margo.

I "humphed" agreement, and went inside for my oversized purse. Peering into the interior, I inquired, "How are you getting along, Uncle James?"

It's a little dark in here, my dear. Funny how different that phrase sounded, coming from my uncle. *But otherwise just fine.*

I should explain that after considerable experimentation, we had managed to attach Uncle James to just one letter, *and* fold him up and put him in an envelope for safe-keeping.

As we climbed into our transportation, Mom had a sudden thought and asked, "What about your car, Jamie, I thought it was just the battery?"

"Uh," I temporized, "it needed some other things done, so I just left it until after we got back."

Mom seemed satisfied with that "explanation."

The ride to the airport was uneventful, except I felt like a teenager going to the prom. Even though I could afford it, I don't ride in many limos.

AIRPLANE RIDE—also uneventful. Dennis sat with me and gave me a little more background on his early life. His mother had died shortly after he was born, he told me, and he had never known her. I got the impression that his father was rather remote during Dennis's childhood—"busy with building up his practice" to quote Dennis. Also, that he had been a somewhat solitary child, even though he had had a long-term Nanny whom he had been fond of.

"We got to know each other better when I joined the firm," was his answer when I questioned him about their present relationship.

CHAPTER TWENTY-ONE

onference—something of a disappointment in terms of solving a crime. I met a number of Uncle James's colleagues, but none jumped out at me as murderers. Although I don't know what I expected—someone to look up from a treatise on chloral hydrate and go "Bwaa-ha-ha-ha-ha?"

On the other hand, I was sort of amazed at Kalamazoo. I guess, with that name, I was picturing a couple of gas stations, a general store, and a dingy diner *cum* beer joint. To my surprise and pleasure, the town was thriving; much of it very recent, quite a bit larger than anticipated, and had a certain charm.

The university campus was a tad industrial as far as the buildings went, but the intense green surrounding them softened the image. As a matter of fact, it was MAY in capital letters all over town. Flowers were everywhere, and every lawn was brand new. The Kalamazooans were grabbing at the end of winter with both hands and every seed they could get those hands on.

The conference spread out in more than one of the industrial-style edifices, but the book-dealer stalls were congregated together in just one. Uncle James, now firmly attached to my conference badge, kept up a running commentary on each professional person we encountered, so I surprised more than one or two with my knowledge of them and their businesses. Since all of them regarded me initially with either thinly-veiled pity or thinly-veiled contempt, it was a pleasure to see some of those expressions change (okay, so I *was* cheating. So what?).

Uncle Zalman buzzed around like a slightly demented bumblebee. However, it was obvious that eccentric as he might be, he was also afforded a good bit of respect.

Zalman may look a bit left-of-center, my dear, but he has remarkable expertise, Uncle James admonished.

I was only too conscious of my lack in that regard; although I could certainly hold my own, and then some, among the librarians. That managed to keep my ego from deflating completely. Without Uncle James, however, I would have tucked my tail between my legs and scuttled for safety when it came to the rest of the conference attendees.

I almost did, when a portly, middle-aged matron brought us what I thought was an exquisite fifteenth-century manuscript for appraisal. Uncle Zalman, with what I was sure was a devilish twinkle, said, "You do Jamie, is good practice." Uncle James's chortle was not necessary.

I took the tiny, lovely thing in my hands and gulped audibly. In my head, Uncle James said soothingly, *look it over, my dear, so I can see it, and I'll do the rest.*

I carefully turned the yellowed, parchment pages, and listened even more carefully. I must have looked like Madame Blavatsky in a trance, since I occasionally closed my eyes, the better to hear Uncle James. I, of course, had to open them again quickly so that we could both see, as well.

"Fifteenth-century Flemish," I intoned, "looks like Use of Paris; original binding but someone has cut off the sleeves at a later date and sewn them up. Some sixteenth-century insertions, this illumination and this one; probably sewed up the sleeves at the same time. Calendar missing. I would gues . . ." I pretended to think it over, while Uncle James made the calculation; and I named a price that made her bristle indignantly.

"But I paid much more!"

I shrugged. "Well, that is my opinion, but you can take it to someone else and see what they say. I'm sorry."

She huffed away.

Uncle Zalman gave me an enthusiastic hug and Uncle James gave me a spectral pat on the back.

Well done, my dear.

Uncle James, I thought it was beautiful, and worth much more.

Unfortunately, my dear, what you have to pay for them and what they can be appraised for is not always the same thing. It was lovely in some respects, the Christ in the Winepress *illumination was most unusual, for example, but had been mistreated. She would most probably get less than she paid for it, if she decided to sell. Dealers take a mark-up, my dear.* There was a hint of sly amusement in his voice. *Although prices have risen,* he added.

He went on, *Of course, if she took it apart and sold the pieces separately, she could realize a tidy profit.*

"Uncle James," I gasped aloud, causing some heads to turn in curiosity. I hastily resorted to just thinking my shock.

No, no, my dear, I wasn't serious. I have never done that, nor even suggested it. Books are as important to me as they are to you. Nevertheless, it was plain, that someone had already committed that sacrilege on her manuscript, judging by the missing calendar pages. It's even quite possible that it happened not that long after the manuscript was produced.

You mean, as long ago as the fifteenth or sixteenth centuries?

Yes, my dear, venality, or perhaps necessity, is not new. Then again, the owner at the time may have been simply 'up-dating,' if the sixteenth century insertions are a clue.

You mean making it "relevant?"

Exactly so.

It's a wonder we have anything left, I observed.

Indeed, my dear, a miracle.

"So, you're the new one," a grating voice spoke behind—and above—me. "Think you're up to it?"

Uncle Zalman made an inarticulate, but contemptuous noise, and I turned to confront Mr. Grating. He turned out to be at least 6' 4," with an impressive paunch that suggested an intimate acquaintance with either the dinner table, or the bar stool, and a florid complexion to match. He wore an expression of perpetual discontent on his face—turned-down mouth, deep grooves between his brows, and canyon-like lines around said mouth. Needless to say, I was not drawn to his charm.

"That remains to be seen," I responded coolly, "and you are?"

Another, *Well done!* from Uncle James, who was already filling my head with details about Grating.

"I'm Jack Graber, although that probably doesn't mean anything to you, *yet.*" The slight emphasis on the last word made my lip curl.

"On the contrary Mr. Grat . . . , uh, Graber, you're . . ." and I reeled off the info Uncle James was feeding me.

Grating's eyes widened, but he managed a sneering, "Then you know I'm a tough cookie."

"I'm sure you think so, Mr. Graber," I replied as smoothly as I could, "but I'm not positive which one of us you're trying to convince."

A chill ran up my spine as I realized I could be insulting a murderer, but doggone it, I really don't like being patronized. It had something to do with the fact that he had about a foot and a half on me.

Anger flared briefly in his eyes before he dismissed me with a "We'll see."

After he strode off, accompanied by my mental drum roll which tickled Uncle James, Uncle Zalman tsk, tsked, and commented, "Meshugge! Crazy to think he's hard biscuit."

I bent double with laughter and nearly sent Uncle James tumbling.

"Jamie! You are needing care."

"Certainly, Uncle Zalman," I sputtered.

AFTER THE SESSION, when we met for dinner, I described Grating.

Mom hmmmed, "An unfortunate manner, no doubt, but that doesn't necessarily make him a murderer, Jamie."

"Oh, I know, Mom. It was more likely to make me one."

Everyone laughed at that, but Margo inquired, "Any others that look good as prospects?"

"Not really," I admitted, "one or two of them I wasn't crazy about, Brigham Bryson, for example."

"Brigham Bryson," Margo echoed, "what kind of name is that?"

"One whose parents obviously wanted a girl; that's why

they hung Brigham on him," I shot back, then added wickedly, "of course, mine must have wanted a boy."

Mom gave me a light slap on the wrist, and addressed the letter, "You were named for a much-loved relative."

I don't know about Uncle James, but I did the 'red-as-a-beet' routine. Margo gave Mom an impish, all too knowing grin, which caused the same reaction from Mom.

Dennis cleared his throat, and looked a little red, himself. "This was mostly a fishing expedition, rather than a trapping one. I think we have to see them in their native habitat to get a better idea"

"Let's see," was Margo's sarcastic offering, "if you just throw in something about being a Great White Hunter; you could enter the bad Hemingway contest."

Dennis managed a sheepish grin, although his eyes flashed ice blue. "Uh yeah, I guess that came out a little more, uh, metaphorical than I intended."

Margo gave him a winning grin and he sent the full wattage back to her; which I rather meanly noticed caused her to blink several times.

"Dennis is right, though, about seeing the suspects in their natural habitat, uh, that is, work places. Unfortunately, not all of them are in the Los Angeles area." I sighed, "Graber and Bryson are, of course."

"If they're not all in the LA area, doesn't that kind of let them off the hook?" Margo wanted to know.

"They certainly could have been in town, but you're sort of right. At least, it makes it a lot harder to investigate them."

Mom shook her head, "Jamie, I remind you, it's Sergeant Randon who is doing the investigation."

"I realize that, Mom, but he doesn't know what we know;

and he doesn't know how we know it. He's going to need some discreet help."

Margo interposed, "Wait a minute, what about Specternet?'

"They haven't been all that useful, so far," I objected.

"That's because they didn't know there was going to be a murder, naturally. If they had, they'd have been looking in the right direction. All we have to do is have Uncle James ask them to deliberately look at the ones on the list who are not available to us." She beamed triumphantly.

"It might work," I conceded, reluctantly.

THE FEW DAYS of the conference flowed swiftly, and I surprised myself by actually enjoying it. With my otherworldly assistance, and I include Uncle Zalman, I was getting a (very slight) feel for the job. At least enough to feel that I had potential in that direction. Fortunately, I looked good, and appearance counts for so much, don't you think?

Since Uncle Zalman was continually urging me to look around, I went to several of the sessions, picking and choosing among the subjects that interested me—which actually turned out to be an overwhelming amount. Never having been an expert on the Middle Ages, I was blown away by the diversity of topics from which to choose. I found myself frustrated several times when three or four really interesting-sounding papers were presented at the same time in different places.

I was bemused to discover that one entire session was given over to urine—that was a must-see. The speakers were a lot wittier about pee than I would have expected—but then the subject does seem to lend itself more to humor than scholarship.

One of the papers at the session had the improbable title of "Amorous Humors, Humorous Amours, or Urine Love." Do professors make puns? Really! The artistic examples illustrating the topic were illuminating (well, I do. Make puns, that is), as well. I had no idea chamber pots figured so prominently in art.

I also spent several delirious spare moments wandering from book-stall to book-stall; slavering over the magnificent illuminated manuscripts; wishing for hundreds of thousands of dollars to purchase every one I saw, and coveting each and every new book to go along with them. Only the thought of Uncle James's wonderful library at home, kept me from demonstrating my kleptomaniac tendencies.

Mom was blissfully in her element. She had majored in French and minored in art, in college, and knew a lot more about the medieval period than I did. She amused herself by attending as many sessions as she could squeeze into a day, and brimmed over with enthusiasm every evening. Some of them we sat in on together, and I was continually amazed at how familiar she was with the subject matter.

We frequently browsed the book stalls together, too. I got my love of books from her—and was glad to see I wasn't the only one who would have stooped to larceny if possible. Since, as I said, Mom was also an artist, even though she spent her working years teaching French in a high school. So, the illuminated manuscripts sent her nearly into a state of Nirvana. Well, I guess that's the wrong word, since Nirvana is the absence of desire, and she sure was desiring.

Breaking down, finally, she bought a modest couple of single leaves, even though she disapproved of the fact that they were the product of book desecration.

She 'tsked' over it until I said, "Mom, the sacrilege has already been committed. You're saving the leaves from getting lost, or suffering further damage."

She didn't really accept my rationalization, but stopped fretting (outwardly, at least).

Margo had looked up the local covens online, and had hooked up with one of them. During the day, she managed to keep busy, like the rest of us, with sessions, book dealers, etc. She even took her turn in the stall with Uncle Zalman and me, but she was missing for a couple of our dinner get-togethers; spending those evenings with her new-found friends and returning with a satisfied expression.

Since he didn't have any real role, Dennis tended to hover, actually making himself kind of a nuisance. He insisted on accompanying me to every session Mom didn't attend, also hanging around the stall from a discreet distance, setting my teeth on edge.

I caught Uncle Zalman sending a few looks like "Get lost!" Dennis's way, but he didn't say anything.

TOWARD THE END of my stay, I had gotten a puzzling text from Randon telling me that my gas tank had been filled with sugar. He had gotten it fixed, and was sending me the bill. That part wasn't puzzling, at least. What was the point of sugar? Just a warning? *This is what I can do* message? I decided to shelve it until I got home. I had enough puzzles to contend with every conference day, as it was.

Nevertheless, it tugged at the back of my mind, and invaded my dreams. Giant sugar bowls marched like the Sorcerer's apprentice's brooms in *Fantasia.* They were menacing in their number, and ridiculous in their roundness, parading across a landscape composed of a cross between the Western Michigan campus where the conference was being held, and my former apartment bedroom (well, it's a dream, don't quibble).

I managed to put it out of my consciousness during our very active days.

WITHOUT HELP from my real (sort of) and adopted uncles, I would have been a babbling idiot, but as it was, I came across as almost intelligent. In gratitude, I planted a big, red, kiss on Uncle James's envelope where he resided at night, eliciting a *tee hee* from inside.

The last couple of conference days gave me a surprising feeling of actual competence; and I came to like a number of my literary compatriots, with the exception of Grating. He seemed to be everywhere I was, constantly dropping sneering asides along with hints that *he knew that I knew*, something more than I was letting on. Since that was actually the case, I wondered how he could possibly have guessed.

Brigham Bryson also "bumped into" me repeatedly, so repellently unctuous I felt I needed a shower after every "casual" meeting. He, too, continually made reference to some "deal" he felt he had. Uncle James assured me he was unaware of any such thing.

At the final session, I was surprised again by the fair number of acquaintances I had made who came up to shake my hand, tell me how sorry they were, and how glad they had met me, since they felt I was a worthy successor to Uncle James.

"It's all you, Uncle James. Without you I'm nobody," I unconsciously said aloud.

Jamie! came an unexpectedly stern exclamation. *I want you to stop whining, and simply accept that you are as able as I to carry on your part of the business. Yes, there are a few things to learn, but Zalman can teach you easily.* A slight exaggeration, but I didn't point that out since I was busy cringing. *Stop acting the poor-little-me maiden—the intelligence is yours. Use it.*

Uncle Zalman cocked his head, as he saw my face go white with shock. Surveying me with shrewd little eyes, he guessed, "James give you the 'what fors'—is good. Spanking needed sometimes, even with very good child."

I put my head on his shoulder, uncertain whether to laugh or cry. A couple of deep breaths later, I straightened up, planted another kiss on Uncle James's envelope, and admitted to the whiner accusation. *You're so right, Uncle James, after all, I do have a degree, or two, and I did earn them.*

And you are self-reliant, my dear, you have picked yourself up after disappointments, more than once. Furthermore, you have never leaned on your parents, either financially or emotionally, or asked for more than their love.

Tears welled in my eyes at his praise, as unworthy as I felt to receive it, and I quickly blinked them back before someone saw. *Thank you,* I thought simply, and set to assisting Uncle Zalman oversee the packing up of our things.

CHAPTER TWENTY-TWO

I was feeling a bit depressed after the bustle, and, yes, camaraderie, of the conference. Of course, there was "Grating," that one very unpleasant fellow member. Then there was that one other slightly (very) icky Brigham Bryson. Nevertheless, if all the unpleasant people in the world were murderers, there wouldn't be many of us left. Otherwise, they all seemed perfectly normal, and friendly—if occasionally a bit condescending. Having a mentor in my purse was darned useful, under the circumstances. I hesitated to use words like damn, also under the circumstances. I had to admit however, it didn't put us any closer to zeroing on an obvious perp.

The three out-of-town Names-on-the-List had seemed inoffensive when I spoke to them. However, since I had no prior knowledge of them, I couldn't judge, nor write them off.

Once home, we set a dearly departed, or two, to keeping tabs on them, and a couple of vaguely suspicious revelations had turned up. One of the San Francisco coterie had been in town at the time of Uncle James's almost accident, and had rented a car similar to the one he had described seeing. Another had tenuous ties to a small grocery. As he owned the land and building it was on, he could possibly have come up with beef *aqua vitae.* Both ties were long shots, but possibilities. That was all we had. It seemed very little to go on, and I felt discouraged as I added the above to the meager amount, of "clues" we had already recorded.

Most of the "suspects" rated a "Why?" after their names, I realized when I went over them for the umpteenth times. Graber and Bryson were easier—greed being uppermost. Their *really* suspicious knowledge, of an unnamed object, put them at the top of the list. Of course, the same might be said for the Out-of-Towners, except they had not even hinted to me of any untoward knowledge.

Graber and Bryson went to the top; and the Out-of-Towners went to the bottom, just above Uncle Zalman.

Dennis? Well, maybe he needed money after his divorce. He lived what looked like a moderately high life-style. Also, there had to be a great deal of out-go maintaining the spectacular offices of Ackbury and Ackbury. I had to give him a central position.

The same motive might be applied to his Dad. Although, that really seemed like killing the Golden Goose, since Uncle James had been a highly lucrative client for a lot of years. He had given every evidence of continuing in that mode had he not shuffled off in untimely fashion. I gave Ackbury, Sr. a spot slightly above the bottom, but below Dennis (tough as that was).

I threw my pencil across the room in frustration, and gave it all up for the time being.

I HAD BEEN summoned to revisit those frightfully proper

offices, of my suddenly acquired lawyers, to address certain ramifications of my business inheritance. There, Dennis's Dad oozed all over me like Vaseline—smarmy compliments intermingled with subtle hints that I was too stupid to be out alone. The difference between Dennis's charm (okay, I was a little biased) and Dad's smarm made me wonder how they could have come from the same family.

I asked Dennis if he had been adopted. He gave me an odd look and hedged a bit, "Not as far as I know."

"What does that mean?" I gave him the odd look right back.

He hesitated for an extended minute, making me wonder if it was a taboo subject.

Finally, he replied, "Well, as I told you, I never knew my mother; she died when I was only a couple of weeks old. Congenital heart condition, I'm told."

"And your Dad never remarried."

"He's pretty much of a workaholic, as I said. After my mother died, I guess he just substituted that for women. He's had the occasional date, but nothing very exciting. He says I take after her, but I've never seen a picture."

"What!" I exclaimed. "He's never shown you anything?"

"No, he said he threw out everything after she died—too painful. He's apologized a few times, said he wasn't thinking ahead, just an emotional response. It's okay, I guess. I understand."

Something told me it wasn't okay, and he didn't understand at all, but I said nothing; just shrugged noncommittally.

◆

LATER THAT AFTERNOON, I spoke to Uncle James about it.

"What was Dennis's Mom like?

I really don't know, my dear, I never met her. Their marriage was evidently a whirlwind romance, at least from what I hear. Plus, they were married barely a year before she produced Dennis, and then died tragically in a matter of weeks. I was living in Paris at the time, and had partnered up with Zalman. By the time the two of us had returned to the States, the whole business was already a year in the past.

My gosh! Uncle James, that was pretty quick!

Yes, my dear, but probably for the best.

How can you say that? I was astonished at his unusual lack of concern.

There was an extended pause before Uncle James answered, *Dennis's father was always very tied up in his work, and not easy to get along with. Set in his ways from an early age. It was a surprise to hear that he had gotten that involved with someone that quickly. He did, however, often say he wanted children.* He added, a bit critically, *an heir to carry on the dynasty.*

Well, even if it didn't go well after all, divorce seems easier than death!

Uncle James clucked, ruefully. *Seeing things from the other side, as I do now, my dear, I'm not sure about that.*

I "humphed," making him chuckle.

Changing the subject, I suggested, *Uncle James, I think you should see my list.*

A list, my dear?

I mean of all the people who had possible motive, means, and opportunity.

Unfortunately, my dear, that includes a number of your newest, um, acquaintances, and . . . he hesitated *. . . possibly, your relatives.*

I felt doused in a metaphorical bucket of ice-water as a thought struck me.

Mom's been keeping in touch with you. Not a question, and not quite an accusation.

Just for the most important occasions, my dear. Zalman and I... well, we've been, Uncle James paused, as if embarrassed, *ahem, observing your progress, independently.*

You've been spying on me, all my life?

Humor, tinged Uncle James response, *In a word, yes.*

I had to chuckle at his unvarnished admission, then the chill flooded over me again.

But Dad... Dad never knew?

Jamie! When I said relatives, not for one moment did I mean to suggest your father—my brother! Uncle James, far from an idiot, had read my face correctly, and made the mental leap before I had even really formed the idea myself.

The entire desk quivered with emotion. I dropped limply in the desk chair and laid my head on the cool desk surface. A slight draft of air ruffled my hair.

I was thinking of Zalman, my dear, not either of your parents. No, your father never knew, but I don't think he would have really minded. I felt his assurance was more for his own benefit than mine. Thinking of Mom's side of the story, I wasn't nearly as sure, but I kept that to myself.

The next minute I leaped and shrieked as the desk phone shrilled right beside my ear.

"Who's that?" I yelped, aloud.

You'll have to answer to find out, Ms. Whitehall.

My uncle's use of my assumed name reminded me that I was now a business, and that this number was one of those on my new business cards.

I grabbed the receiver—it was an honest-to goodness, dial-type candlestick phone—and croaked, "Whitehall and Percheff, this is Jamie Whitehall."

A cautious and rather prissy voice said "Ms. Whitehall," doubtfully, "this is Brigham Bryson."

I grimaced, picturing that individual in my head. Stilt-like legs, hair of no particular color and a nose that approximated a beak; he resembled a wading stork, but not the cute Disney variety that brought babies. It was only too easy to remember storks were raptors, when we met.

"What can I do for you, Mr. Bryson?" I inquired briskly.

A desk drawer opened and closed with an emphatic bang. Uncle James's opinion was not exactly a secret.

Trying to keep the laughter out of my voice, I continued, "You'll forgive me, I'm really quite busy.

The prissy voice assured me insincerely that "Of course," he understood, and would "only detain me a moment."

"I did not want to take advantage of your grief, Ms. Whitehall, but after seeing you at the convention, I assumed you were taking up the reins, so to speak."

"You assumed correctly, Mr. Bryson," still brisk.

I represent a, um, a client who is *very* interested in vintage correspondence. Your uncle and I were discussing a sale just before he, uh, passed on."

"I'm afraid I have no record of that, Mr. Bryson, and my partner, Mr. Percheff hasn't mentioned it at all."

"Actually, Ms. Whitehall, he didn't know."

"Didn't know?" I let incredulity creep into my voice.

"No, this was a rather, um, discreet transaction between your uncle and myself—my client wished to remain anonymous."

Did I mention, that at forty-five, I'm old enough to have

taken shorthand? I was scribbling away furiously for Uncle James's benefit, since I didn't think I could handily explain to Boresome, uh, Bryson, why he had to be on the speaker. The phone may have looked like a period candlestick, but it had all the up-to-date bells and whistles.

"I am unaware, Mr. Bryson, of any vintage correspondence in our inventory at the moment, but I will certainly check. However, I am sure you are mistaken, since my Uncle kept excellent records, even though he could not have foreseen his demise. Even if Mr. Percheff had not been apprised, there would have been some reference to your assumed transaction."

"Oh, it's perfectly all right, Ms. Whitehall, I understand your caution, but you can speak freely. Your uncle and I had discussed the matter at length and had come to an understanding."

So that was the 'deal' he kept hinting at.

"I am speaking quite freely, Mr. Bryson, and I have no idea what you're talking about. Whatever 'understanding' you may have thought you had with my uncle was not reflected in his instructions, er, that is, his records. Good day."

"Now see here..." I cut him off before I saw what he expected me to "see here."

Well done, my dear! You certainly silenced him efficiently.

I'm a librarian, Uncle James, we're professional shushers.

Uncle James gave a slightly inelegant snigger.

I decided to go over my "list" again.

I sat for a moment, Bryson's peculiar knowledge concerning a letter made him move to the top of the list—at least for the time being—of potential murderers. His creepy demeanor didn't help, so I hoped I wasn't just being swayed by my dislike.

I also considered Grating, er, Graber. He hadn't mentioned

a letter, but his obvious hostility toward me was also peculiar. Was it just contempt for what he assumed was my inexperience (little did he know)? Furthermore, he seemed to possess some knowledge he really shouldn't have. I dismissed the contempt theory, since his frequent communications had taken on an aura of genuine menace. *You're getting overly paranoid, Jamie,* I told myself firmly.

And Dennis—in spite of his demonstrated attraction for me, and his rapid acceptance of Uncle James, not to mention his eagerness to help—what did I know of him, really? I was reminded of my earlier suspicions. Was that my intuition, which I seemed to be developing rather late in life, or just good sense (also a late development)?

How about his Dad? So different from Dennis, but parents don't necessarily turn out clones. *You are so like your mother, my dear,* the memory made me smile; Mom had all the good sense.

Uncle Zalman? Impossible. Well, at least implausible.

What about the witnesses? Although Uncle James thought they were too far-fetched to consider, they had to be on the list. The postman could probably be ruled out. It was difficult to imagine him manipulating the post office into giving him that route just so he could murder my uncle, after several years of stalking him with junk mail. On the other hand, the gardener presented a slightly less remote possibility.

The out-of-town booksters? Again, difficult to place them in the picture; but if a large amount of money was at stake, arrangements could certainly have been made. I inwardly winced at the thought of what anticipated money could do to people— tear families apart, impel to theft, abuse, murder—I shivered. I'd always had enough (more, as a matter of fact), and had never felt the need for anyone else's. So, putting myself in the mind of a killer, who might have, was almost impossible.

I gave up on chewing over the list, since it hadn't gotten us any further forward, as yet. I just brought up another source of irritation.

Uncle James, isn't it about time you told me what the letter is about—from whom, to whom, saying . . . what? Furthermore, it's sitting in a P.O. Box, and vulnerable there, but you won't let me get it, or even go near the place. How can I . . . we . . . find out who wanted it enough to kill you, if I don't even know what it is?

You know that it's a letter, Jamie—one that would not only confirm many rumors, but also, revise history. That's all I want you to know, for now.

But why is that, Uncle James?

I think—no I know—I have put you in danger, and I can barely forgive myself. I could have let sleeping dogs lie, however, you would have been in danger just by being my heir. Nevertheless, with the exception of the phrases I managed to emphasize in my letter to you and the will, I haven't—at least I hope I haven't—given anyone any indication that you know anything. I wouldn't even tell you this much, except it appears you will be getting more inquiries about correspondence. He went on sadly, *I'm afraid I am discovering that it's almost impossible to keep a complete secret, heart's dearest, so the less you know, the less chance that you will be a target.*

Uncle James, that's the most . . ." I choked off what I'd been going to say; but then, exasperation and frustration got the better of me, and I let it all out.

Uncle James, didn't it occur to you, that if you thought someone would go through your stuff and read it, it might not have been a good idea, to tell me in another letter that you had something really valuable, and you had been murdered for it?

A long silence. Then, *Oh, Jamie, I must be a senile, old idiot! I thought I had everything figured out. How could I have been such a fool! I thought no one could tamper with the seals and not be obvious. All they needed was my desk, and one of my envelopes.*

Things started slipping off the desk onto the floor, in an avalanche of dejection.

Uncle James, Uncle James, it's all right. Anyone who would stoop to murder in the first place, would simply have assumed I knew it all, no matter what you did. And the same thing goes for Uncle Zalman, I added.

I pulled out his desk drawer and gave it a hug. *Actually,* I comforted him, *it's better that they know I know. I might have told somebody. Like the police, for example, and that might provide some protection. Moreover, it's certainly better for me that you warned me in advance.* The drawer remained silent.

After some quiet consideration, I said, *I didn't have to take the job, you know, I didn't need the money and I didn't have a clue about the business.*

Why did you do it, Jamie? Wistfully.

Because you wanted me to. It occurred to me that that was absolutely true.

The papers in the drawer leapt up and bestowed on me what I was sure were the gentlest of kisses.

CHAPTER TWENTY-THREE

kay, back to the list. I filled Uncle James in on what I had been thinking without him hearing.

I'm moving Brigham Bryson to the top, I announced to Uncle James.

Hmmm. I'll admit he's not my favorite person, but I have difficulty seeing him soiling his hands.

He knew about the letter. I reminded my uncle.

It seems to have been even a more open secret then I imagined.

I think Graber knows, too, although he didn't come out and say so. He certainly wanted me to know he was a "hard biscuit" as Uncle Zalman put it.

Uncle James's laughter proclaimed his delight.

That's two, and I've decided Dennis and his Dad make four. How about the will witnesses? Doubtful I guess, but I've put them down for five and six. The out-of-town book dealers you told me about are seven and eight, even though they never inquired about any "correspondence."

And Zalman, put in Uncle James, reluctantly.

Try as I might, I just couldn't see Zalman, the Gnome King (I apologized in my head, but really . . .), knocking Uncle James on the head, dragging his body to a car, driving to the house, dragging Uncle James out again, and into the office. I said as much to Uncle James.

He might have had help, Uncle James offered.

What from, a forklift? I inquired sarcastically.

Don't get mouthy with me, young lady, admonished my uncle with obviously pretend indignation. It came to me that he must have felt we had a real relationship if I thought I could "talk back."

I reluctantly added Uncle Zalman to the list.

I would have to suffer a broken heart for eternity. Another broken heart, he amended after a pause. *For eternity,* he said again, as though I didn't get the time span the first time around, *if it were Zalman.*

I sighed. "Was the letter worth it?" I wondered that aloud, but thinking, *Another broken heart?*

I thought it worth a great deal, my dear, but one death, particularly mine, he added ironically, *and two "almosts"— never.*

How did you come by it, Uncle James?

I purchased some books from the estate of an elderly gentleman, who had no heirs who could be found. Improbable as it may sound, I found the letter while I was looking the books over. It was inside a volume of the Man in the Iron Mask. Not a particularly valuable book, but a client of mine wanted an old copy for his daughter—a child who actually likes to read, and historical novels, at that. She already had the other D'Artagnan romances, and, her father wanted to complete her collection with a fairly inexpensive, but at least vintage, copy.

I marveled at a child of that caliber, before I asked, *what were you going to do with it—the letter, that is?*

Publish, was my uncle's succinct answer.

Elaborating, he went on, *As I mentioned, the letter, if genuine, would confirm a number of historical rumors, as well as put a number of noses out of joint. Plus, make something of an uncomfortable change in history books. However, it was not such a bombshell that the course of history was going to be forever altered, etc. etc., etc. Just a very interesting curiosity, and potentially quite remunerative. I would have had it authenticated, put it up for sale, added to my reputation, along with adding to my estate for you, Jamie.*

Uncle James, don't you think we should make the letter public? Make a big deal out of authentication, and all that?

Before he could answer, another thought intruded. *Uncle James, if I write a letter, can you sign it?*

Whaa?

I explained my dilemma with Randon. *I can't possibly tell him everything, and I can't show him the real letter,* I concluded.

I see the problem, dryly. *I don't know, my dear, I can move some things, but frankly, I haven't felt the need to write.*

I visualized the "Hello, Spectral, give me Heaven" routine, and gave a little shudder.

Back to your original question, my dear, I think we should sit on things as they are for a bit longer—of course, I've already been wrong in my thinking.

I shrugged, *Maybe, you're right, it's so hard to know what to do . . .* I stopped short, sure I had a brilliant idea.

Can't we ask more of your friends to ask some of their acquaintances? The dearly departed, that is.

Ask them what, heart's dearest?

If they saw anyone around the house when you were killed? Are you positive they don't know anything?

My dear, that's one of the first things that came to my mind when I discovered I was looking down at a very deceased me. I put out what you might call an APB.

And?

As I have already said, my dear, we are not omnipotent, any more than we were in life. It seems no one was paying any attention. I can only see what I could see in life, and they can only do the same. To witness my murder, one of us had to be looking directly at the spot where I got "whacked," and there was no particular reason for that to be the case. The same thing holds true for any loiterers.

I grinned at Uncle James's use of "whacked," but heaved another sigh. *That would have been too easy.*

'Fraid so, I could hear Uncle James's answering grin. *Now as to your second question, whip up a draft of an amended letter, and we'll see how well I perform as a poltergeist.*

Well, pretty successfully, I'd say, since you managed to create quite a cyclone, a time or two.

Mmmm, yes, smugly, *although I haven't tried to manipulate anything that required, what you might call, my "small muscles."*

Well, give it a shot, Mr. Schwarzenegger. See how your ectoplasm works on little things like pens and paper.

I let Uncle James dictate a second letter to me, carefully leaving out the reference to the "valuable object." Merely (merely!) stating that he felt someone wished him ill, probably due to some vague "business transactions" which may have made him some enemies. The whole thing sounded rather weak, but added credence to my fib of having dismissed his misgivings. The part about my being "so like my mother," we let stand. Knowing what I now knew, they seemed the greatest compliment, and the loveliest words, he could have said to me.

It took several tries before my uncle could manage to make a pen stand upright; and many more before he could kind of grasp it. We had to stop more than once to rest, since both of us were becoming exhausted (evidently ectoplasm has a limited shelf life).

Finally, I suggested, *if I hold the pen, Uncle James, do you suppose you could make my hand write your name?*

An excellent idea—once more into the breach.

I felt the warmth of his hand covering mine—funny, he *felt* alive, no icy grip, or frigid aura surrounding him. I held the pen loosely in my fingers, relaxed, and made like Bridey Murphy. Again, we had a few false starts, mainly because I relaxed a little too much and kept dropping the pen. Trying to be more like Goldilocks rather than Bridey, I got it "just right" at last, and produced a fairly reasonable facsimile of his signature. I just hoped Randon wasn't going to call in a handwriting expert; I didn't want to have to explain that my uncle had a tad more difficulty writing now that he was dead.

CHAPTER TWENTY-FOUR

 tap on the office door told me Margo had returned.

"C'mon in," I directed.

"Hi, everybody," she saluted us as calmly as though she greeted the departed on a regular basis (maybe she did—who knew?) "Whass'up?"

I filled her in on what Uncle James had told me about finding the letter, and then showed her our fairly abbreviated list of suspects, only two of whom we wanted to be murderers (well, not wanted, but you know what I mean).

"How about the heir?" she asked.

"What air?" I responded, wondering if she wanted to open the windows.

"No, no," she corrected in exasperation, "heir, H. E. I. R."

"Who?"

"The heir who couldn't be found."

"We don't know if there even was one." Then I went completely still, "That's what Ski Mask was looking for! The *Man in the Iron Mask!*

The absurdity of what I had just said hit me only a beat after it hit Margo, and we screamed with laughter.

It wasn't that funny to me, observed Uncle James. Then he added, *you two are like having a gaggle of teenagers around.*

I relayed his commentary to Margo, who said, "Was that gaggle or giggle?"

We dissolved in laughter again, proving him only too right. But hey, if you can't be a teenager with the BFF you've known since your childhood, then when?

"Anyway," Margo returned to her original question, "what about the possible heir? I don't think you can count him or her out; especially after your encounter with Ski Mask."

I shook my head. "How can we possibly find a missing heir that nobody else could find, and pin a murder on him or her, when no one could find any trace of an heir in the first place?"

"I suppose it *could,*" she emphasized the word, "be just coincidence that an intruder would go for the books. It *might* be reasonable to think Uncle James *might* hide something there; but it does seem suspicious."

I nodded.

Uncle James concurred. *Anyone knowing me, or the business as a whole, would know that would be the last place any of us would stash something really valuable. That's something only amateurs, forgive me, would do. If there is an heir, he or she may have put the letter in the book in the first place—which might indicate unfamiliarity with the business, but familiarity with the collection.*

"But it's just as possible, or even more so, that the elderly gentleman did it himself."

Uncle James acknowledged that it was so.

"So, we're no farther along, because Ski Mask probably assumed you either hadn't found the letter yet, or you might have left it where it was until you decided what to do with it."

"But how did Ski Mask know?" Margo pointed out, reasonably.

"He must have put it there." I offered; then shook my head at the idea.

It's possible, but a stretch to think that I wouldn't have examined the books, or that I would just have left it lying around.

"Hmmm, yeah; but if he thought he was fast enough—and you were dead . . ."

Uncle James made a wordless, but thoughtful, noise.

Again, I relayed all of this to Margo.

"I agree with Uncle James that anyone knowing the business would know he wouldn't be so careless, but I bet Ski Mask was just covering all the bases. Or, maybe he hadn't heard the rumors going around, about the 'something valuable.' It's possible he isn't connected directly to the business, and hoped to get there first. That is . . . ."

Margo shook her head, "More than a tad confused, but, yeah, basically I get your reasoning. But," she returned to the original point, "he had to have known what he was going for, or he wouldn't have gone for it."

"You have the right of it," I conceded

"Thank you, Shakespeare."

I noticed we had stopped carefully referring to him or her, and had just settled on Him. While it was just possible that Ski Mask was a definitely burly lady, my impression was certainly masculine.

Margo addressed the air, "Uncle James, what about those guys who witnessed your will?"

I remembered, "Oh, yeah, the ones with the theatrical names—Gleason Marden and Quincy McNair."

My gardener and the postman.

"Yes, of course, but why did you ask *them*, Uncle James?"

They seemed to me to be the most impartial witnesses I could find, as well as convenient. Besides, the gardener had been recommended to me by the same gentleman from whom I bought the Man in the Iron Mask, as well as the rest of the collection.

"What! You had the *same* gardener?"

Yes, a long, dismayed pause. *Until now I never gave the connection a thought. Although, he really seems like a long shot as a suspect, since he wasn't named in the gentleman's will. Plus, they had only the barest of acquaintance, since Gleason had only worked there a short while. He was very diligent, however, which is why he was recommended.*

I gave the two of them some consideration, trying to fit either witness into the role of murderer—too many loose ends—and finally concurred.

"Well, unless the postman went postal, or the gardener absolutely hated Double Delight roses, I guess we can forget them."

Margo disagreed, although she conceded that the postman might be a long shot, "But the gardener could be the heir, so they should both stay on the list."

"I think you're getting obsessed, or you've been reading too much Dickens. Uncle James just said he wasn't named in the will."

"Of course not," she threw back with asperity, "he was unknown, and was trying to keep a low profile.

I made a poo-pooing noise.

"It could happen," she insisted. "Furthermore, how many gardeners are named Gleason Marden, I ask you?

"Only one that I know of, but that doesn't mean anything.

Mom's old gardener was Harold Dahlia, so there."

"I totally forgot about him," we tee-heed again in remembrance.

Serious once more, Margo persisted, "*Mr. Somebody* knew that letter was in the book. Even if he isn't the heir, the gardener could have seen the old man put it there. I'm almost convinced he figures in here somewhere." Seeing my dubious expression, she added, "this might be a 'knowing.'"

I threw up my hands, when she "knew," she knew. I used to be skeptical, but now I was talking to my uncle's shade as cozily as I talked to Margo. So, could I believe one and discount the other? Of course, she was only "almost" convinced, so it wasn't a "knowing" yet.

"We need to look at motives," I observed, totally unnecessarily, from the expression on Margo's face.

"Duh!" she retorted.

I ignored her, "Money seems to be the answer with Graber and Bryson, and maybe the out-of-towners. Don't you think, Unc?

There was a surprised and, I could tell, tickled pause before I got an answer.

I would think so, Jamie. I would think that was case for most of the suspects. Although, I suppose there could be professional jealousy. Graber and I have had our fallings-out, on more than one occasion. This happens in any occupation. It rarely leads to murder, however. The last was desert dry.

"Does that mean it does, sometimes?"

He produced a short hah, hah, but gave me a serious answer. *As with many professions, it's more often trying to murder a rival's reputation.*

I thought about his reputation, and inquired bluntly,

"Would it really have killed yours if everyone had known about you?"

After a bit of consideration, he replied, *It, was more or less an open secret among some of my colleagues —we recognized each other, you see. However, it was not something one ever admitted to among our straight friends. I am sure a number of them were aware, but didn't let it hinder our business relationships. If my secret came out, it might not have destroyed my career but, if they knew for sure, it would have made some people treat me in a different way.*

I "humphed" with indignation, but let the subject drop.

"What about Dennis and his Dad?"

As suspects, my dear? There was a tinge of amusement in his mental voice.

"Of course, you knew what I meant," I accused.

Again, a feeling of amusement, but after a pause another serious answer, *That, would be a little more complicated, I guess. Nevertheless, money, and prestige would apply there, as well. Dennis might want to emerge from the shadow of his father to prove he was equally successful, as well as astute. Furthermore, his father could wish to add a little more burnish to his already glowing reputation. He has always been a proud man.*

I mused grumpily for a bit about male egos, before I asked, my uncle, "Do you think there is a possibility of a missing heir?"

Margo put in, "*I* think so."

"If it's not an absolute knowing, it's just your opinion." I said loftily.

She grinned and pointed out that's all we had so far.

Uncle James acknowledged that was all too true.

I slumped. "Unless somebody walks into the office and announces, 'By the way, I killed the last person I did business with here,' it looks like that's about all we're going to have."

"Uh, huh."

On that ground, I puzzled, "The two things don't seem to go together."

"What two things?" Margo was equally puzzled, since my, "two things" didn't seem to go together, either.

"Ski Mask wanting to get the letter from the book, because he knew it was there. *And,* so many people in the business knowing about it. Sort of," I admitted. "But they didn't know it was *there.* So, how do *they* know one thing, and how does Ski Mask know something else? Why do so many people know there's a letter?" I went on, addressing my uncle directly. "You didn't even tell *me* that at first. On the other hand, perfect strangers—well," I conceded, "not strangers to you, but to me—seem to have the scoop?"

I'm at something of a loss, dearest, because I didn't even confide in my lawyers. I can only think it must have something to do with the owner, himself.

"It's the heir," Margo stated emphatically, when I relayed Uncle James's words.

"I told you, you're getting obsessed."

On another tack, she opined, "Sergeant Randon wouldn't be too pleased if he knew we were butting in."

"Mom said that, too, as you know, but Randon hasn't met Uncle James."

"So how do we drop a few hints without looking like we're guilty?"

"Thank you for the 'we.' I appreciate the support, but I'm going to be the one who looks guilty."

"No, you had to have some help. It would take two of us to move the body. Or even just position it, if this is the spot."

We enlarged on the subject until Uncle James was convulsed at our earnest discussion of whether we could have pulled off his demise.

If you two seriously intend to go in for crime, he suggested, *pick on someone your own size.*

Margo and I were both incensed at his doubting our abilities.

We chewed the list over a little more before giving it up as a lost cause for the day.

"Let's tackle it again, tomorrow," Margo said practically, "we need dinner. Fish, it's supposed to be brain food."

I shrugged helplessly. The whole thing was just too confusing. Too many of what seem to be Red Herrings. An entire school of them, as a matter of fact, and they don't seem to be brain food.

Margo shrugged, too, and Uncle James heaved a sigh (since he didn't need to breathe, that must have taken some doing).

◆

BEFORE I WENT to bed, I had a few more questions for my uncle.

Uncle James, what do you look like?

Thought you'd never ask, was the cool response.

I didn't apologize, I only continued, *I've just been picturing Dad, maybe a little grayer.*

He gave one of those for-my-benefit sighs. *A lot grayer, Jamie, my hair turned white in my late twenties. I was pretty much the same coloring as your father when we were young.*

I got my auburn hair from Dad, so I could easily picture that. Otherwise, that was about it, even I could see that I was more like Mom.

Do you look alike? I mean, did you?

He gave a snort, *tough to decide on a verb tense, isn't it? I haunt, therefore I am.*

I laughed, but persisted, *well, do you?*

More like Hal than a Deco desk, he answered facetiously, but added, *our coloring was similar, dear, but I actually looked more like your grandfather, and Hal resembled our mother. Richard and I looked more alike, I feel.*

I determined to go over our old photo albums at the first opportunity. Uncle Richard might give me some idea.

Does Mom . . . I hesitated, *did she keep any pictures of you, do you think?*

Silence. Then, *She, said not, Jamie.* His sadness was almost a third presence in the room.

I was going to tackle Mom on that one, too.

CHAPTER TWENTY-FIVE

I surprised my parents by saying I was coming to dinner for a second night in the week. I made the excuse that I had checked a book out of the library that I was sure Mom would love.

My parents had brought me up with a strong Protestant ethic, or maybe Catholic guilt, since their religious preferences differed. Due to their exceptionally comfortable position, Mom could have hired an entire staff of servants, had she cared to. Instead, she simply settled for a cleaning woman who came in once a week. As far as cooking was concerned, Mom held sway over the kitchen like Victoria over the Empire. Getting her to share recipes with me had been like pulling teeth, but she had caved reluctantly in the end. I knew that was my best shot at getting her alone, since she barely allowed Dad over the threshold.

Seizing my chance in the kitchen, I brought up the very uncomfortable subject of the pictures. Were there or were there not? When I did, Mom stared at me, unblinking for a *long* time. At last, just when I was afraid I had mortally wounded her, she admitted, "Just one, darling."

She raised her voice a bit, "I just bought a pair of the cutest shoes. Come upstairs, while the potatoes boil, and take a look, you'll be green with envy."

She hustled me out of the kitchen and up the stairs. Once in their bedroom, she continued with the ruse. In fact, it wasn't so much of a ruse. She had bought new shoes, and I *was* green.

"Try them on," she directed, still a little louder than usual, after I had let out the requisite squeals of appreciation.

While I did, she went to one of her own paintings hanging on the wall, took it down, and pulled a small snapshot out of the back, where it had been hidden under the lining. It was so much like an old movie, that for a moment, I almost laughed.

Laughed, that is, until I got a good look at the photo.

It was a picture of a bride and groom, framed under a bower of roses. I knew the beaming bride well. She was standing beside me. The groom . . .

I raised my eyes. My face must have been gray-green, because Mom looked alarmed.

"You were married!" I whispered.

"We got right up to the altar, Jamie," she responded with more stoicism than I would have thought possible, "and just a bit beyond,"

"Oh, Mom!" I didn't know which was more heart-breaking—the wedding itself, or that she *could* be stoic. If I hadn't known Mom for forty-five years, I would have expected the burden of that now long-ago tragedy to have crushed her like a used soda can.

Then I noticed something. In the dappled sunlight spilling into the bower, the groom's hair was decidedly reddish.

'My hair turned white in my late twenties' came back to me.

Dad's voice floated up the stairs, "Hey, you two, are we going to eat?"

Mom ran to the banister and called down, "Sorry, we got carried away with clothes."

Dad's laughter echoed up.

Thrusting the picture into my hands she ordered, "You take it, Jamie."

I protested, but she was adamant. "You *must*. It's what I want."

Given that, I could only accept.

The rest of the evening was one of the longest of my life. I choked down my food as though I were starving, rather than otherwise. I also kept up a running barrage of conversation that made my father give me a questioning look.

I'm afraid I'm babbling, folks," I "explained." "I'm exhausted. I had no idea owning a home was so much work. I don't know how you guys do it at your ages."

I knew that would deflect my father's curiosity.

"Our ages! Why let me tell you . . ."

I escaped while he was still defending the septuagenarians.

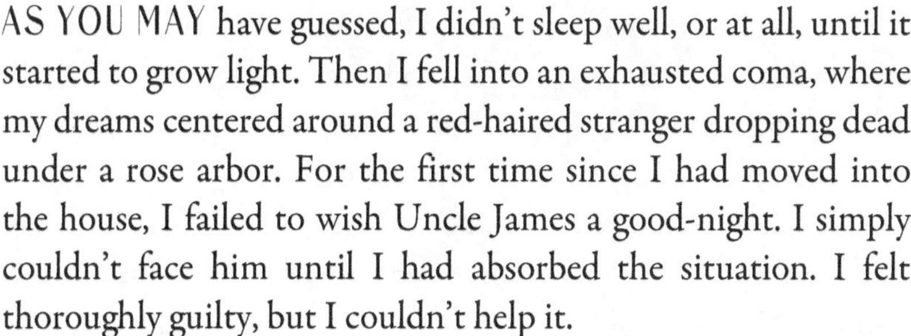

AS YOU MAY have guessed, I didn't sleep well, or at all, until it started to grow light. Then I fell into an exhausted coma, where my dreams centered around a red-haired stranger dropping dead under a rose arbor. For the first time since I had moved into the house, I failed to wish Uncle James a good-night. I simply couldn't face him until I had absorbed the situation. I felt thoroughly guilty, but I couldn't help it.

I avoided him in the morning, as well. Marking time until,

still reeling from shock and sick at heart, I could take my nice, new, somewhat-forged letter to Randon, with whom I had made an appointment for the afternoon.

Somewhat to my surprise, he was looking a bit more spruce than usual. His hair was combed, his tie was spiffily in place rather than hanging askew, and his suit looked as though it had actually seen the inside of a dry cleaner. If I had more of an ego, or had been less depressed, I would have thought he dressed up for me. As it was, I discarded the thought, and just decided he had had some sort of mildly formal police occasion. I *did* notice, in a disinterested way, that the blinds which covered the glass that looked into the rest of the station, were down.

After reading the letter over—not once, but twice—he gave me a dissatisfied look.

"So, what about this made you feel it needed to be 'burned?'"

I stared at him wordlessly. *Okay, Jamie, now what story are you going to cover your story with?* I thought. I mentally clutched at various straws, before deciding on Stuffy Ageist as the best road to drive my getting-to-be-car-full of fibs down.

"Uh, I decided it was some sort of mental problem of my Uncle's. I never met him, after all. I just knew he was old. I thought, perhaps . . ." I let myself trail off, hoping I didn't sound just as stupid as I felt.

"You though that a successful businessman, who was worth a great deal of money, was suffering from incipient dementia?"

I blinked at "incipient," somehow that didn't fit with Rundown's generally rumpled demeanor.

"Well, yes, of course that doesn't *necessarily* follow, but as I said I didn't know him. Memory loss, or possibly paranoia, can come on fairly suddenly, I've heard." I really sounded just as stupid as I felt.

Randon sat back in his chair, and gave me one of his penetrating stares. I couldn't keep myself from cringing in my chair, as though the lights of the third degree had just turned on over my head.

He ran his hand over his chin (which looked freshly shaved), never taking his eyes off me. Just as I was ready to confess to everything including the theft of the Mona Lisa, he sighed, and said, "Would you like a cup of tea?"

My explosive burst of laughter, which startled him as it escalated into near hysteria, had him leaping up from his chair. He pounded my back as he exclaimed, "Sweetheart, what's the matter?"

This sobered me immediately. Indeed, I became so sober I burst into tears. Okay, murder, especially mine, plus my *really* guilty knowledge, makes me emotional.

After a moment's amazed paralysis, Randon picked me up in his arms, carried me to his chair, and rocked me the way you would a fretful infant. I continued to weep uncontrollably. Partly in delayed reaction and partly because I knew with a dreadful certainty, that I was going to have to add him to the already out-of-control list of Uncle James's acquaintances. Furthermore, I *really* couldn't tell him about the wedding without more hysteria.

When I subsided to hiccups, he placed me gently back in my chair, and again asked, "How about that tea?"

I nodded miserably.

The tea revived me a bit, and I apologized profusely. Seeing I seemed to have successfully thrown off my psychotic tendencies for at least a few minutes, Randon inquired mildly, "Would you like to tell me anything?"

"No, but it looks like I'm going to have to. You won't be

able to solve the murder until you've met the victim."

Randon looked apprehensive, since I appeared to be regressing; but I assured him with a dismissive wave of my hand, "No, I'm not going to be hysterical again, and yes, I'm serious, but not crazy."

He continued to look doubtful, as well he should, but I went on, "Can you take a little time to come with me to the house?"

"Your Uncle James's . . . ?"

"That's the one. I need to show you . . . well, let's say there are some things I haven't quite disclosed. I promise I will behave in a sane and responsible manner." I managed a slightly watery grin.

He picked up his hat.

AT THE HOUSE, we repeated the same scenario I had already run through with Margo, Mom, Uncle Zalman, and Dennis. Any more additions and Uncle James was going to have to get a Specretary to handle his Spookmail.

Randon was silent so long I started to worry about his heart. Was he going to have a seizure? He had stood through-out the entire demonstration, but now he sank in a chair and just went on being silent. The papers on the desk curled up at me, inquiringly. I shrugged. We waited.

Finally, he regained his feet, crossed to where I was standing, lifted my chin and kissed me long and thoroughly.

Dizzy and nearly breathless, I blurted, "Uncle James says, *get a room.*"

Instantly horrified, Randon promptly doffed his battered hat and did his own profuse apologizing to the desk.

Stammering, he repeated, "I'm so sorry, Sir, so sorry... I totally forgot myself. Please forgive me for my utter lack of decorum (Decorum! That was right up there with incipient; there was more to Randon's upbringing than met the eye). For a minute..." He trailed away, in such obvious distress that Uncle James snorted, making the papers jump on the desk, which in turn made Randon jump.

Tell him I understand. It's not often you fall in love with Madame Blavatsky.

It was now my turn to be flustered. Forgetting *myself*, I yelled out loud, "No, no. we're... it's... he's..." and gave up, since I had no idea what we, it, or he actually were.

A quiet voice in my head observed *I call it as I see it, my dear*.

I didn't know whether to pump my fist in the air, or return to the uncontrollable weeping.

CHAPTER TWENTY-SIX

ack in the living room, I showed Randon the original letter with its glowing rubrics. To my vast relief he agreed with me that it couldn't possibly be entered into evidence. Still hatless, he ran his hands through his hair as he spoke; undoubtedly thinking there wasn't *much* that could be.

"Who else knows about this?' he demanded, suddenly.

Blushing furiously, I told him.

His aghast—I use that word deliberately, in this case—expression spoke volumes.

"You mean I'm number six?"

"Uh, yes, I'm afraid so."

"SIX people are talking to a dead guy?" Randon's voice had gotten a little high.

"It would seem so."

"Your lawyer knew, and not me?"

"Yes." This seemed to aggrieve him more than anything.

Randon fell with a plop onto my couch, and buried his face in his hands. I knew how he felt; everyone but Dennis had taken it much better than I had. Mom, Margo, and Uncle Zalman had accepted without so much as an eyeblink. In Randon's case, it appeared to be Uncle James's response to the kiss that convinced him.

Without raising his head, Randon mumbled, "Okay, he's dead, and you're talking to him. Now what? You think I can tell the Captain that?"

"Why do think I didn't tell *you?'*

In my mind's eye, I pictured an endless stream of uniformed cops, queuing up to get the victim's take on his own murder.

"I agree, it's awkward . . ." I began.

"AWK . . ." Realizing he sounded like a rock concert attendee, he lowered his voice, and continued with unconvincing mildness, "Yes, Jamie, it's awkward."

By mutual, if tacit, consent, neither of us mentioned the kiss bit. Now *that* was awkward.

"I don't suppose your uncle saw, heard or even smelled anything? Anything I can use, that is?'

"He didn't see anything and neither did anybody else."

"Anybody else?" on a rising note.

I explained the Spooknet, "They have to be specifically looking," I finished.

Randon had resumed his former rundown appearance. "I also don't suppose he could tell me exactly where he was when he was murdered?" he asked hopelessly.

"OMG, I totally forgot to ask him if he remembered! Wait here."

I dashed back in to Uncle James and put the question to him.

There was a moment of hesitation before Uncle James answered, *I think I was here, Jamie. At least I've decided I must have been, but as for when, I couldn't say with any surety.*

Here! You couldn't have been here! You said you weren't when I asked before! What's changed? I demanded. this was definitely going to throw a monkey-wrench in Randon's works.

Yes, I know. Now that I know you so much better, heart's dearest, and I've been around the Afterlife a bit longer, I've gone back and thought things over very carefully. There is a period of time when things seemed to go more than a little blurry. Odd, that . . . he mused. *However, after careful reflection, I think I was—well, at least now, I'm almost positive—right here, at home, when I was killed.*

I ran my hands through my hair in frustration; then it dawned on me that I had forgotten to let Uncle James in on the Beef Blood Herring. He was as confused as I was, as we all were. That would only add to that confusion.

That was the problem; then the emphasis in his statement struck me. *You weren't here before that, I already know that, but you were somewhere else—with someone else . . .* I let my guess trail off.

Yes, heart's dearest, I'm afraid I rather glossed over that part when I told you the story previously. Does it make a difference?

I knew what he meant by "that part," and I knew what he meant when he said "now that he knew me better," but he still needed reassurance. He wasn't referring to the Where, but to the Why. Cravenly, I'm afraid I carefully avoided asking about the Who.

Of course not! I said emphatically, *but it makes a big difference to Sergeant Randon.*

I now brought him more or less up to date about the blood issue, simply telling him it was nonhuman.

It doesn't seem to make much sense that I can see, Jamie.

However, I do see that I have made it harder for the Sergeant by not being entirely straight-forward. I didn't want to needlessly involve, er, others.

I acknowledged that was certainly the case but tried not to blame him too much, since he hadn't known how I would react to his, um, activities. So, I just said, *I know, Uncle James, we can't figure it out either. But you obviously had to have been somewhere else, since you thought you weren't here, so you weren't really.*

I let that go when Uncle James made a funny noise, and switched back to the main point, *The murderer must have been covering his tracks, but how does that do it?*

Well for one thing, of course, he would not be expecting me to be telling you where I was. Therefore, he must have had a reason for making it look as though I were killed somewhere else, rather than just after arriving home.

I repeated to Uncle James, what I had already said to Mom. About the murderer wanting to look like he couldn't have been here if he was seen, but somewhere else where he had an alibi all set up. He agreed that was a definite possibility. However, he reminded me that, if so, the murderer contradicted his own set-up.

Uncomfortably, I decided I had to tackle the Who question. I didn't want to sound accusatory, but he had made a couple of wrong decisions; thinking he was being protective.

Uncle James, what about the, uh, friend, you were, uh, visiting?

Even without seeing, I could imagine Uncle James slightly squirming. My parents wouldn't have liked to be asked that kind of question, either.

Well, he sounded just as embarrassed as I was. Some things you just don't discuss with younger relatives. and the darned subject just kept coming up! *It was actually a new acquaintance, dear, more of a 'getting to know you' kind of thing.*

Nobody connected with the business?

No, someone with a completely different sort of expertise—a scientific background, as a matter of fact.

Well, someone with a scientific background would know about chloral hydrate.

Even I do. Besides, we hadn't known each other long enough for him to have an eye on my money.

I relayed the info to Randon, causing him more exasperation. "I'll still have to get a name from your uncle and do some investigation. I can't just take his word for it." He shut his eyes for a moment, when he heard what he had just said.

I begged him to be very discreet.

With that he gave me an exaggerated rolling of the eyes, and jammed on his hat with the air of a man about to enter a joust. Rising abruptly, he strode out into the hall, throwing over his shoulder, "I've got to think about this."

Realizing, as he reached for the doorknob, that he had come with me in my car, he turned and added, painfully, "As soon as you drop me off."

Whadoya know? Cops can blush, too.

The ride back to the station was conducted in what passed for a dignified silence. Getting out of the car, Randon leaned in my window and threw out, "Let me know if anything comes in by Spectergraph."

GOING HOME, I dreaded, for the first time, my forthcoming private conversation with Uncle James. I hadn't, as yet, prepared myself. I knew that was never going to happen, anyway. I now understood what people meant when they talked about "steeling" themselves. I was sure my next visit to the dentist was going to be expensive, since I was afraid I was gritting my teeth to nubs.

Walking back into the office, I swallowed hard and said, "Hi, Uncle James, I'm back."

Let's have it, was the terse rejoinder.

Obviously, he hadn't missed my slight neglect from the night before, he had just refrained from bringing it up, until now. Just as obviously, my expression, which I was sure looked like a felon on his way to the gallows, must have been *something* of a tip-off.

Silently, I reached in my purse and then laid the photograph on the desk. It felt like I was stabbing Uncle James through the heart for his second murder.

To my complete shock, amazement, disbelief, and a slew of other expressive nouns, the photo rose in the air, and spun as merrily as a pinwheel.

Oh! Jamie, came my uncle's deliriously delighted thought, *she kept it!*

Spectral kisses rained on my cheek. My hair was tossed by a zephyr of unbridled joy; while the desk chair twirled like a demented carousel. It felt like a private screening of *The Invisible Man Returns.*

All of this was so unexpected, I was frozen in position, with my hand still out.

I finally stammered aloud, "You . . . you . . . you're happy?"

Happy! Oh, Darling! I doubted he was addressing me.

More soberly, he continued, *Yes, I was afraid she had put all reminders of that unfortunate event out of her mind forever. It means she has forgiven me!*

"Can you . . . would you . . . tell me about it, Uncle James? I couldn't, that is, I didn't have a chance to ask Mom."

Hal. Not a question. He knew my Dad was the obstacle.

"Well, yes," I admitted grudgingly. I felt like we were all engaged in a conspiracy against Dad.

Uncle James read my face. As everybody seemed to do. Honestly!

Your father is not only a good man, but he loves your mother very much, and better than I ever could. It was a long time ago, but it would still hurt him.

I sat down in the desk chair and laid my head on the desk. After a moment, I raised it to ask, "How about you?"

He hesitated, *I'm not sure how to explain it. If you don't . . .* he broke off for a minute, before he said, *there is a conflict.*

"Uncle James," I exclaimed, "isn't that kind of an understatement?"

He gave a melancholy whisper of a laugh, *well, I guess.* Finally, he gave a kind of humph, and tried for an "explanation." *I did love your mother just as much, Jamie, and I almost convinced myself that it would be all right, forever. At the last, well . . . actually . . . more than the last minute, I realized I couldn't deny myself—there was, uh* (was it my imagination, or did the desk look redder?) *someone else, and I knew it would never be all right. That's really what your father couldn't forgive, dearest.*

"But, Mom?"

She knew I loved her, it was easier for her to see the truth and know I was right. She knew I would never, ever, have given her up, if I hadn't been right. At least she knew it, intellectually, but emotionally . . . I was so relieved when she fell in love with Hal.

"Why did you wait so long? You were actually married!"

Sadly. *I thought I could have my cake and eat it, too, Jamie.*

But it would have been—I would have been—so wrong.

"What about your marriage?"

It was annulled.

I took in a long breath, feeling like I hadn't had any air for quite a while, and reverted to thought.

I'm angry, and I'm sad.

I know, heart's dearest.

But—I guess I understand, too.

There was a whoosh of air, which scattered papers on the desk.

Ectoplasmic sigh?

A slight titter from my uncle, *Best I can do with the equipment I have,* he responded in the same manner. A pause, then he ventured, *I was worried . . . that you . . .*

Nah, if Mom doesn't blame you, how can I? Then I quickly added, *You, said I was like Mom.*

He easily understood what I didn't say.

◆

IN LIGHT OF that conversation, what's a girl—okay, that's stretching it a bit—to do? Talk to Mom, of course.

I headed for my folks' house and, with the lamest of excuses, whisked Mom away over Dad's protestations, and took her back home to Uncle James.

CHAPTER TWENTY-SEVEN

'll just gloss over the short meeting between Mom and Uncle James while the photo waved in the air like a Fourth-of-July banner. She says she doesn't hear him, but you'd never know it. I thought it best to wait in the living room after a quick glimpse of the above.

After she came in, smiling her usual "Uncle James smile," I brought her up to date on the latest episode of *The Middle-Aged and the Clueless*. She sat with a slight frown on her face before saying, "That poor man."

Which one? I thought.

I squirmed in my chair as she went on, "I well know what a secret like that can mean. For Sergeant Randon, it could mean his job if anyone knew he was involved with someone who was part of an ongoing investigation. Not to mention, that he believed she was communicating with the dead. For James, his secret would have meant subtle ostracizing and the death of his reputation. The problems are not unalike, Jamie."

"Mom," I protested, "we're not really involved—all he did

was give me a kiss under emotional pressure. I mean he felt emotional pressure. That is . . ."

Mom waved me to a halt. "Jamie, I felt his immediate attraction to you when he impounded your car."

"Impounded?"

"You didn't think I believed the breakdown story, did you?"

My mom, more of a witch than Margo.

"What are your feelings, darling?"

"Mom," I threw up my hands, "I just don't know. Dennis . . ." I didn't know how to finish that sentence.

"Forty-five, and still alive," observed my mother with a quirk of the lips.

"Yeah, Mom, Angelina Jolie's always been my role model."

My mother laughed heartily at that, but said, "seriously, darling, choosing between two very eligible men pales in comparison to the Sergeant's problem with having a not-so-departed, murder victim. As I pointed out, police departments don't always look kindly on outsider intrusions, especially paranormal ones."

"Some departments have psychic consultants."

Mom made an impatient movement.

"Well, what else could I do, Mom? Uncle James was murdered, and he is still sticking around. I couldn't keep it from Sergeant Randon any longer; that would be like abetting the crime. Besides, if Dennis knows . . . ."

"You believe in equality between suitors," Mom broke in.

I looked at Mom without answering for a time. When she said she "well knew" the magnitude of the problem, she wasn't just giving me the "I feel your pain" routine. If anyone knew how easily secrets could ruin lives, she was one of the ones.

Even now we were keeping a big one from my father that still had the power to hurt and harm.

Like Dennis, Mom read my face, saying what I knew was true, "Sooner or later we have to tell your father, darling. That's going to be very difficult."

Difficult! I felt a shrinking inside my chest. Besides, Dad might have . . . No! I firmly repressed that thought before it grew into a Name-On-The-List.

"I don't know how we're going to do it, Mom."

"I'll think of a way when the time comes," assured Mom.

Crossing my fingers, I only hoped it was as easy as it seemed when I was a child, when Mom could always figure out the right way to do everything.

Changing the subject, in a way, Mom asked, "Why don't you tell me the car story, Jamie—the real one, that is."

I filled her in. Her face went white, but otherwise she paid calm attention, and only remarked on Sergeant Randon's thoroughness. For the life of me, I couldn't remember if he had ever told me his first name.

I mulled that over—I seemed to be doing a lot of mulling in the last couple of weeks. Maybe if I had done more mulling in the past, I wouldn't have had those two failed marriages. Nah, I'd just have married some other idiots. Randon didn't seem like an idiot, but then, neither did Dennis, and he and I were on a first name basis. Since Randon had kissed me just as enthusiastically (I felt my face flaming as red as Hester's letter, at the remembrance), surely, we could consider ourselves close acquaintances.

Mom had been watching me during this entire procedure, and shaking with silent laughter. "Jamie, don't ever play poker."

"I guess I should compare myself to the old newspaper

joke. Since everyone manages to read me like *The Times*." I resisted the urge to stick my thumb in my mouth like a two-year-old.

"There are worse things," my mother replied mildly.

"I know, Mom, but I'm forty-five, for Pete's sake! You'd think I could manage a touch of mystery."

You seem to be doing all right without it," Then her face clouded, "You're right, though, it could be a problem under the present circumstances."

She went white again, as she realized that the "present circumstances" meant that it wasn't only eligible bachelors who were after me.

A knock startled us both. "Jamie, it is Zalman," sang a voice.

I hurried to let him in.

"Uncle Zalman, why don't you have a key?"

Since the house was also a place of business, it didn't make sense for one partner to have to announce himself to the other.

"I had—before trip to hospital. I lose."

I absolutely gelled in place. "You mean . . . someone *else* has it now?"

Zalman stared, stricken. "Oh, Jamie, I am not thinking, till you say. You are in more danger, and I am letting it happen."

I patted his arm to console him, all the while thinking furiously, *that's how Ski Mask got in—just opened the door.*

"I'm going to call the locksmith, right now, we'll have all the locks changed immediately, and get you a new key."

"No, no," he protested, "they will take again. I cannot stop them. You have only key," he paused, "and policeman, too."

I knew he was right. Tiny and elderly, Uncle Gnome King was no match for a murderer. We would just have to work out some schedule, so that I was always here to let him in, day or night.

"Come in the living room, Uncle Z., Mom's here."

His face lit up and he practically panted like an aging Chihuahua.

"Ah, Lily, always so beautiful, so beautiful, so like Jamie," he enthused, giving her a kiss on both cheeks.

Mom's grin was full of affection for her old friend, and told me a great deal about who might have communicated with whom during the years I was growing up. Uncle Zalman as Mercury, or Gabriel, I couldn't decide which. I stifled an internal giggle trying to fit him into either mold as the Messenger of the Gods.

Leaving Uncle Zalman showering my mother with blandishments, as though he hadn't seen her in years rather than days, I put a call into the locksmith. A female voice answered and told me perkily that someone would be there immediately—immediately between then and five, that is. I promised Miss Perkette I would definitely be here and waiting, and rejoined the Odd Couple.

Zalman was regaling Mom with the latest from the world of the printed page and Mom was, amazingly, asking knowledgeable questions with every appearance of interest. I felt something of a pang of jealousy at the years I had missed. I shook it off. *Water under the bridge, Jamie.*

I thought, sadly, of Dad. It wasn't like him—at least not as I knew him—to be so intransigent.

Mom stood up. "Jamie, let's talk to James and see if there's anything—anything—he can tell us. For one thing, if he was killed here, we know there must have been a good bit of *his* blood," she shuddered, but soldiered on, "so the cow blood doesn't mean what we thought it might . . . or does it?"

"I just told him about it, Mom . . . well, more or less. He didn't have any idea."

She gestured impatiently. "But it has to mean something."

"Well, if it was intended to confuse, it's certainly working."

She nodded, but waved her hand with that impatient gesture again. "No, there's more, I'm sure of it." She continued to stand, "Time, it's got something to do with the time of death."

"Yeah, Mom, that's what we thought already, but what? He was found in the morning by his gardener—*Gardener!* flashed through my head—and his housekeeper, but he was killed the night before."

"How closely was the time of death established?"

"Uh, I haven't the foggiest; and Uncle James is even foggier."

"Ask the Sergeant, that's something he should be at liberty to tell you."

"Gosh, Mom, we can ask Uncle James when he first saw himself. He can pin *that* down pretty much to the second."

"Yes, Jamie, but the police don't have his input," she corrected me, with exaggerated patience.

I apologized for mouthing off and Uncle Zalman tittered. "Mama is still having authority."

You've got to know my mother, she's only one inch taller than I am, but again, Queen Victoria could have taken lessons.

WE TROOPED into the office, which warmed significantly. Mom got that beatific look on her face that proximity to my uncle gave her. But, like everyone who couldn't actually hear him, she addressed the air near the desk. "James, is there anything more you can think of that poor Sergeant Randon can possibly make use of."

It's hard to think of anything when you're here, Lily. Then . . . *No! No! Scratch that, Jamie!*

I knew that thought wasn't meant for me to hear. It had gotten past his careful control.

Mom was looking at me oddly. I hastened to say, "He's thinking, Mom."

Tell Lily, I've been going over and over this—and I remember a few more details. I was here, standing by the desk, drinking a cup of tea . . .

I broke in, "Tea! Did anybody say anything about tea? Nobody said anything about tea! Was there a teacup?"

I jabbed my thumb into my phone while the others stared. Did I mention that I had put Randon's direct line on my phone? I stood and tapped my foot in aggravation as his voice told me he was unavailable, but to leave a message. I did, adding ASAP, firmly.

That's the last I remember, Uncle James continued, amusement in his voice. I relayed that to my audience.

Mom laid both hands flat on the desk, and pressed a little of that authority on my uncle, "*before* that, James."

An exasperated noise from Uncle James, who must have wished for a slightly more immediate presence than a desk, since he was definitely at a disadvantage with Mom leaning on him.

The day went like any other, calls, appraisals, sales, purchases. Mrs. Denby, she's my housekeeper, was here for a second half-day instead of her usual one. Her daughter's getting married and there were some fairly expensive details, I gathered. So, she was looking for extra money. I noticed she had changed the rug here by the desk for the one in the hall. I had simply assumed it was because I had spilled a bit of tea a day, or two, before. Otherwise, it was routine—oh, yes, a couple of calls from Graber and Bryson, trying to winkle more information from me about the letter. I, uh, went out for a while, and, as I said, at the end of the day, I was drinking another cup of tea—and then . . .

My phone rang. Randon.

"Tea, was there a teacup?" I burbled. "And a rug?"

"Jamie, what are you talking about?" Randon asked with the same exaggerated patience my mother used.

"Can you come to the house? This might be something important."

Slight hesitation, "Half an hour."

CHAPTER TWENTY-EIGHT

rue to his word, the Sergeant was there in twenty-nine minutes, looking, if possible, even more rumpled than usual. Seeing I was a group and not a solo, his face got as expressionless as his tie.

"Okay, what's this all about?"

I explained. "Uncle James said he was drinking tea, uh, then, and the rug had been switched."

Randon pinched the bridge of his nose. "Looks like we need to reinterview a couple of people. How about the funeral? Where's he buried? Sorry, Sir," with a nod to the desk.

"James is wishing cremation. I am only one there, except lawyers."

"Cremation," Randon groaned. "I had a hunch I should never have released the body. Sorry, Sir," another salute to the desk.

Mom was skewering Uncle Zalman with her eyes. He gave her a pleading look, "James is wanting no trouble for you, Lily. Then I am in hospital, and cannot tell you."

Mom nodded, but said nothing.

Randon motioned me out into the hall. Lowering his voice, he almost whispered, "You think he got chloral hydrate in the tea, don't you?"

"Don't you?"

"That's a possibility, but now, it doesn't look like we can prove it. You do know that still doesn't definitely mean he was killed here? If, the killer wanted," he pinched the bridge of his nose again, "for some reason to kill him somewhere else . . . Aagh." I expected him to burst into a chorus of "Can't Get No Satisfaction."

He looked at me with an indefinable expression. "I've got to go, I'm playing hooky from another case, as it is."

◆

HE PHONED ME late the next day. He had talked to Gleason Marden, the gardener, at the station, going over Marden's previous statement about finding Uncle James. Marden repeated essentially what he had said before; disclaiming any knowledge of any sort of dishes.

The Sergeant had also spoken to Mrs. Denby on the phone and had asked her to come to the office, so that he could show her the rug Uncle James was lying on, to see if she could identify it. While he had her on the phone, he had asked her the same question about dishes that he had asked Marden. She answered emphatically if there had been any, she would have washed them immediately. I could feel Randon's inner groan at that news. However, it confirmed the suspicion that there was something amiss with the teacup and that it had been spirited away by the murderer.

"The perp not only took the teacup but the original rug with Uncle James's blood on it. Then he substituted another one and doused it with cow!" I was struck as hard as Uncle James, "that's what the beef blood was all about! So, we can definitely say he *was* killed here but the killer wanted to cover that up, and make it seem he was killed somewhere else."

"Very good, Miss Marple! Except that we don't know that for a certainty until I talk to Mrs. Denby about the rugs."

"But the teacup makes it look like it, and there *must* have been two rugs, or there'd be two kinds of blood. The substitution still doesn't quite make sense."

"Well, yes, good thinking again, Miss Marple," he acknowledged grudgingly.

I smirked smugly, even though he couldn't see me.

"Sorry to pull the rug out from under you, Sergeant."

He groaned and then inquired rather wistfully, "Why don't you use my first name?"

"I don't know it," I admitted, feeling foolish. One of those pauses where I was sure he was pinching the bridge of his nose again. I could see a habit developing.

"It's Philip—Philip Cole Randon. My mother's maiden name was Cole. She always called me by my middle name."

"Cole is nice, it suits you. I wouldn't want to use her special name, Philip."

"No, I think I'd like you to call me Cole." The slight emphasis on *you* made me shift uneasily. I'm not used to *too* much attention, and two guys was too much.

"Uh, well, if that's . . . I mean . . . if you don't . . ." I ran out of ways to phrase it. I wasn't sure I was ready for baby names.

A funny noise on the other end told me Rundown (all

right, *other* people's baby names) was reading my mind. "If you'd rather stick to Sergeant."

"Cole, it is," I snapped.

"Hey, it shouldn't cause a fight. Call me whatever you want." His voice was aggrieved.

"I apologize profoundly, Serg . . . , Cole," I stammered. "I'm having a case of nerves, I think."

He apologized in turn. "Jamie, believe me, I understand. You wouldn't be real if you weren't. Most people never come close to a murder, and even fewer, well," he hesitated, "don't experience what you already have."

"Aren't targets, for one thing, and don't talk to the dead, for another, you mean."

"I didn't want to say it that bluntly, but yes."

I allowed him to think the problem was about Uncle James, and not about a two-guy dilemma, I have some pride, after all.

We had a few more minutes of conversation and he started to ring off. Belatedly, I remembered to tell him about Uncle Zalman's key. A huff of breath told me he was slouching back in his chair, pinching his nose again.

"You mean, all this time, you've been a sitting duck." he said wearily.

"I had the locks changed."

"But anyone could have gotten in until yesterday."

"Well," I felt that old tingle up the spine, wishing it meant lust and not unbridled fear, "yes, they could have."

"Are you at home?"

"No, I'm at the library, I have to work here sometimes."

"Stay there, I'm going to follow you home."

"But . . ."

"Stay there!"

I ended the call, bewildered.

ONCE AT HOME, we went through the same drill as I had with Dad and Mom. Rundown (I'm trying, I'm trying), threw out all of my food, even the unopened boxes and cans. When I protested that I had just bought them, he just gave me a disgusted look and went on with the disposal derby. Then he insisted on accompanying me to the store for replacements. He actually tried to pay for it, but I drew the line.

Home again, he inspected all the replacement locks, trying them repeatedly until he was satisfied. After that, he went through my rooms with the demeanor of Sherlock Holmes at his OCD best. I expected him to say, "You *see,* Watson, but you do not *observe.*"

Finally, having deemed everything as safe as he could make it, he made his departure. Yes, I said, "Goodbye, Cole," and breathed a sigh of relief.

CHAPTER TWENTY-NINE

hen we all, except Mom, gathered that evening—including Dennis, whom I had invited to a home-cooked meal—I brought everybody up to speed. I had already gone over everything with Uncle James, who found the suggestion that he might have been poisoned before he was conked, inexplicably amusing.

That's put me in the same class as Rasputin, he announced, somewhat smugly. *I had no idea I was so durable.*

My dinner companions were equally amused when I told them what Uncle James had said.

"Get serious, folks," I admonished, "murder is no joke."

Demurring, Dennis observed, "Your uncle has an amazing capacity for balance, considering his circumstances." (Talk about understatement!) "If he can see humor in it, more power to him."

Still uncomfortable, I nevertheless had to agree.

Reading my mind, or more probably my face, he hastened to add, "Not that I see humor in any of it, especially . . ." he let that thought hang in the air.

"Jamie is being right, not funny. I am losing best friend, nearly losing Jamie."

I patted Uncle Zalman's shoulder, "But he's still here."

"He cannot always stay, Jamie," Zalman protested, his face a wrinkled apple of distress.

"I'll go get him and we can enjoy him, now," I suggested.

I brought back his envelope to the table, and set him at the head of the table. Strangely, by tacit consent, we always left that place vacant.

"Good evening, Sir," said Dennis formally.

We brainstormed the rest of the evening and got no further than before.

Margo held out for the missing heir. Zalman leaned toward Graber. Dennis sort of concurred, "Or that other guy with the funny name."

"You mean Brigham Bryson?"

"Yeah, that one."

I didn't say what I was thinking—it was something I hadn't even hinted to Uncle James. I couldn't make myself ask the questions I most wanted the answer to, *What about the past, Uncle James? Were there jealous lovers? Were there rejected lovers? Were there frightened lovers?*

I caught Dennis watching me. "What's wrong, Jamie?"

Shuddering, I evaded the question, "I just feel we're missing something—too many somethings."

"Someone, you mean."

I didn't answer, but he read me easily.

"Someone he used to know." He leaned on the last word, subtly.

"Who's up for dessert?" Rising, I changed the subject.

Dennis followed me, "I'll help you bring it out."

Not wanting to make a scene, I gave in and let him accompany me to the kitchen. I expected the third degree. What I didn't expect was what I got.

With a smothered exclamation I couldn't translate, Dennis wrapped both arms around me like an anaconda, and, pressing me to the back of the kitchen door, proceeded to kiss me like a man drowning. After a few seconds, I was the one drowning. I had somehow forgotten how to use my lungs, and very quickly my knees followed suit. If he hadn't been leaning into me with the full Monty, I would have slithered to the floor like that same anaconda.

Finally regaining some sanity, and in desperate need of air, I pushed him slightly away. Only slightly, I'm not crazy—and did a little gasping.

He must have noticed what I had noticed; because his face pinked, and he moved in the dessert direction, clearing his throat. "I guess the plates should go in now." Giving me a hint of dimple, he added, "Well, you did ask who was up for dessert."

Not giving me a chance to retort, he grabbed two of the plates, and headed for the door. It was lemon meringue pie, and I fully expected the meringue to heave a sigh and melt over the sides of the plates (of course I can cook; I told you I had Mom's recipes).

Odd looks greeted us as Dennis led the way back to the dining room. "Sorry," I apologized breezily, "had to repair some of the meringue—too warm in the kitchen."

Margo rolled her eyes, and said "Mmmmn."

Uncle Zalman, bless his heart, was perfectly content with my explanation. "That is looking very good, Jamie."

WE CHATTED desultorily for another hour, lazily chewing over the odd idea that the murderer wanted/didn't want everybody to know that Uncle James had/hadn't been murdered here/elsewhere, coming as usual to no conclusion, and then Dennis excused himself.

"Early morning. That was delicious. Many thanks; I don't get many home-cooked meals, anymore."

Zalman gave me enthusiastic kisses on both cheeks, and excused himself, as well. That left Margo, who stared at me with arms folded.

"What?

"It certainly seemed to be 'warm in the kitchen.'"

I flushed unbecomingly, nodding toward Uncle James's envelope. She subsided, but I knew the subject was only on hold.

"Just what did go on in the kitchen that your uncle couldn't know about?" she persisted, after I had said goodnight to Uncle James and restored him to the desk. "Obviously," she went on, as I sat there wordless, "Dennis wasn't just inquiring about the best tool to whip egg whites."

Reluctantly, I gave her the scoop on the kitchen episode, which didn't make any more sense in retrospect than it did when it happened.

"I thought he might have wanted to grill you about Uncle James's past."

"Yeah, me too."

"I don't want to sound incredulous, but why is this sort of thing happening to you, now?"

"What do you mean to *me, now*?" I demanded, affronted.

She hastened to assure me that she was not referring to either age or looks, but rather right in the middle of a murder investigation.

I shrugged. I couldn't explain it either.

She then announced she was jealous and going to bed.

"Wait! What!"

She continued out and I heard her close the bedroom door firmly.

IN THE BATHROOM, as I brushed my teeth before bed, I gazed at myself in the mirror. I like to claim a multiplicity of talents; but I wondered if I could now add "vamp" to them. Shaking my head with a spray of toothpaste, I decided that was stretching it quite a bit. The unease was back, in spades. But even if Dennis had an agenda, I couldn't figure out Randon. I just couldn't make myself use his mother's name for him in my own mind—Randon was safer. Freud could have made a lot out of that psychological twist.

CHAPTER THIRTY

———•———

In the morning, I confronted Margo about her "jealous" comment the night before. I didn't forget to offer a cup of real cocoa when I did so, however.

"It's been a while, you know," she sighed.

I sat back in my chair and stared at her for some minutes, at a loss for what to say. Yes, it had been a while—for both of us, as a matter of fact. Her last relationship lasted twelve months, and looked as though it was really going somewhere. Margo's never been married, and has a gift for picking needy, broke, overaged adolescents (my opinion), who were even worse choices than mine. This time, the guy actually looked promising. He was a professional who actually made his own living, then just vanished without even a goodbye. Unlike her usual self, Margo was completely closemouthed about it; refusing to discuss it entirely. In the two years since then, the subject had been *verboten,* and I was taken aback by her raising it.

"He didn't like it that I 'knew' things, you know," she finally offered, breaking the silence.

"You mean he just walked out because he couldn't face the

possibility you might 'know' something about him?"

"I think so."

"Then there must have *been* something and you're better off without somebody like that."

"I guess." Then as though the dam broke (cliché, but appropriate), she gave me the whole story, finishing with, "There was something, I could tell, but I didn't care. I knew it wasn't something bad that he had done, just *something* he couldn't talk about."

"Ummm," I responded, unconvinced.

"What's really a wild coincidence, is that he was a clerk at Ackbury and Ackbury for a short while."

"Whaaa?" I started up out of my chair. "Why didn't you say so before this?"

"It was only for a couple of months; just a coincidence."

"You, of all people, telling me 'it was just a coincidence.' Whaddya, crazy?"

Eyes wide, she regarded me, speechless.

"You're right, how come I just blew that off? I always say there's no such thing as coincidence. You know I always say that."

I agreed. She always says that, it irritates the heck out of me.

"Why would I . . . ." she floundered, waving her hands in distress. "Why would I just kind of 'forget' Tim worked there?"

Tim Manning, I thought, *that was his name.*

Margo was still fretting. "I guess I just didn't want to think about him at all, so I just walled that off conveniently."

"I think it was a painful subject, and you didn't really want to give it much thought."

"Maybe," she was the one unconvinced. "Or maybe it was a spell."

I snapped to attention. "Oh, come on, now you're really reaching." She was, wasn't she?

"Well, it really was *very* convenient."

"Then, how come you suddenly 'remembered'? Do spells lose their potency over time, like aspirin?"

"You're making fun," she pouted. "You need to take these things seriously. Especially now."

I had to admit she had a point. Nevertheless, I shrugged it off, "I have to get to work." I had cut my library job down to two days a week, but they were still looking for someone permanent to replace me.

"Yeah, me too, and there's a coven meeting tonight. Can I talk you into coming, this once?"

She always asked, and I always said no. I knew Wicca was benign, careful of the environment, believed in equality, etc. etc., but it still made me uncomfortable.

She got a little twinkle, and asked, "Would it make you feel better if I called the coven a 'grove?'"

"Just a bunch of friendly anti-rowans?"

She gave me an irritated look, "You know there are two sides to the rowan thing."

I chuckled, and apologized. She has a rowan-wood wand, and is sensitive about the tree's reputation among some Wiccans for warding off witches.

AT THE LIBRARY, which was having a slow afternoon (yes, we actually have busy periods), I thought about the "coincidence," and decided to give Dennis a call.

His voice brightened when he heard my voice, but then took

on a defensive tone. "You're not going to bawl me out, are you?"

"I'm of two minds, but that's not why I called. Do you remember Tim Manning?"

"Sure, he clerked for us for... I think only a couple of months. He was studying for the bar."

"Studying... he wasn't a lawyer, yet? How old *was* he?" I remembered him as graying and getting slightly paunchy, but still attractive.

"Forty-eight, forty-nine—I'm not sure exactly. He was making a career switch. Why?"

"Well, actually he used to date Margo, and then walked out on her. His name came up today, and she told me he worked for you."

"Walked out on her... same with us. Just took off without even a kiss my... er... a goodbye."

"You mean he said nothing about quitting?"

"No, just didn't show up for work one day. We never heard from him again."

"Didn't you think that was odd?"

"Of course. We tried to trace him, but got nowhere. His family said they had gotten a letter saying he had decided to go to Europe and bum around for a while, take the bar later. Midlife crisis, I thought. We let it go after that."

"Margo didn't hear a thing."

"Well, it was probably a lot easier to write to his family than to break off with a steady girlfriend."

"Men!"

Dennis laughed, "I've seen women do the same thing."

I reluctantly acknowledged the truth of that.

"How did his name 'come up' anyway?"

"Margo mentioned him. She was really broken up when he

walked out and wouldn't talk about him at all for a long time. I think she's finally getting over it, and moving on."

"Good, how about dinner?"

Again, that little niggle, "Mom and Dad are expecting me tonight—it's my regular Thursday."

"Tomorrow?"

"I'd love to."

"Seven?"

"Great." I hung up, oddly uneasy. For some reason, Margo's words kept echoing in my head. *Maybe it's a spell.*

Oh, come on, Jamie, that's ridiculous.

WHEN I GOT HOME, I found a message from Randon asking me to call ASAP. At first, I decided it could keep until morning; then curiosity got the better of me and I did as bade. To my dismay, his first words were "Sit down, Jamie."

Alarmed, I stammered, "No, no, what is it?" I was terrified that it might have been Mom, or Uncle Z., or Margo. Even though it wasn't any of them, it was almost as bad,

"Mrs. Denby didn't show up at the station at the appointed time. I waited for two hours, then I drove to her place and found her." He was silent for a minute, "She had probably been dead from the night before. We'll know more after the medical examiner has looked at her."

I did sit down then, heartsick, and frankly, scared out of my wits.

After a long silence, I finally got my breathing under control, "Was it, by any chance, chloral hydrate?"

"We don't know that either, until the report." A grim

addition, "It was more like your uncle, Jamie, she'd been struck from behind. Fractured her skull…" The last said so low I could barely hear it.

I gasped in response. "How does HE know?"

Understanding me immediately, he replied, "I don't think he *knows*, Jamie, but he could guess that she might have noticed the rug."

"Then, the gardener could be a target, too."

"We'll have a man patrol around his place, and keep an eye on things."

"I'm going to my folks for dinner." After this news, I wanted him to know where I was.

"Go straight home from there," he ordered, "I don't want you making any detours.

"I promise—I mean that."

I SHOWED UP at Mom and Dad's just in time to see Dad driving out. He waved and announced Mom had forgotten something at the store.

"Back in a flash, Squirt."

As I suspected, Mom had sent him on a wild grocery chase, so she could inquire about the case, and just incidentally, Uncle James.

We were sitting on a Hans Wegner couch—sleek, spare, but uncomfortable—facing a genuine Eames chair that had been in the family before I was. That was Dad's favorite. There were pieces from Noguchi, well, one piece, the coffee table. more Hans Wegner—Mom's favorite—in the dining room, etc., etc., etc. Mom is enthusiastically mid-century modern, which always struck me as strange. The whole house was a veritable treasure trove of museum-quality fifties-style.

I tell you all this because it was so far from Mom's personality. Even as a child, I had found our décor a trifle stiff and cold. Too straight up-and-down, too sharply angled, no lolling, except for Dad's Eames chair. Mom, on the other hand, was warmth itself, *and* graciousness, *and* understanding; I couldn't have asked for a better adolescence, for example. Where my friends were constantly complaining about how their parents didn't understand them, I never had a complaint. Well, maybe she understood me a little *too* well.

Maybe I'm reading too much into furniture, but now that I know her story a little better, I see some symbolism there in her choices. No Deco, nothing to remind Dad of his brother, but as close as she could get.

I told Mom what had transpired at dinner the night before, and even about Dennis; but carefully kept Mrs. Denby out of the conversation—at least for now—and tried to be amusing.

She sighed and got that thoughtful look. "You're a big girl, darling, but I'm going to say 'be careful' anyway."

"I know," heaving a sigh in my turn, only my sigh had a lot more heft, if you catch my drift.

I continued with my tale, filling her in about Margo and the strange disappearance of Tim Manning.

Mom frowned over that one, too. "That's too much of a 'coincidence'"

"I think so, too. But his folks got a letter."

"They must have been fairly elderly."

"You're only seventy, Mom. They didn't have to be *that* old."

"All the same, it seems rather callous of him."

"Maybe they didn't have a very close relationship."

Mom shook her head, but before she could say more, the arrival of Dad put an end to the conversation.

Dad kissed me on the cheek, with his usual, "Looking good, Squirt," and handed Mom the totally unnecessary jar of mayonnaise.

I maintained my pose of just the usual night-with-the parents as long as possible, but excused myself, as soon as I could, without looking like I was running away.

CHAPTER THIRTY-ONE

s I drove into my driveway, I was greeted
by an odd sight—the gardener's pickup
was still parked in front of the garage,
blocking my way. To my dismay the house was dark, Margo
was evidently still at the coven meeting. I didn't realize until
then how much I was counting on her being there. *Should have
stayed a little longer with the folks, Jamie.*

The hairs on my arms stood up like pickets in the fence;
when I noticed the curtains billowing out of the open (open?)
office windows as though the house was in full sail.

Not being one of those heroines who insist on descending
into a darkened basement where you *know* something horrific
is waiting, I immediately hit Randon on my phone. Message
machine. Swearing under my breath in frustration, I left a
"please call, immediately," and hit Dennis's number. Same story.
Same message.

Okay, I *wasn't* one of those heroines, but I decided I *had* to
do *something*. The curtains had me really worried.

I aimed my headlights at the front porch so they lit up the

door. Trying to look in every direction at the same time, I stepped cautiously out of the car, leaving the motor running. Positioning my various keys between my fingers like brass knucks (I read articles on women's self-defense), I headed (okay, scampered) for the front door, looking like a running back avoiding a tackle.

To my amazement, I got the key in the lock on the first try. I flipped it, kicked the door open, and reached inside for the hall light. Big surprise—no light.

Roundly beating myself up for not bringing the flashlight out of the car with me, I did the football run in reverse, jumped back in the car and slammed the door, locking everything up.

I sat there for a while, breathing hard. Once again, I hit Randon's number. Once again message machine. Once again, same message.

Once again, Dennis. Once again, same story, same message.

The curtains were now roiling in a frenzy. Uncle James was working up a full head of steam. Did that mean "Come in," or "Stay out?"

I pounded my hands on the steering wheel in a frenzy of my own. I decided, "Once more, into the breach," remembering Uncle James's quotation. Repeat performance, only this time with the flashlight tucked under my arm.

I crept into the house, sliding along the hall wall. The office door was open, and even in the bare light I could see the room was a mess. Books, papers, tchotchkes, including the desk drawers, were everywhere on the floor. I screamed, "Uncle James," my voice breaking into a sob. Thanking God, I heard him in my head.

I'm all right Jamie, but you need the police. And, you need to get back in the car immediately.

This was an order. One more touchdown run, and I was back locked in the car.

I was on the phone, hysterically begging Randon to call, when not one—but two—familiar cars pulled up at the curb, and not one—but two—familiar figures leaped out.

I became *really* hysterical then, with maniacal laughter.

They found me, bent over the steering wheel, laughing until the tears poured down my cheeks.

"Darling..."

"Jamie, baby..."

At that, the tears turned into real sobs, and I pointed wordlessly at the front door.

Randon whipped out his gun; and, to my total shock, so did Dennis. Randon gave Dennis a look, but didn't waste time on foolish questions like "You got a permit for that, Counselor?" He just raised an eyebrow and led the way into the house. I followed.

Inside, both men gave involuntary grunts, at the devastation wrought in the office.

"Your Uncle...?" Both asked simultaneously, then gave each other peeved looks.

I was tempted to burst into real laughter this time.

"He said he was okay."

Randon pinched his nose, as usual. "You came in the house?"

Dennis shook his head in silence.

"Well," I started, defensively, "I...."

Randon held up a hand. "Don't explain."

Dennis rubbed a hand over his face. If I didn't know better, I would have said he was trying to smother amusement. Mildly, he inquired, "Can you talk to your uncle now?"

"Yes." *Uncle James, what happened? Did you see?*

I suggest you tell your friends to look carefully around. I didn't see much, since a great deal took place out of the office, but I know there was more than you see here.

Didn't you see who did this?

He was completely disguised. Wearing padded clothing and a ski mask. Boots with heels on his feet, his height was difficult to determine. He came prepared not to be recognizable.

I repeated what Uncle James had said.

Randon turned to Dennis. "You take the upstairs, I'll take the down. We'll both do the outside."

Dennis looked like he wanted to protest, but simply nodded and headed for the stairs.

"You," Randon addressed me sternly, "don't move an inch."

Uncle James gave a smothered chuckle.

After Randon had started his search, Uncle James admonished me, also sternly. *You should never have come in alone.*

I saw the curtains.

They were intended to warn you to stay away, and call someone.

I did call them, but all I got was their voice-mails. I had to know if you were all right.

A deep sigh from Uncle James; which, of course, could only have been for my benefit, *Jamie, dearest, I'm dead. I cannot be injured further.* In spite of himself, the situation, and his annoyance with me, my uncle couldn't suppress a *tee-hee*.

In spite of myself, I couldn't either.

Randon walked back in to find me patting the desk and giggling into the air. "You all right, Ms. Whitehall?"

I blushed. "Uncle James made a joke."

Randon rolled his eyes. Dennis spoke from the doorway. "Nothing too unusual upstairs, that I could see. A few books on the floor, but not so bad. Not all over the place." He glanced at me, knowing my feelings about the books.

Randon bristled a bit. I got the idea that was because Dennis knew anything about my upstairs, but only growled, "Okay. Let's take the yard."

"I want to come, too."

"You stay here!" came from both men.

I bristled.

Jamie! from Uncle James.

I subsided.

After they had gone out, Uncle James added, *You, need to let them be heroes, Jamie. They know you're brave, but they . . . well, they're a little like schoolboys vying for the prom queen. They very much want to show off, and you must let them.*

I hugged the desk.

CHAPTER THIRTY-TWO

———•———

The sound of the backdoor slamming, and two pairs of rushing feet interrupted us.

Randon came first, on his phone, followed on his heels by a white-faced Dennis.

"We found the gardener," he explained.

The desk chair slid gently and unobtrusively behind me. I sat down, not needing to ask what that meant.

Randon was off the phone by that time, and added, "No sign of a struggle. We ... uh I, figure it could be chloral hydrate, again." He paused for a beat, and went on, "Something strange, though, about the body." He glanced at Dennis, and stopped abruptly.

I was conscious of a roaring in my ears. "But how ... ?"

"Remains to be seen," Randon was grim.

"You can turn on the lights now," Dennis put in. "The intruder had tripped all the switches in the fuse box, before he came in." He was equally grim.

"I changed the locks." I whispered.

"Old house, old windows," surmised Randon with an air of

superiority, "slid a tool in and pried the window lock open is my guess. Tomorrow, I'll have some guys fit all the windows with those locks you just attach on the inside."

Dennis shot Randon a glower.

There were fumbling noises, then, "Oh my God!" Margo's voice sounded from the hall, just as I flipped on some lights, revealing the havoc.

"Come in, and sit down," Dennis said quietly. "There's some bad news."

Since Margo was still in her Wiccan attire, I had to force down an insane desire to break out in a chorus of *Don't Nobody Bring Me No Bad News.* I felt every bit as unreal as Dorothy.

Randon, was more practical. "Let's get cracking on the kitchen."

I let out a loud groan, knowing exactly what he meant.

Margo held up a restraining hand. "Hold it just a minute," she ordered, "a little explanation, if you please."

"He'll tell you," Randon nodded at Dennis, and strode off to the kitchen.

Dennis had been white-faced; now he resembled an old-fashioned thermometer. I could hear Uncle James making soft, snorting sounds, and knew he was trying not to laugh at the Testosterone Twins. Through gritted teeth, Dennis explained the situation to Margo.

Just a tad snottily, I put in, "I suppose you knew it already?"

Margo, to her credit, ignored my tone and answered simply, "No."

Feeling ashamed of myself, I sighed, "We probably should have guessed."

Dennis looked surprised, and inquired, "How do you figure?"

I started with, "Well," and then froze with my mouth open.

Margo got it immediately, "The other witness.... Oh my God!"

Randon chose that moment to rejoin us, "I didn't..." Looking from Margo to me, he was instantly alert. "What?"

"Quincy McNair," Margo and I almost screamed, simultaneously.

No fleas on Randon. He addressed the air, "Mr. Olivian, the address?"

It was already on the desk.

Randon read it into the phone—APB, I assumed—and headed for the door. Just outside the office, I grabbed his arm before he could leave. "What something strange?"

Randon disengaged my hand and reported tersely, "Still looked 'arranged,' but he was laid out neatly, face-down."

With that enigmatic "explanation," he strode out the door.

———— ◆ ————

DENNIS, EVIDENTLY feeling he had to assert himself somehow, ordered me to get more garbage bags, and told Margo to help him in the kitchen with the usual throw-away routine.

I slapped my forehead in despair. I had just purchased some really good-looking short ribs and a rather expensive roast, not to mention all the staples that went out in the last purge.

Dennis, not needing to read my mind this time, assured me—insisted, really—that it was "all on him, and no backtalk." Adding, "I'll give you the cash, you take it to the store and spend it. All of it. That way you'll know it's safe."

I leaned my head on his shoulder for a minute, realizing he was perfectly aware of my repressed suspicions where he was concerned.

"Thank you," I whispered.

He understood. Darn the man, why did he have to be so intuitive?

I handed him two garbage bags, and he and Margo got busy throwing away the rest of what looked like absolutely innocent food.

"We can't even give it to charity," I bemoaned the waste.

"Yeah," Margo agreed, "it's killing me, too."

"That's the problem," Dennis twinkled, "it's liable to kill them."

"Kind of takes the edge off charity, doesn't it," offered Margo.

This struck me, nonsensically, as incredibly witty, and I started to laugh uncontrollably. Once I got started, Margo and Dennis joined in, and the three of us roared for some moments, until reality set in again.

The unmistakable sound of a police cruiser engine brought us up short. Peremptory raps on the front door sent all three of us scurrying to open it. Randon stood there, looking as though he might cry.

"Too late," was all he said at first, grimly.

When he had recovered at bit, he explained that this death wasn't as neat as the others. The body hadn't been "laid out" the same way as Uncle James, or presumably the gardener, and it was obvious the chloral hydrate had caused wracking convulsions before the victim had succumbed.

"It does that sometimes," he finished, miserably.

I was the one who cried. I didn't even know the victims, actually, but I felt their loss as though they had been my best friends.

DENNIS AND RANDON left together, after trying futilely to out-jockey each other for last place. I had gotten so tired of their middle-school posturing, I thought they'd never leave; and Margo had long ago departed for her bed after a useless attempt to hide her giggles.

I felt thoroughly drained, thoroughly pissed-off, and profoundly sad. It didn't matter that I had scarcely been acquainted with any of the three; I felt as guilty as though I had snuffed them myself. I said as much to Uncle James.

If anyone, my dear, should feel guilty, it is I, he observed sadly, *this is all due to my foolish desire to make a splash. If I had simply announced my discovery, admitted I was still searching for proof of authenticity, and let the chips fall where they might, we would have been spared this horror.*

I was torn between sobs and guffaws to hear the original murder victim recriminate himself for being murdered!

I finally said, *you don't know that, Uncle James. I think there's more going on than just the obvious. It can't simply be all about wanting to be famous.*

Perhaps, my dear, he agreed, absently.

Ah, was his next comment.

What?

I just got a message.

Facespook! The hairs on my arms rose and saluted.

One of my friends reports that he saw a figure, dressed like my visitor, near Quincy's apartment. Driving a red Cadillac crossover.

The hairs on my head joined my arms.

Dennis! Wait a minute. Can't be. Can it? The timing seemed all off; but then I couldn't raise him on the phone. Wait another minute. What was the time of death? For all I knew, he could have been dead for days. Wait again. Why now? Why weren't they killed when Uncle James was?

I dropped my head on the desk, as the room seemed to spin out of control. I felt Uncle James's warm presence and a couple of spectral pats on the back.

This smells a little fishy, my dear; a bit too much of that "obvious."

I looked up, feeling better. Of course! Who disguises himself completely and then drives an immediately recognizable car? I was pretty sure Dennis could figure that one out. Men might be idiots in some ways, but that was really stretching it.

Exhausted, it was now closing in on 3 AM. I patted the desk and bade Uncle James, good night. After waving to the patrol car that Randon had ordered to keep an eye on the house, I fell into bed. Expecting to fall asleep immediately, I found my thoughts whirling around the trilogies. Repeating Uncle James, Uncle Zalman, and me, Denby, Marden, and McNair, like a mantra, until my dreams took over, and I was Goldilocks being chased by the three bears.

CHAPTER THIRTYTHREE-

———•———

Promptly at 8:30 AM, Randon was on my doorstop. The doorbell sent me flying from my bed; stumbling toward the hall, while still trying to get an arm in my robe, and gasping in horror when I peeped through the peephole and determined the identity of my visitor.

The doorbell shrilled several more times as I dithered. Margo's screamed "Answer it!" from the top of the stairs forced me to open the door. Did I mention there was actually a small, but as usual, elegantly Deco-furnished bedroom off the library? Margo had claimed it for her own. There is such a thing as too much togetherness.

Randon, appearing as usual Rundown, took one look and bent double. Well, so I don't wear Prada to bed. Nevertheless, his glee was excessive.

The next minute, he had gathered me up in his arms, carried me to the kitchen, and plunked me in a chair.

"Sit there, I'm making breakfast."

After he had stoked me with scrambled eggs, bacon, toast

(with honey), and hot tea, he ordered, "Go brush your hair."

I scurried from the room, in a manner reminiscent of a fleeing cockroach.

Like a whirlwind, I brushed hair and teeth, applied lipstick and donned jeans and tee-shirt. Still dizzy from lack of sleep, I hoped I had attained Presentable. Glamorous was definitely out of reach (usually).

I clattered back to the kitchen, where Rundown was cleaning up. He smirked when he saw me, but went on loading the dishwasher, his sleeves rolled up. To my everlasting dismay, the sight of that domestic scene undid me completely, and I wailed like one demented.

Once again, I was swept up in his arms; but this time he was the one who plunked in the chair. With the barest of sound, he whispered, "I love you, baby, one day you'll have to decide."

I cried harder. Two men were bad enough; two who read me went from sublime to unbearable.

When I was finally wept out, I just sat there; knowing I should climb off his lap, but unable to summon the energy.

Another gentle whisper, "Did you know you snore?"

My eyes flew open. The clock over the stove said 10:30.

"Wha . . . ? Wha . . . ?"

I leaped to my feet; had a dizzy spell and plopped back down.

Snarky laughter, "If this is your usual morning routine, I'm glad I'm forewarned."

I leaped up again, and resisted the urge to brain him with the teapot.

Some of that must have showed on my face, because he sobered and said, "I know, it was a bad night. For me too, I feel like I should have seen it coming."

"That's the way I feel, but I also think there's more to it, that we don't know."

"Like, maybe, everything?" Randon gave me a quizzically raised eyebrow.

I waggled mine in response.

By tacit, but mutual, consent, we ignored his whispered declaration. He, I'm sure, out of embarrassment. For me, it was total panic.

Could you love two people? Or even one? I barely knew either of them. I got heart palpitations just thinking about love.

My eyes must have widened at this thought, because Randon frowned and said, "What's up?"

Stuttering, I covered hastily, "I just remembered, Uncle James got a message."

Randon winced, "You mean, from the 'Great Beyond?'"

"Yes, via Facespook."

"And?"

I hesitated, conscious that I might be aiming a spotlight directly at Dennis.

"Well?"

"It's a little, well, delicate."

"Out with it."

"The messenger said he, or it, or whatever, saw a figure dressed exactly like the one who broke in here..." My conscience smote me.

"This wouldn't have anything to do with a certain red automobile, would it?" Randon leaned casually back in the chair.

My chagrin shone as brightly as my crimson face.

"I heard about the car from witnesses across the street; they saw it pulling away in a hurry."

"You already knew, and you didn't say anything," I stated accusingly.

"I spoke to Ackbury about it already. On the surface, he seems to be in the clear. He was in meetings most of yesterday *and* in the evening. He says," slight pause, "that's why you couldn't get through to him last night. I didn't see any reason to worry you. If he wanted to tell you, he could. He shrugged, "I'll be doing a little more checking, of course, but the meetings can be verified. His car could have been used without him missing it, any of those times."

I didn't know how to respond. Alphonse and Gaston came to mind. There they were, oh, so politely trying to best each other; but nothing underhanded, mind you, all according to the Marquis of Queensbury. Why did I want to slap both of them silly?

"Don't you need a fob?" *Can you 'hot-wire' modern cars*, I wondered?

"Ackbury told me he 'lost' one of his right after he got the car. Didn't give it much thought, just paid for another one." Expensive, that.

"Were you ever married?" I asked suddenly.

He blinked, startled by my abrupt change of subject, then grinned.

"No, I was engaged once and . . ." he let the sentence hang for a bit before continuing, "I did live with one or two." He shifted, uncomfortably, in his chair.

"One or two?" I inquired dryly.

He had the nerve to look smug. "The police *never* reveal their sources."

I gave him a sour look.

"Hey! Wait a minute. I think I heard about a couple of husbands along the way."

"Well, okay, there were one or two."

His grin widened, then turned both curious and hopeful. "What made you ask?

"You know a lot about me because you had me investigated. All I know is that your Mom called you Cole. It doesn't seem fair."

He shifted again, "You were part of a probable homicide investigation, Jamie."

"I know that" I sighed, "but it all seems," I trailed off.

"Invasive? I'm hip."

I smiled inwardly. If there was one word that *didn't* describe Rundown, that had to be it. I appraised him, wondering what word did. Steady? Reliable? Sounded too dull. Unexpected? I remembered the tea in the drawer. Deep? I considered his vocabulary, plus the *one or two* relationships.

"Well?" His challenge broke into my musings.

"Oh! I'm sorry, I was just thinking about the 'probable' part," I covered hastily, no sense feeding his ego. "There's no probability, anymore."

He looked grim. "And so far, we're not getting anywhere. The longer we go, the colder the trail, and the harder it gets. And the will witnesses, *plus* Mrs. Denby!" he smashed one fist into the other palm, making me jump.

"It wasn't your fault."

"Yes, it was. I had the wrong angle at the start. I know better than to start out with an angle. I started with you, you know," he stared at the floor, "then I sort of focused on that lawyer of yours. He seems to be in the clear." This was accompanied by a sour look.

"But the will actually pointed at me. Since it *wasn't* me, there shouldn't have been any *obvious* reason to kill *them*." I sighed, "Mrs. Denby, though, she would have known about the rug, but even then . . ." I trailed off, not sure what 'then' was. "Dennis . . . well, I don't know, he's still on *my* list." It made me extremely uncomfortable to admit that, but it was true.

Randon looked slightly amused at my italics. "Yeah, well, *obviously* there was a reason. Damned if I can figure out what, however. You're the only one with the red-letter motive."

"Hah, hah."

"Okay, feeble joke. Seriously, what was there about the will that could have fingered someone else?"

"I can't imagine, and neither can Uncle James. He left everything to me and never mentioned a single other bequest to anyone except $2,000 to the housekeeper. Not to Uncle Zalman, or my mother; he didn't even give the gardener anything. That might have been his motive, but now he's dead."

"And she's dead, as well. As suspicious as my job makes me, I don't think I would have seen her poisoning your uncle's tea and whacking him over the head because she didn't get more."

I agreed that even though stranger things had happened, it seemed unlikely. "So, the killer, himself, is narrowing the field of suspects. That seems really crazy."

"Except that, crazy as it seems on the surface, he—or she, but I don't think so—must feel they could somehow lead us to him. Mrs. Denby we already know; we just can't pick up the connection to the will witnesses. Yet," he added firmly.

"I keep thinking . . ." I was suddenly reluctant to voice my thoughts, a feeling of disloyalty sweeping over me.

"Out with it."

"Uncle James . . ." I gulped.

"Am I going to have to wring it out of you?"

"Mom said he had someone . . ." for the third time I choked.

"And, of course, that someone was a guy. When he was young, that might have been enough to *possibly* ruin his business, and his reputation, if it got around. You're thinking that 'someone' still feels the same pressure, and killed him because it was going to come out in some way. I've already given that considerable thought; and I think it's a good possibility; maybe doesn't have anything to do with his business."

"Why didn't you say?" I was fretful.

"You seem to be very protective of Mr. Olivian, who doesn't seem to be that concerned in the same way."

"How do you know?"

"I don't mean to put words in his mouth, but he's dead, Jamie, it doesn't matter what anyone thinks, now." He made that uncomfortable shift another time. "Besides, there were rumors before he died, which I followed up. If you remember, I already knew that he was gay, not only because Percheff knew. He was very discreet, but . . ." he shrugged.

"I've only known him a short time, but I love him," I said.

"Of course, you do. And it's only too evident that he loves you." He got a quizzical expression, "I can't believe I'm talking this way about the deceased." His expression changed to one slightly on the sly side. "Does he say anything about me?"

"Oh, for Heaven's sake!" I retorted. "What do you expect him to say?"

He looked crestfallen. "I just was hoping he approved of me."

I slapped my forehead. "Were you going to ask him for my hand? I have parents, you know."

He looked even more crestfallen, "That was ridiculous; I admit it."

"Forget it. I sometimes feel he and Uncle Zalman are my guardians, myself. I also have to remind myself that I'm forty-five, and not a teenager."

His grin returned, "I have to remind myself of that about you, too."

I threw a dish towel at him. He fielded it and got a dangerous look. I started to back away toward the office, but he caught me before I reached the door.

I was smothered in another one of those embarrassing full Monty embraces. Minutes, or maybe hours, went by. I was just going down for the third time when he abruptly released me. Jamming his Fedora on his head, he stalked out the front door.

CHAPTER THIRTY-FOUR

That evening I sat at Uncle James's desk, glumly and guiltily aware that my uncle's murder had somehow receded into second place as a problem, while juggling two guys somehow occupied the forefront.

It's not all, or even a little bit, about you! I thought, *well, maybe a little bit,* I acknowledged, to myself, *I was almost offed, too.*

So why, said I to me, *are you stewing over your love life. Not getting killed just might take precedence.*

Uncle James, carefully *not* intruding, was silent as the grave (so to speak), while I moped. Finally, evidently feeling I'd been childish long enough, he ventured a question.

Want to talk about it?

I jumped. *Uncle James, I thought you didn't read minds.*

He chuckled. *Don't play poker, darling.*

I've been told that before, I conceded grumpily.

Warmth enfolded me; as close to a real-life hug as arms from the Great Beyond could manage.

It's what makes you you, my dear, and so many of us love you . . . a wicked snigger.

Oh, Uncle James, I haven't forgotten what this is all about; I've just never been in this position before. It makes everything so much harder.

There are no easy murders, my dear, he said gently.

Umph, I responded. *I know! But we're not getting any closer to the murderer, and time is passing. Add that to trying to keep the Testosterone Twins apart . . .* I sank down in the chair, and kicked my feet.

You look like you did when you were five.

I laughed and sat up straighter, *You, mean I'm acting the way I did at five.*

Something like that.

I gathered my courage around me and forced myself to ask, *Uncle James, could it be possible . . .* I choked and started again. *Do you think it's not just about the object you discovered, but something, I mean, somebody . . ."*

Uncle James broke in, *you are referring to my checkered past, my dear.*

My face flamed.

I know, my dear, as I've said, it isn't easy to talk about sex with an elderly relative, especially, if it's slightly offbeat sex. There was stifled amusement in his mental tone.

Well, yeah, it's not so offbeat, I'm cool that you're gay . . . .

Oh, goody, the amusement grew.

All right, make fun. I mean it, I just don't know how else to put it. But you certainly are right-on about the sex part. I wouldn't ever talk to Dad about . . .

A chortle. I'm surrounded by snarks.

More seriously, he took up the subject. *I have explored that issue myself, my dear, the truth is I just don't know. There weren't that many, well, relationships, in my past. Two are also deceased, one still alive, but it was an amicable parting. We are still on excellent terms and have considerable residual affection for each other, we just grew apart.* The feeling of a shrug, *perhaps my, well, checkered past,* a slight snort, *is a connection. And it might be connected to my discovery, as well. I'm just not seeing how at the moment.*

And you're sure the live one can't be involved?

I can't be positive, Jamie, but I would very much doubt it— or at least, I wouldn't want to think so. Which might not be a good thing, he added reflectively.

Curiosity got the better of me. *Unc, are you in touch with the ones who've passed on?*

A roar of laughter. I'll say one thing for Uncle James, when he laughed, he laughed.

Actually, heart's dearest, they have greeted me. However, while we still know affection for those we have cared for, there isn't quite the same feeling.

My face flamed, again, *I didn't mean to pry.*

Uncle James ignored me. *I probably shouldn't be spilling secrets about my afterlife situation. Of course,* he continued ruefully, *I'm stuck to the desk, so I don't really know all that much about it, myself.*

I laughed in turn, then returned to the subject. *There must be some connection; or, er, they must, well what could . . .* I gave up, frustrated.

Uncle James switched topics, *Jamie, you have got to recover the "object," as you put it.*

Don't you think, I gulped, *someone is watching the box?*

They can't watch it all the time, Jamie.

They could hire someone.

Uncle James was quiet for a moment. *Hire someone, yes, that's what we'll do. Hire a messenger to retrieve it, so you're not seen near the box, you or any of your family.*

How about a policeman?

Plainclothes, and not your friend.

Yes.

Sounds good.

Energized, I hit Randon's number. Expecting to leave a message, I was surprised to hear his voice, "Hi, Jamie."

I stuttered for a moment and then ventured my request.

"Yeah, I think we can do that. I'll set it up tomorrow."

He rang off without a goodbye, which left me staring at the phone.

Margo's voice interrupted me.

"Thought I'd find you here. Hi, Mr. Olivian."

"We're brainstorming again. So far, all storm, no brain."

"How far did we get?"

I summarized.

"So, once we get the 'object' what do we do with it?"

"Uncle James?" I said aloud.

I'm not sure, yet. Wait until you've looked it over.

Margo sighed "We've had one definite murder and two almosts, three more out-and-out murders, *and* at least two break-ins. It's gotta be hot stuff. But why kill for it? Wouldn't throwing a whole lot of money at it, or for it," she considered, "work just as well?"

"Did you tell anyone about it, Uncle James?' I again asked, aloud.

No, my dear . . . well . . . I did say something to the effect I was on the trail of a discovery.

"Uncle James!" My voice rose.

"What, what?" screamed Margo.

I just said to a colleague that I might have found something important.

"Why didn't you tell us?" My voice hit a high C.

Because the colleague is deceased, my dear. He was in the hospital dying, at the time.

I conveyed the info to Margo, who slapped her forehead.

"Did you describe it?"

I gave him a bare outline.

"Could he have blabbed to anyone else?"

He was very ill, Jamie. It was the last thing on his mind, I'm sure. I was simply trying to make conversation and distract a good friend I was losing. Distracting myself, actually. A glimmer of humor, *I didn't expect to join him, so soon.*

What did he die of? I asked, suddenly suspicious.

Congestive heart failure, dear, he had been ill for some time—no, it wasn't chloral hydrate. I was with him when he passed, as a matter of fact.

"Oh! Uncle James! How sad!

I filled Margo in. Always empathic, tears filled her eyes.

THE DOORBELL RANG, making the two of us jump, and the pens on the desk rattle.

I looked at the clock. Almost nine at night, a little late for most casual visitors. I practically tiptoed to the door and looked through the peephole. Randon?

I threw open the door. Behind Randon stood a fresh-faced young cop, almost rigidly at attention.

"Okay, here's what we'll do." Randon pushed past me, motioning to the young man to follow him.

The young man gave me a helpless look and said "Sorry, Ma'am," as he trod on Randon's heels.

I stood back, shaking my head.

Randon strode into the office, started to say, "Good evening," to my uncle, realized his error, and stammered a lame (and belated) greeting to me. "Uh, uh, Ms. Olivian."

I grinned inwardly at the 'Ms. Olivian.' So did Margo, behind his back, as she vanished.

He started outlining his plan for picking up the 'object,' from the P.O. Box in a very loud voice.

Stifling a giggle, I interrupted and reminded him that *I* was neither elderly, or deaf, and that *everybody* in the room was quite capable of hearing him. Privately, from his behavior, I wondered if he had put something in his tea.

He halted, seemingly confused, and continued with his "inside" voice.

"How does that sound?" he finished.

It sounds to me as though your young man finds you a distraction.

I mentally gave Uncle James an elbow in the ribs, and answered Randon, "It sounds okay, Sergeant. I just can't help worrying."

The so-called "young man" looked distressed. "He's coming right straight back to me," Randon protested.

"I know, but if someone's watching!"

"This is going to be at night, Ms. 'Olivian,' fairly late at night. We just have to take the chance that he hasn't hired a twenty-four-hour surveillance team. And," he went on, jerking his head in the direction of his actually young companion, "he's going to be in plain clothes, not a uniform, and isn't connected to you."

"I know, Sergeant, and you're very kind. It's just that . . ."

"I understand, Ms. 'Olivian.' Four people have already died, and this might be the reason."

No, it isn't four, it's three and three. Uncle Zalman and I were meant to be part of the first trio. I heard an answering *Hmmm,* from my uncle.

Rundown, as though *he* had heard me, as well. With his back to the younger cop, gave me a look that almost melted my shoes. I think I actually staggered a little.

Hmmm, thought Uncle James, again.

I gave him another mental poke.

"We're good with tomorrow night, Ms. 'Olivian?'"

"Oh, yes, certainly, Sergeant."

"Good." He turned to his young feudal serf, and said, "I'll be out in a minute, Wozenski. Just want to run over it one more time with Ms. Olivian."

"Yes, Sir." The young man practically clicked his heels and departed.

Randon took my hand, said dreamily, "Good-night, Sir," and kissed my hand about the same way a remora kisses a shark.

"Good night, uh, Cole," I emphasized the *good night,* steadying myself against the desk.

He took the hint and vamoosed.

◆

COLE? IS THAT his name?

Uh, well, yes, not exactly . . . his middle name, it's what his mother called him.

I see.

Well, he asked me to use it, what could I say?

You certainly couldn't use your pet name for him.

I thought you didn't read minds.

No, but as you pointed out, I'm not deaf, either.

I realized I'd probably been indiscreet in his earshot.

Uncle James, what is the thing we're getting?

You know it's a letter, Jamie.

Yes, but how can it be that important?

It's revealing, my dear, as I said. It confirms some rumors, and upsets others. People like their history tidy, and that's all I'm going to say for now.

I kissed my fingers and patted the desk.

I like my sleep tidy, so I'm going to bed.

Another warm hug and he said, *Goodnight.*

CHAPTER THIRTY-FIVE

ll the next day, I was utterly useless. I fielded calls. One from old Grating, who I was seriously considering removing from my list, since he just screamed to be a murder victim (mine; that is).

He was unbelievably accusing me of using my influence (yeah, right!) to have him blackballed from some honorary society or other. He stubbornly refused to accept my assurance that, except when we were actually on the phone, I never gave him a thought.

The accusations went along with thinly veiled hints of "holding out" on him in certain mysterious "transactions" (aha, the letter again). All this was making me wish for Margo's possible witchy powers to inflict serious hives. He hung up in high dudgeon when I said all future communications would be through my attorney, eliciting a spectral pat or two from Uncle James.

I also had to deflect something similar from Bryson, the Stork, still trying to convince me he had a deal with my uncle, as well as a couple of others whom I had never heard from before. One caller being on my list as an out-of-towner. The word was most weirdly getting around, actually adding, albeit rather weakly, to the suspects on the list.

While I managed to handle the above annoying instances with some degree of intelligence, generally I had to call people back and correct what I had just told them. I screwed up the billing, until Uncle James literally sucked the pen I was twiddling, out of my hands, with one of his small-scale whirlwinds. Then he scarily proceeded to shut down the computer (pet gremlins, maybe?).

Jamie, go do something else!, he ordered.

I started to apologize, but he repeated, *Go!* Then added, *I'll take messages.*

My hair stood up, and I squeaked, "Huh?" then realized I didn't really want to know.

Margo strolled in, saying casually, "Half-day birthday for party for one of the bosses' kids," and then gave me a sharper look.

"What's up? You look like the Bride of Frankenstein."

I patted my hair back down. "I'm going shopping," I decided, "I'm taking a half-day, too."

Margo heaved a dramatic sigh, "And you need company."

Did I mention, clothes bore her?

"You're damned right."

"Poor choice of words."

Uncle James chuckled.

The state of my psyche was such that I didn't even change my clothes. Of course, I was again wearing my Audrey Hepburn Capris and ballet flats, so I felt presentable enough.

DRIVING TO MY favorite vintage shop, I gave Margo the lowdown.

"You need your Mom to come to dinner, tonight. *Without* your Dad."

"What excuse."

"You're trying on clothes you bought and want her opinion. That would bore him silly—me, too," she finished.

"Works for me."

I called Mom before I went into the store.

"I *need* you tonight, Mom. Tell Dad I'm getting your opinion on clothes."

Bless my Mom, she didn't raise a single objection, or ask a single question. "See you at six, Jamie."

In the meantime, I really did shop, and spend I might add. For one thing, I acquired a Schiaparelli design from approximately 1939. I was sure it was a knock-off (surely, it had to be) and cost way more than I usually spend on knock-offs, but I couldn't resist. I didn't know where I was going to wear it, yet, but I didn't care. It was sea-foam green, with a draped capelet in tangerine. Sleeveless, ankle-length, and fit every curve (all right, I don't have too many of those, but it fit what I had).

Finally, Margo demanded, "Donuts," in a tone that brooked no refusal. I agreed, and we headed out with my many packages, and Margo's single one. She had surprised me and bought a DRESS, in a lovely shade, somewhere between apricot and salmon, that made her skin glow, forties-style, which was darling on her curves, and swirled around her like a ballerina's tutu. A suspicion crossed my mind, but I held it for later.

We stopped at the market for groceries and headed home.

"Tell me exactly why I need Mom?"
"She's going to read the letter, of course."
I stared at her, baffled.
"Watch the road!"

CHAPTER THIRTY-SIX

om showed up promptly at six, but Wozenski still had not returned. I knew it was too early, but I couldn't help looking at the clock every five minutes as we ate. Mom stood it as long as she could, but then dropped her fork in exasperation, and demanded an explanation.

"I don't want to say, just yet, Mom. Can you wait a little longer?"

She gave me a look, but nodded.

Margo had gone off to one of her meetings, giving me a meaningful look when she left.

It was almost ten before Wozenski showed up on the porch, wearing a jacket that proclaimed Pizza Hut prominently, AND, holding a large, flat cardboard box. I rolled my eyes and let him in.

He offered the box with a flourish, and whispered, "It's inside."

My grin must have flustered him, because his face got as red as the Pizza Hut lettering.

"Thank you, Officer Wozenski, you've been most helpful and most kind."

He got even redder, and muttered, "My pleasure, Ma'am."

I sighed—Ma'am, yet! Well, I wasn't quite old enough to be his mother, but almost.

I took the box into the living where Mom was waiting.

"Pizza, Jamie? But we already ate."

"This is a little different, Mom."

Her gaze became astute, "I take it this is what we've been waiting for all evening."

My heart fluttered in my chest. "This is it, Mom."

I opened the pizza box and took out an envelope of Uncle James's cream-colored stationery. I wanted to handle it like I'd handle an asp, or maybe set fire to it, unread. Nevertheless, I took a deep breath and opened it. Inside was a far older piece of cream-colored parchment. I carefully unfolded the ancient document and surveyed it with something like hatred.

Handing it to Mom, I demanded, "You read it," did I fail to mention it was in seventeenth-century French?

Mom gave me a look, but acceded. After all, she *had* majored in French.

Mon cher, cher, ami,

You have protested the necessity of the little plan I outlined to you. Stating I could not love you if I asked such a thing. How wrong! How wrong!

It is because of our love that I ask. Who else could I trust with the burden of this secret? Who else could share it with me?

Know that my feelings for you will never change, in spite of the new role you will be playing. But you also know that the king must have an heir, and the Queen is not too displeasing, eh? Especially for one who has the "Spanish manner" as you have.

I do not wish to over-dramatize, mon cher, but the future of France is in your hands, as will be, one hopes, the Queen.

I remain, as I always will, devoted to you, but I must put France first, in my duty, if not in my heart.

It was unsigned and I stared blankly at nothing for a moment before realization dawned. I yanked Mom out of the living room and into the office.

"It's Richelieu! And he's got a lover!" I practically screamed into the air.

There was silence on the paranormal front for a moment, and Mom got the expression she always got around Uncle James. Then... *Yes, Jamie. Now, can you guess the identity of the other unnamed?*

I went cold with the implications of the epistle. "It can't be Mazarin?" I spoke out loud for Mom's benefit.

Exactly.

"But that means..."

Yes, it means that the rumor of the Queen's involvement with Mazarin was not a rumor, nor the dubious parentage of Louis XIV.

"And it opens a whole new can of worms," I stated with emphasis.

That too.

I knew the outlines of the Mazarin story. He was evidently hand-picked by Richelieu to be his successor. He was also rumored to have had an affair, and perhaps a secret marriage, after Louis XIII's death, with Anne of Austria, Louis XIV's mother. AND to be the father of Louis, himself, since the royal couple had been married some twenty-three years with no eggs in the basket, although there were reported miscarriages. He also seemed to have something of a checkered past. Born Giulio

Mazzarini, he was an adventurer, as well as a heavy gambler. Considered quite a gallant with the ladies, he may also have had a prior wife, A failed priest, he had dropped out of the seminary, then was mysteriously "promoted" to cardinal after a diplomatic coup to his credit, etc., etc., etc. All this was well-known to historians, but, a '*cher ami*' of Richelieu!

In my mind I pictured portraits of the "Red Eminence," as Richelieu was dubbed—the aquiline profile, so like a hawk, the autocratic gaze, watchful, but somehow detached. Trying to imagine it alive with passion for anyone, or anything, even France, was beyond my abilities.

"That's going to make some historians unhappy," I mused, "but why is that a motive for murder. Given our penchant for sex scandals, these days, I'd think it would be well-received among the gossipy set. And I'll bet there are plenty of those with history credentials."

Mom and Uncle James both snorted.

But there are those who cannot bear to see their "facts" overturned, my dear. Love him, or hate him, and there are strong opinions on both sides, Richelieu's life appeared to be well-examined.

"But you know he had a reputation for being devious."

Well-deserved, it would seem, dryly.

Feeling like a UN interpreter, I had also been saying Uncle James's half of the conversation out loud, so that Mom could get all of it. I looked at Mom and thought Richelieu wasn't the only devious one, whose life appeared to be "well-examined." Then I mentally spanked myself, Mom had a right to her personal life just as I did. It's just hard to imagine your parents, or relatives, as characters in an almost Greek-style tragedy. I knew she loved Dad; she demonstrated that every day. However, it was nothing to what she had felt, and still felt, if her face was telling the truth, for Uncle James. And, in spite of what he *knew* to be *his* truth, he had, for a moment, stepped out of himself to feel for her.

"People are so complicated," I said out loud.

Yes, my dear, and for some, what would seem like very little to us, can impel them to crime. Don't forget, a potentially large amount of money enters into the equation. Our murderer may simply be motivated by greed, without any other underlying reason. Religion, as well, can also be a powerful motivating force, many people are extreme about their beliefs. If revealed, this relationship would be very disturbing for a great number. Remember, Richelieu was a Prince of the Church, a Cardinal, as was Mazarin.

"Yeah, and didn't he rise kind of suddenly?"

Indeed, although not entirely surprising, given what we know now. Was that a pun, my dear?

I realized what I had said, and turned beet-red. "Uncle James," I expostulated, shocked.

Mom looked a little red, herself, and tittered like a teenager, when I repeated, "a pun!"

I know, my dear, eighty seems very old to you, because it's hard to remember that eighty-year-olds were once young. I didn't mean to shock you, with my rather naughty sense of humor. Although that was definitely mild, compared to what I know of today's youth. However, as usual for you, uncomfortable coming from an octogenarian uncle.

"Uh-huh," I agreed; then felt more than a little put-out that Uncle James evidently felt I was Miss Priggy.

"James," Mom broke in, "what is Jamie supposed to do with the letter?"

I think it would be best to send it right back to a safety deposit box, where it will be out of reach of those who want— no—who have been trying to get their hands on it.

"Wozenski can't deliver pizza backwards."

No, but one of the other young men on the squad can rent a new box, and store some other inconspicuous item.

"Aargh! This is crazy! Why don't we just put it out for everybody to see?"

There's a murderer running around loose, Jamie, he needs to be found first.

"But if we make it public, he won't have any reason to go on murdering."

How about revenge, heart's dearest?

I swallowed hard; that little insane twist had escaped me. "If he couldn't have it, I couldn't, either—or . . . if he thinks I know . . .

Very possibly.

CHAPTER THIRTY-SEVEN

The morning went as usual, with the usual harassing calls from Grating and Boresome. I reminded Graber that I would only communicate through my attorney and hung up in the midst of his—increasingly crazy—rant.

Uncle James spectrally shook his head, and commented, *I don't understand that man. His ex-partner was a very congenial, as well as professional, person to deal with. That's probably,* he mused, *why he's an 'ex' partner.*

Graber had a partner?

Yes, the business used to be Graber and Manning.

"Manning," I whispered.

Yes, fellow named Timbrel Manning, with Graber for several years. Decided to become a lawyer.

Oh my God! Uncle James! I put him swiftly into the picture.

This puts a whole new light on things, Jamie.

I'll say!

I immediately called Randon, who had to know the contents of the letter anyway, before it did its disappearing act once again. After giving him the Graber news, I filled him in to Uncle James's new plan. In my mind's eye, I could see him doing the Vulcan nose-pinch.

"Guess we'll have to give Graber a little closer look. A lot closer, that is. Your uncle wants to put the letter *back,* now?"

"Well," I said a little defensively, "it's probably the safest place."

"I don't read French," he commented enigmatically.

"And?"

"I only have your word for what it says."

"You have my mother's word," I responded in a huff.

"I'm not insulting your mother, I know she's reliable, but the Captain doesn't know that."

"What does that mean?"

"We need an official translation."

I went rigid, "Oh, Cole, we can't!" I didn't even realize I had used his first name, spontaneously.

There was a rather strange noise on the other end of the line; then he cleared his throat and went on as though I hadn't spoken.

"It can be done by a plumber."

"What?" I interrupted him with a shriek.

"Take it easy, not a real plumber."

This time, I pinched *my* nose. "Run that by me, again. I'm not keeping up."

He gave a brief bark of laughter, and explained. "You have a leak under the kitchen sink, you call a plumber; he comes and just happens to be an expert in seventeenth-century French. *Voila!*"

"Does this sound a little over the top to you?"

"Does this whole case sound a little over the top to you?"

I deflated and agreed he was probably right, but still demurred. He reminded me that not days, but weeks, had gone by since the first murder, and that the chances of catching the killer were fading by the hour. I literally threw up my hands, sending the cell phone into the corner with a crash.

When I retrieved it, still functioning, I heard him shouting wildly, "What's happened? Are you all-right? Answer me?"

I assured him I was fine, just a slight accident with the phone. I hoped the blinds were still down in his office, picturing an entire squadron of men in blue observing their Sergeant having a hissy-fit.

"Ahem, my apologies, Ms. Olivian, I was afraid you had been attacked."

I cut off a gurgle of laughter, and thanked him for his concern, hoping he hadn't accidently activated the speaker-phone.

"Back to what I was discussing, Ms. Olivian." I assumed he was no longer alone. "That will be all, Wozenski. I'll go over your report as soon as I can."

I gave another gurgle, but held the phone away from me, so that he couldn't hear.

After getting the details down pat, I hung up, feeling not just uncomfortable, but absolutely panic-stricken. I was sure Uncle James was right, and the letter was safer in a box; but was I safer? Was Mom? Uncle Zalman?

I WAS BEGINNING to build up a fine head of paranoia steam, when Uncle Zalman, himself, arrived.

"Good morning, my beautiful Jamie," he greeted me breezily.

He lost a good bit of the breeze when I told him about the letter, and its contents. Uncle Zalman might be old and speak like someone out of a forties' comedy, nevertheless, I had come to understand those superficials covered up a shrewd and alert mind.

I showed him the letter, and he read it, frowning ferociously the entire time (does everyone read archaic French, these days?). I studied him while he read. When he finished, he handed the letter back, still with the same thunderous frown, but with no comment. I got the feeling he saw something that escaped not only me, but Uncle James, as well.

"Uncle Zalman . . ." I began.

"Must think, Jamie, then say. What is on agenda, today?"

I let it go for the time; and outlined what I felt important. I was aware, of course, that my darling Uncle Gnomish was indulging me. Letting me think I was knowledgeable enough to know what was "on agenda," all the while carefully guiding me like a preschooler.

I regarded him as we took care of various items "on agenda," and finally asked, "Uncle Zalman, where are you from?"

He gave me a delighted smile and I was smote, guiltily, with the thought that this was the first I had actually asked him anything about himself.

"I am being born in Poland. My father is engineer—he is getting job in Germany. We are moving when I am baby. Live there for some time. War is coming. We see early. We are running. We are running to America; live with cousin.

"When was this, Uncle Zalman?"

"Was 1938. My father is sending us ahead; is coming later.

I felt a chill, sure of what was coming.

"He work, he write for a while, then nothing." There was silence for a long moment. "My mother is getting job in dress factory. She is knowing how to sew. We move away from cousin, start pretending to be Catholics."

"Catholics!" I exclaimed, unbelieving.

"Yes, is strange. They are wanting me for altar-boy. I am knowing a little Latin, so I think, Yeshua, he is one of us, why would *he* mind?"

I smothered a laugh, and marveled at his matter-of-fact acceptance of such a complete one-eighty.

"After war," he continued, "Mama is wanting to go home—look for Papa. Poland is no good. Communists. We go to Germany. Live there, rest of time. After a while, is okay to be Jews again. Speak Yiddish, German, Polish sometimes with Mama. I am forgetting much English. My father," he shook his head in sorrowful negation, "we do not find."

I hugged him, and he returned my hug; giving me a kiss on the cheek. "But I have James, and you."

"How did you meet Uncle James?'

"Was in Paris. I am forty; work with books, like now. I meet James that way. He offer me job, rest is history."

I grinned at his attempt at an Americanism.

He grinned back, and took on a mischievous look. "But you are being born and we are coming home to you. We see in hospital, when Daddy is not there."

I was stunned, "You've known me from right after my birth."

"*Natürlich.*"

I shook my head in turn, "Uncle Zalman, you're a caution."

"Is so," came the complacent response.

"I wish I had known you two sooner."

Zalman frowned, his face furrowing again into a thousand wrinkles, "Was not good idea, at least not until you are grown-up."

I reminded him that I had been grown-up for some time, and that Uncle James had to die before I knew him at all, "And," I added," you're eighty-five. I might have missed you entirely."

He acknowledged that was so, then beamed, "But, did not happen."

I had to agree, and hugged him again; then sighed and asked, "Uncle Zalman, do you think I'm ever going to know the business, while you're still around to help?"

He waggled a finger at me, "Uncle James is still around, who says I am going anywhere? You are future, Jamie—Ebook—James and Zalman, we are old manuscripts on vellum."

Uncle James laughter joined my own.

CHAPTER THIRTY-EIGHT

As, according to Randon's "plan," the day progressed, and I waited for the "plumber," I was becoming so agitated I was forgetting to breathe. Both of my darling uncles were urging me to "take deep breaths and slow down, Jamie," but I was as wired as a guitar string. I wanted to get, what I was rapidly considering a loathsome object, out of the house. At the same time as I wanted to glue it to my body so it couldn't ever be seen.

When the doorbell shrilled, I leaped and squealed, my heart racing, like a condemned prisoner being collected for the gallows. Heeding my uncles' admonitions, I took three deep breaths, and tottered to the door. Through the peephole, I saw the *soi-disant* plumber, accompanied by a discreet van, which was parked in my driveway. Randon had assured me that the "van" would contain more than plumbing accouterments.

I admitted the plumber, who threw me a casual greeting as he headed for the kitchen. To my surprise, he shut off the water to the sink, and proceeded to inspect the pipes underneath.

"Ms. Olivian, I want to show you where the leak is coming from."

"Whitehall."

He gave me an enigmatic look as I bent to look at the 'leak,' but merely whispered, "Bring me the letter."

Going along with the gag, I straightened up and asked, a little too loudly, "Can you fix it right away?"

He answered from the depths of the underside of the sink, "Might need to order a part."

I could hear the phone ringing in the office. I excused myself and went to answer. No one.

I thought you might need an excuse to come back to the office, was Uncle James smug offering.

How did you know? You can't leave here.

Asked a favor of a "friend," he has been watching.

I made an "ulp" noise; I still hadn't gotten used to the Spectral Generation, nor the fact that Uncle James, and presumably the rest of them, could make phones ring, curtains wave, etc. I rubbed the goosebumps down on my arms, and stuffed the letter down the front of my tee shirt.

Hmmm, remarked Uncle James.

I ignored him, and returned to my "plumber." Squatting, I pulled the letter out and handed it to him. "Hmmm," was his remark.

Taking a handkerchief out of his pocket, he spread it on the under-sink floor, and carefully placed the letter on top. Whipping out his phone, he took a generous number of pictures, explaining *sotto voce* as he did so.

"We may have to enter this into evidence, but the Sergeant didn't want to until it was absolutely necessary. A scan might jeopardize the object itself; so, this will do for the time being."

At my patent distress, he went on, shrewdly guessing the cause, "I know, Wozenski knows, and the Sergeant knows. We're keeping it quiet for a while, until it has to come out."

I stifled the impulse to hug him wildly, and just thanked him for his understanding.

"Sergeant's orders, Ma'am," a slightly roguish expression passed over his face and was quickly gone.

"Looks like I'm going to have to order that part, Ms., uh, Whitehall," he pulled his head out of the sink. "I'll probably get it tomorrow, and bring it by to finish up."

"Thank you. I'll be here."

Returning the letter to its previous resting place, which caused a couple of blinks, I went back to Uncle James.

CHAPTER THIRTY-NINE

I restored the letter to its temporary home in the safe, and gave Uncle James the low-down. *I'm assuming he's going to read the letter from the pictures and fill Randon in. I'm pretty sure Mom was accurate,* I remarked on a rising mental tone.

Your mother was a straight A student, my dear.

I know that, Uncle James, but she majored in contemporary French, not seventeenth-century.

It's not all that difficult, dearest, to extrapolate in reverse.

Since I had taken just enough French to get my master's, I had to take his word for it. Well, my expertise is in Latin, so there.

In the meantime, Dennis called and told me he still had some papers for me to sign with regard to the estate, and since he was going to meet another client, he would swing by on his way back to the office. True to his word, he arrived about two hours later with the documents.

I GLANCED IDLY at the sheaf of papers Dennis had pulled out of his briefcase—on top was a memo signed with the initials AJA. "Who's that?" I asked without real interest.

"That's Dad, of course," he replied the same way, as he shuffled the papers, searching for the copies he wanted signed.

I frowned. "Those aren't your initials."

"Naturally."

"But aren't you a junior?"

"No, Dad didn't want that. Since he's sort of obsessed with France for some reason, I'm named for the patron saint of Paris, St. Denis, and Cardinal Mazarin—Jules. Actually, that's my real first name; I use my middle."

A sick feeling, like aspic making its way down my back, froze my breath. In barely a whisper, I asked, "What's your father's name?"

"Armand Jean—he's named for Cardinal Richelieu."

Giving me a look, he continued, "What's the matter with you, you've turned green?"

"I . . . I think it's my lunch . . . I suddenly feel really queasy."

All solicitude, he set the papers on the hall table, and threw an arm around my shoulders.

"Come on, let's sit down."

He led me into the living room and carefully lowered me to the couch.

The queasiness was all too real. My head whirled with a welter of conflicting emotions and speculations.

"I think I'm going to have to lie down, Dennis," I said, only partly an untruth.

"Lie back on the couch and put your feet up," he ordered. "I'm not leaving until Margo comes home."

I prayed for her to come soon.

"I'll go into the office and lie on the settee, there. Uncle James can watch over me," I ventured lamely.

"Jamie, he's dead!" he retorted with exasperation. "He can't lift you, if you fall." Running his hands through his hair, he fumed, "How can we be having this conversation. I'm actually arguing whether your dead uncle can pick you up off the floor."

The absurdity struck me and I gave a weak chuckle; then remembered why I felt faint in the first place, which gave fresh fuel to the nausea.

Dennis had been watching me, as I went from green to red to green again, like a stop-light. He took a step toward me.

"Jamie," he began in seductive tones.

Just at what might have been an interesting moment, the doorbell rang. Dennis strode to it with an inarticulate gargle, threw it open, and revealed Randon on the other side.

I groaned inwardly. Just the complication I needed.

He glowered at Dennis and demanded, "What's going on?"

Dennis drew himself up, and replied with exaggerated dignity, "Jamie felt ill, and *I'm* tending to her."

"Well, she doesn't look so hot after *your* tending."

Mentally slapping my forehead, I renewed my prayers for Margo's return.

As the TTs glared at each other, Margo (bless her) chose that moment to walk in—emerald velvet cape swirling, humming, and waving what looked like Harry Potter's wand. Both men stopped glowering and goggled instead.

"*Expecto patronum,*" I offered.

"Oh, for heaven's sake, we've been having band practice. I can't play an instrument, and I can't sing, but I'm spot-on as a Bandmaster."

"Band practice," muttered Rundown, feebly.

Dennis flashed his klieg light grin and inquired, *"Night on Bald Mountain?"*

Margo laughed and answered, *"In My Garden,* for one. It used to open the *Firestone Hour.* At least that's what I've heard, it was before my time."

Randon perked up and grinned, as well, "I've seen old kinescopes of that show. Loved it." Then he started to laugh uproariously.

I'm not generally telepathic, but I knew exactly what was going on in his mind. Picturing a mass of hooded Wiccans, performing an old standard from the previous century, was too much for him.

"We're doing this for the Senior Center," Margo informed him, testily. Since several of us are Herbalists, we thought it was appropriate."

Both he and Dennis, who had joined in, sobered immediately, looking properly respectful.

I sighed, and asked, "Did you have something on your mind, Sergeant?"

"Uh, oh yeah. I wanted to know if Wozenski, uh, checked everything out satisfactorily, the other night."

"Yes, thank you," I replied formally, "he was most efficient. I appreciate your concern, and I also appreciate your recommending a good plumber. Now, if you all will excuse me . . . ." I rose and headed for the bedroom, leaving the TTs no choice but to leave.

Margo said, "Goodnight guys, I'm off, too," and started after me (she *does* read minds).

Bowing to the inevitable, the men left, each one trying to be the last one out.

"LET'S HAVE IT." Margo stood with her arms folded, baton at the ready, as though she were about to use it to get me to 'sing.'

"We've got to go back to the office," I forestalled more questions.

She blinked, but followed me silently.

In the office, I closed the drapes, after scanning the yard and checking the French doors, making sure they were locked.

What's up, my dear, came Uncle James's mild inquiry.

Tersely, I told both of them, finishing with, "It can't be Dennis, because he told me the whole story with no problem."

The silence stretched so long, I was getting anxious, when Uncle James's heartbroken, *No! Oh, please no!* echoed in my head, then, *I never knew that Dennis was using his middle name. I didn't ever hear another one. I should have seen . . . I should have guessed . . . I just didn't want to believe . . . How did he know?* There was agony in his tone.

Margo didn't need telepathy to come to the same conclusion I already had, and tears ran down her cheeks.

"What do we do now, Uncle James?'

His reply was ragged with pain. *Give me tonight to come to terms with it, my dear, and we'll work out a strategy in the morning.*

I acquiesced and propelled Margo out the door.

Once outside, we fell weeping into each other's arms.

"Oh Jamie, how horrible for him—horrible twice over."

"Yes, and he's tried to protect their secret all these years."

Then I froze. "Mom! What if You-Know-Who thinks Mom knows?'

I dialed Randon, who answered on the first ring.

"Get a squad car to Mom's quick.

Bless that man! He hung up without a word. In the distance, I heard Sirens—yes, more than one.

The front door opened silently.

CHAPTER FORTY

argo and I froze in place. Framed in my lovely doorway was Dennis's father, the usual pasted-on smile, that failed to reach his eyes, on his face.

"Ah, two lovely ladies, I'm so pleased to find you both at home." He raised the old-fashioned, but lethal, revolver in his hand. "Have I interrupted a sad occasion? I discern traces of recent tears. Perhaps our little witch has had a premonition?"

"I've had a premonition all right, you old creep. I see you marching to the gallows."

"The gallows, my dear?" He made me want to slap him when he used that expression. "A bit passé, don't you think?" He gave a weird whinny that frayed our nerves, "But then witchcraft is a bit medieval, isn't it?"

"You can't possibly think you can get away with two more murders," I stated with a lot more confidence than I felt.

"Ah, my dear," again, I resisted the urge to charge at him, gun or no gun, "these will not be murders, just unfortunate accidents. This is an old house, with old fittings—an uncertain furnace, a leaky hot water heater. Gas is so easily ignited."

I blinked. *Surely,* he knew Uncle James had made certain everything in the house was totally state-of-the-art. I kept silent, however. Only then did I notice that Margo and I, as if on strings, had been edging imperceptibly in a circular movement toward the office door. Dennis's father had been unwittingly keeping pace with us.

"You mean to blow up my house?' I sputtered, torn between outrage and the need to keep him from noticing our snail's pace revolution around the entry.

"It's not *your* house," he snarled, "it's James's. You have no place here."

"He left it to me." I reminded him quietly.

"It's all because of that woman." His voice rose, almost to a shriek.

For a minute I thought he must mean his late wife, and then realization dawned. "Mom!" I gasped. "But that was over . . ."

"It was never over." Spit flew from his mouth.

We backed up a step, simultaneously.

"He never loved *me,* the way he did her. But I almost fixed that—and shortly, I will have it all taken care of."

I felt sick, but wanted to keep him talking as long as possible. I read extensively, I know the drill—just a little farther to the door . . . .

"But, what did the letter have to do with it?" I asked disingenuously.

"Ha! You saw the names. I knew you would know, when Dennis told me you talked about it. Besides, Zalman knew my name; *everyone* would have guessed. They would have seen . . . I couldn't have that . . . my reputation . . . I have a reputation!" His voice hit falsetto again.

Uncle Zalman! I added one more item to the list of things *I* was going to kill *Dennis's father* for.

"Okay, but there's something I don't understand," I began.

"Only one?" He gave that unnerving whinny, again. "I would have guessed much more," nastily. "For example, you never did know about the cattle ranch, did you?"

I mentally slapped my forehead, I did that a lot, it seems. I remembered Dennis saying "Dad has his fingers in a lot of pies," and "we used to ride at the ranch." I had simply, and stupidly, kept assuming "ranch" was a euphemism for a couple of horses and a glorified vacation home.

"You had cows? That's where the blood came from. But why did you use it?"

"Don't you see? I wanted people to think he was killed somewhere else. I wasn't supposed to be here. I had an alibi for elsewhere, so if I *were* seen here, I wasn't responsible."

I shook my head at that convoluted logic.

"But that doesn't make sense," Margo burst out.

He gave her a look of withering scorn. "Of course, you wouldn't get it. If he was killed elsewhere, I couldn't have done it because everyone knew I wasn't here."

"But, as soon as they tested the blood, they knew it was from a cow."

He snorted impatiently. "Of course, do you still not understand? That meant he *was* killed here."

We looked blank.

He made another sound of exasperation. "If anyone saw me here, I already had an alibi for my presence elsewhere; therefore, they couldn't have seen *me*. Of course, I was disguised," he added.

"Ingenious," I managed, wondering if all crazies sounded

so crazy. He still wasn't making sense to anyone but himself.

Then I chilled; since I was already in igloo territory this took some doing, as a lightbulb went off in my head. I knew why Dennis's Dad had substituted beef blood for human—he was leaving his signature! That wasn't crazy, well it was, but it was the insanity of pure spite. He wanted *Uncle James* to know who did it, even if he thought Uncle James couldn't *really* know. The revulsion I felt at that realization almost sent me to the floor; only knowing that Uncle James was on the other side of the door kept me upright.

To keep him crowing about his genius, and my mind off the above, AND because I genuinely wanted to know, I asked, "You were obviously Mr. Ski Mask. Since you really knew Uncle James well," I mentally gagged at the thought, "you must have known he didn't hide things in books. Why did you break in here?"

"Simple, my dear," I winced at the familiarity, "I put the letter there."

I goggled, "You! You put the letter in the book?"

He sneered, "I can't imagine why your uncle thought you could handle his business. So slow! Of course, I had every intention of retrieving it before he found it. It's just unfortunate that he chanced on it first."

"But how did you know about it in the first place?"

"Idiot! I was the old man's heir, obviously."

"Huh?" both of us shrieked, in unison. In spite of our situation, Margo poked me in the ribs.

His triumphant sneer grew broader, "I was his lawyer; that should be obvious, and drew up his will. Since he had stated that he had no relatives—and after his death we could find none—his will gave some of his estate directly to charity; and instructed me to auction off the bulk of the rest for the same purpose. However, there was also a provision giving me the letter. The old man thought I could make it public and realize the profits. He was grateful to me, you see," his pride was horrifying. "When I read it, I knew it could never happen. No one could ever know. I made sure that bequest never got into the final version of the will."

"Who was going to connect it with you?'

"James, of course."

Tears welled in my eyes, "But he would never have told anyone, and if you had only asked, he would have destroyed it."

"I couldn't take that chance. Killing him was very difficult, after all we had been to each other, but it was necessary, you see. Besides," and the craziness was back in his eyes, "you look just like Lily."

I willed strength back in my knees, because I could feel them buckling. I had never had hate directed at me with such palpable force, before.

Margo broke in for the first time. "What about Tim?"

"Collateral damage, my little witch. He was unfortunate enough to have seen the original draft, and knew the final version was different. I assured him that the old man had changed his mind, but, again, I couldn't take a chance."

"So, that was it." Somehow, she seemed relieved.

Graber and Bryson don't know how lucky they are, I thought. They were probably next on the agenda, and would never have had even an inkling to warn them.

We had reached the office door in our snail-like perambulation. I *very, very* slowly eased my hand back to the handle.

"And the chloral hydrate, that was just to make Uncle James sleepy?"

"Certainly, and I didn't want him to feel any pain when I hit him."

"Very thoughtful," I muttered, the nausea welling back up.

"Well," he said indignantly, "I loved him. I gave my wife the same consideration."

Sparkly lights were flashing in front of my eyes. Sternly ordering myself not to faint, I turned the handle, slowly. Margo was pressed up against me like Chang against Eng. I gave her a poke and the two of us fell back against the door and dropped (literally) into the office, where the lights had mysteriously gone out.

A loud bang, sounding like the Last Trump, and a splintering of glass was followed by swearing. Margo and I were crawling as fast as possible (actually, faster, my knees felt like they had grown wings) to a spot behind the desk.

Dennis's Dad, meanwhile, had found a lamp, and turned it on.

"Now, now, ladies, what can you possibly hope to gain by this useless little maneuver? You can't get past me. You can't reach the phone. I know you're not carrying any cells, and you know I wouldn't let you reach the front door."

A quiet, but steely, voice spoke in my head. *I will handle this, heart's dearest.*

The freshly sharpened pencils on the desk stood erect; then rose to eye level. The letter opener took its place below them.

Dennis's father goggled, open-mouthed in terror, as the curtains blew inward, stretching across the desk like strangling fingers.

"Ah, ah, ah," Dennis's father gargled. He fired wildly. The pencils parted to make way for the bullets; then regrouped, forming an arrowhead pointed toward the source of the menace.

Almost happily, Dennis's father raised the gun to his temple and disposed of the last round.

Sobs shook me, but they weren't mine. Uncle James had broken down and wept inconsolably.

Margo and I embraced the desk as tightly as we could and waited.

Randon found us there.

CHAPTER FORTY-ONE

o, where were you," I screamed.

I flew at him, beating my fists on his chest. He tried to answer and deflect my blows at the same time.

"Ouch! Hey! At your Mom's, waiting until she said..." I then had two men in tears.

My strength gave out and my knees gave way. Uncle James had me surrounded with warmth instantly. I felt slightly ashamed, considering the horrible blow he had just received, and gathered myself together (well, kinda).

Randon's chalk-white face, which I hadn't bothered to notice, told me exactly how terrified he had been.

"Sorry," I whispered.

Randon spoke in the general direction of the desk, "Can you ever forgive me, Sir?"

If possible, his face got even whiter.

Uncle James managed a ghost of his usual chuckle (no pun intended), *Tell your young man, that there is no need for apology. If anything had happened to Lily... Your Sergeant had a terrible dilemma, my dear. He didn't know where, or at whom, the next attack would strike. And even on this side, we can't be in two places at once. He also thought you were locked in safely. Unfortunately, all of us failed to understand the sad unbalance we were up against, and how clever desperation can make one. Armand (his voice broke on the name) just managed to procure another key by theft or subterfuge—possibly Dennis's unwitting assistance.*

Randon was staring at me, bug-eyed through all of this.

I drew a deep breath, "He says..." I couldn't go any farther. The nausea I had been suppressing the entire time overwhelmed me and I raced out the door to the downstairs powder room.

After I ceased retching and threw cold water on my face, I staggered, hair dripping, back to the office, where I was comvulsed with sudden fury.

"My office! Uncle James's office! Our office! He's ruined it!" I wanted to rain blows on the corpse, as well.

Margo had disappeared; she returned with a steaming cup. "Drink it!" she ordered.

Naturally, it was cocoa, with more chocolate than I'd ingested in probably ten years. The "beige" was as dark as race-track mud, and almost as thick.

I tossed it down like Jack Daniels. I felt better, and not *quite* as maniacal.

Uncle James released me from my supernatural blanket, evidently feeling that chocolate of that quantity could hold me up by itself.

Two guys in white appeared at the office door (when did he call them?). Randon gave a jerk of his head indicating the body on the floor. They quietly went to work.

Randon grasped my elbow and marched me to the living room. Margo discreetly headed for the stairs.

"No!" I almost yelled.

Randon, understanding, reached for her hand, "You, too. No solitaries. Okay?"

She nodded, and blew out a whuff of air.

Once in the living room, Randon motioned to the couch, and obediently, we sat.

"Listen, I know nothing's going to erase what just happened from your minds, but the office *isn't* ruined, the house *isn't* ruined, because they've *literally* got a good spirit and he's going to keep the place good. You've just got to think that Ackbury was sick, terminally in fact, and that fatal illness claimed him. Unfortunately, his illness was like the plague and claimed others . . ." He broke off and turned white again.

The silence stretched, until Margo got up and said, "Cocoa, Sergeant?" and left to fetch it.

He gazed after her admiringly; then returned his focus to me. Dropping to his knees in front of me, he touched my hair so lightly it was like a butterfly kiss.

"If anything had happened to you, I'd have taken the place next to Ackbury.

Horrorstruck, I gasped, "Uncle James couldn't have stood it."

He blinked and looked confused. "Uncle James? Would that be too many of us on the other side?"

He asked in a tone of genuine inquiry which struck me as hysterically funny—I use that adjective advisedly. I screamed insanely with reaction laughter while he held me so tightly, I expected a couple of cracked ribs when I finally came out of it.

Margo, who had obviously been hovering outside the door, entered with two more cups of molten chocolate. After all, she needed it, too.

Randon studied his for a moment; then tipped it up, giving a surprised "Mmmm," as he swallowed. He drank the rest with enthusiasm.

The guys in white peeked in again and Randon excused himself.

Margo plopped down beside me and took my hand. We sat, silently gripping each other's hands.

Finally, she said, "I'm sleeping in your room."

"Are you kidding? We're squeezing into the double sleeping bag; and, we're bringing Uncle James with us."

"I haven't had a chance to scream, yet."

"I promise you at least ten uninterrupted minutes—more, if you want to beat up the pillows."

Randon returned, carrying a desk drawer. "I think I've got him." The papers inside fluttered in response to his unspoken question.

I had to do quite a bit of flopping around before he got the idea.

I quenched a mad desire to be hysterical again, and simply said "Thank you," to Randon. "We're all going to stay together, tonight."

Randon's yearning look suggested more of a crowd than was proper, but he only said. "Good." His cell tweedled and he answered tersely. His face went as ashen as before, and he rang off with a wordless grunt.

He waved his hands in a spasm of distress before he could speak. I wanted to throw myself over the desk drawer to shield it from what I was sure was more horrific news.

"They've got your partner at the hospital."

"Zalman?" I screamed it simultaneously with Uncle James.

"He's in bad shape, they're not sure . . ."

I scrambled from the couch, Margo echoing my every move.

Get in the envelope, I told Uncle James. Heedless of my disheveled appearance, I raced to the hall, grabbed my purse, and was almost out the door before Randon grabbed my arm.

"You two are going with me."

I didn't argue.

AT THE HOSPITAL, we were greeted by a tired-looking young doctor, who informed us that Uncle Zalman was hanging on, but it was touch and go.

"What happened?" We didn't even know what it was.

"Hit-and-run."

Now we knew.

The doctor continued, "A couple of witnesses said they saw a red crossover, but couldn't get a license plate."

I slid to the floor.

Jamie, dearest, Jamie . . . Uncle James's voice brought me to my senses. I opened my eyes to see both the doctor and Randon bending over me, solicitously.

"I think we can be pretty sure it wasn't Dennis, Jamie," was the first thing out of Randon's mouth.

In my semi-conscious state, a golden glow of nobility seemed to surround Randon. If ever a man exuded selflessness, it had to be my darling Rundown. I regarded him with enthusiasm. Then I thought of Uncle Zalman, and my enthusiasm abated.

I struggled to sit up. "I have to see him."

The doctor looked dubious; then nodded.

I saw the reason for his doubt when I entered Uncle Zalman's room. Wires connected him to every manner of monitor. His face was swollen on one side so that he looked like a cartoon version of himself, and bandages swathed his head, Arabian pasha-style.

"It's his head injury we're the most concerned about," the doctor informed me, unnecessarily, I might add. What else would kill him?

"His heart's a little iffy, as well," he added

Well, that answered that.

I plunked myself down by the bed and took Zalman's hand.

"Uncle Zalman, you can't go yet. You've got to stay with us for a while. I've got Uncle James with me, and he says so, too."

The doctor gave me a look that suggested I needed as much help as Zalman. Shaking his head, he rather doubtfully left the room.

After his departure, I tried to will my soul into Uncle Zalman's body.

Jamie, put me on his chest.

I didn't stop to ask why. I just did as Uncle James asked. When the nurse came in to check the monitors, she frowned at the envelope.

"It's a letter from his best friend," I explained awkwardly.

She shrugged, and went off, but not before one last frown.

The tears I couldn't control slid down my cheeks as fast as melting glaciers, and I finally gave way to sobs.

RANDON FOUND ME there and started for me with concern, when he was halted by an irritated voice saying, "Jamie, you are making bed shake."

Randon stood rooted to the spot, arms out and mouth agape, looking ridiculous. I just stared into Uncle Zalman's astonishingly clear eyes with my mouth hanging even farther open than Randon's.

"I have a headache," was Uncle Zalman's querulous complaint.

My uncle's mellow tones, a tad exhausted, sounded in my head, *You, can pick me up now, Jamie.*

Still speechless, I bent to do as he asked.

Rundown finally unfroze from his Statue's position, and muttered, "Headache, he has a headache!"

Whirling on his heel, he strode to the door and disappeared. I heard some muted kerfuffle in the hall. The door reopened to admit a disapproving and disbelieving doctor, who marched authoritatively to the bed. After taking one look at his only recently critical patient, he assumed the same paralyzed posture as Rundown's.

Uncle Zalman must be related to Medusa, was my somewhat demented thought.

"M . . . M . . ." the doctor struggled to form words.

Has the same effect on the tongue. Still bordering on crazed.

"What did I tell you?" Randon demanded belligerently.

The doctor shrugged helplessly.

"I have headache," Uncle Zalman repeated with increasing annoyance, "what is matter with you?"

"I . . . I'll . . . get you something." Hesitant at first, the doctor drew himself up and said more firmly, "I need to examine you first."

Uncle Zalman switched his attention to me. "I have fall?"

"You don't remember, Uncle Zalman?'

"I think I am walking. Is possible I miss step, trip over curb."

I glanced at the doctor with appeal in my eyes. He picked up on my appeal, and told my darling Uncle Gnomish, gently, "You were hit by a car Mr. Percheff; they didn't stop. You're doing," he stopped, momentarily at a loss for words, "much better than we expected; but you have to be quiet and let us observe you for a few days."

"Take care of headache, I am quiet."

The doctor looked at me, caught between laughter and amazement.

"We'll do whatever we can, Mr. Percheff."

He requested, well, more like ordered, Randon and me out of the room.

In the hall, Randon demanded, before I could say anything, "Don't tell me, I don't want to know."

"I can't tell you anything, because I don't know any more than you do. It was Uncle James. Uncle Zalman just 'came back,' because Uncle James wanted him to. He must have told Uncle Zalman he wanted him to go on taking care of me, Uncle Zalman takes that very seriously."

Randon looked dubious, probably at the thought of either of us being able to take care of anybody.

"Well," I went on testily, "what do you want me to say?" I was more than a tad insulted by what I perceived as a slur on my uncle's abilities.

Randon looked confused, "I just didn't think he could do it all by himself."

"Huh?" Now I was confused.

"Your Uncle James," he stated as though that should have been obvious. "I would think it would have been a really tough thing for him to do alone, without running out of ectoplasm— or whatever they use over there."

Giving myself a slap for presuming, *A bit self-absorbed, aren't we, Jamie?* I gave Randon the biggest smile I could manage, and exclaimed aloud, "Brilliant, that's brilliant. He must have called buddies on the Spooknet. Doctors, he must know some of those."

If the spectrally-abled were even slightly responsible for Uncle Zalman's virtual rise from the dead, I was forever in their debt, and ready to embrace them (well, maybe not exactly *embrace*).

Randon smiled back a little uncomfortably, "You *can* ask him, Jamie."

I now looked dubious, "He sounded awfully tired," I recalled.

"There, you see? It was hard work."

"Of course, it was. I'm not arguing. Why are you being so insistent?"

Randon sighed, and visibly drooped, "I just witnessed a miracle; I guess I'm not up to it." He looked more dejected than ever.

"Who is? I'll bet even St. Teresa of Avila wasn't 'up to it.' Have you seen pictures of Bernini's sculpture, she looks completely done-in?"

"Bernini?"

"St. Teresa, you idiot. Bernini was a man." I had to laugh.

Randon actually grinned, wiping away the dejection. "I saw the exhibition."

I remembered the bust of Bernini's mistress—talk about lust in marble—and grinned back.

After a minute, however, my early childhood rose up in front of me, and I swallowed hard. "The nuns said only God could work miracles, are we being blasphemous?"

"Jamie, did you see the same thing I did?"

"Yes."

"Well, then it happened. Maybe God has helpers, too."

I acknowledged that could be the case, realizing that the nuns didn't have any good explanation for Uncle James, and he was certainly a certainty. Uh, you know what I mean.

By this time the doctor had finished with Uncle Zalman. He came out of the room shaking his head like a wet golden retriever. I knew the feeling, even though I was acquainted with Uncle James and the doctor wasn't.

"Except for a headache, Mr. Percheff seems to have sustained remarkably little damage from his head injury." The doctor's voice held a slight whine to it that I sympathized with. "His heart is still not quite what we would like, so naturally, he needs to be here for a while."

"Naturally." Randon and I agreed.

"You can say goodnight, but now I want him to rest." I could see the doctor scrambling to regain his former authority by even the slightest means.

"Of course, Doctor, we understand," I offered disingenuously.

Randon gave me a sideways glance.

"One last peek and then I'll take you home, Ms. Olivian," Randon said formally, also disingenuous.

"Thank you, Sergeant Randon." I offered, keeping the disingenuous going.

WHEN WE ARRIVED at the house, Randon walked me to the door and took my hand. Holding it for what seemed forever, he finally heaved another sigh and walked away without a word.

I put the key in the lock, and then just stood there until Uncle James's voice aroused me.

Open the door, Jamie, it's time for bed.

I started to do as he said, but the door was flung open by Margo before I had a chance. Behind her stood Mom with a baseball bat over her shoulder.

"Whaa?"

"It's about time." Margo yanked me inside like she was reeling in a marlin.

"Margo called me," Mom offered by way of "explanation."

"But what about Dad?" I inquired, horrified. I could imagine, all too clearly, the detachment of police which had shown up at their house.

Mom's face crumpled with pain, "We'll have to deal with that in the morning, Jamie."

"Give us the worst," Margo demanded.

"If you're referring to Uncle Zalman, there is no worst . . . at least not anymore."

Both faces registered disbelief.

"He was critical. You mean he is dead." Mom stated flatly.

"No, Mom, he's actually pretty good. He's not young, so they're watching him."

Mom drew Margo to her, as they both regarded me like an escaped loony.

"Let's go in the office, Uncle James needs a rest. I'll explain . . . or at least I'll try. I don't think he's ready, yet."

I told the story, finally appealing, "I have to go to bed,

Margo and I were going to share the sleeping bag."

"I'll stay here on the couch," Mom declared firmly, brooking no opposition, as if I had any to offer. She did spare just a momentary glance at Uncle James's envelope.

I restored Uncle James to the desk—he had been silent the entire time—but when I wished him goodnight he said with longing, *Tell Lily goodnight from me, too.*

Feeling like the Greek chorus of a tragedy, I did as he wished. Mom answered with a curt "Yes," and shut her lips tightly.

WE RETIRED. All of us slept like the dead, if I may use that phrase, in spite of the events of the night. Emotional exhaustion knocks you out better than Ambien.

AFTERWORD

———•———

The next day was painful. We had to come clean with Dad, of course. A bunch of cops showing up unexpectedly on his doorstep, not to mention Mom's unexplained all-nighter, was certainly a dead (no pun intended) giveaway. And yes, he was angry (all right, furious); but not entirely for some of the reasons we imagined.

"Did you think I didn't know anything was going on?" he demanded of me. "You were nearly killed, Squirt, and claimed you had no idea who it was."

I protested, weakly, "But I didn't."

He made a contemptuous noise, "That doesn't fly, Jamie, you knew about James. Besides, you never mentioned it again, just went on as though nothing had happened. Do you really think I'm such a chump?"

I shook my head, unable to reply.

He looked at my mother, accusingly, "I knew you were in touch with James," he announced through tight lips, "I saw him at the hospital when the Squirt, here, was born, and, I might add, other places."

Mom managed to look astonished, chagrined and guilty, all at the same time.

"And, by the way, I recognized Zalman at James's house. Did you think I didn't, at least, know where my brother lived? I kept waiting for somebody to say something, but nobody did. So, I just kept waiting, and watching, hoping the Squirt knew what she was doing."

We were speechless.

"Why didn't you tell me about James immediately, Lily?"

I jumped in, "It was my fault, Dad, Mom didn't know right away. I kept it from her, too."

"Right away," he echoed.

"Dad, there were circumstances . . . Mom wanted to tell you, but I didn't know . . ." I left off, not sure what I "didn't know."

Dad looked at me for a long uncomfortable moment; then sighed, "You heard the story and thought that my prejudices would get in the way. *And* you thought . . ." There was unconcealed bitterness in his tone, even though he left the rest of the sentence unsaid.

Knowing he guessed at my fleeting suspicions, tears rolled down my face.

Seeing that, Dad softened a little, "Didn't you ask why you were named for him, Squirt?"

I went blank with shock. I was so used to my name being my name, it had never occurred to me.

Dad continued gently, "I guess in your shoes, Jamie, I might have thought the same way you did . . . well, partially, anyhow. I have to blame myself for being a jerk, as well." A hint of humor crept into his voice, "I suppose you could say I've had my consciousness raised."

More sadly, again, he admitted, "Over the years I wanted

to put it right with James, but my pride got in the way. I didn't worry about him and Lily, because, well, you know why."

My mother looked more than a bit indignant at that. "I would never," she began through tight lips.

"Now, Honey, I didn't mean it that way," Dad tried to pacify her, knowing he had sort of stepped over a line, "I know you better than that."

She still looked less than mollified.

"James was special, Lily, I knew I couldn't take his place; I just had to make one of my own; and I knew once I did . . ." he let that trail off.

Her face lit and she gave him *almost* the smile I had seen her give Uncle James.

"Anyway," Dad took up where he left off, "I got over my pride, and made up my mind to see James and reconcile. Just waited until too late." He stopped and his face worked.

I traded looks with Mom.

"Hal," said Mom, "I think you should at least come with us to James's, er, Jamie's house, and see it from the inside. You'll feel a lot closer to James, I know."

Once more, into the breach, I silently quoted.

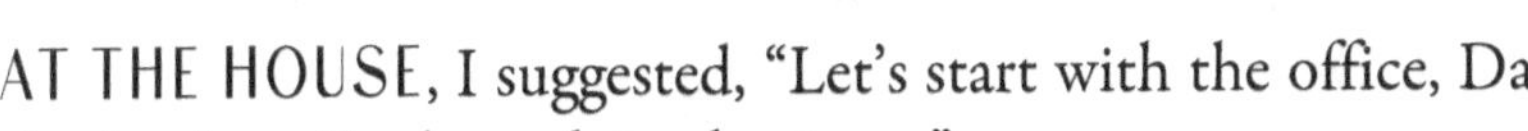

AT THE HOUSE, I suggested, "Let's start with the office, Dad, that's where I've been doing business."

Dad gave me a curious look, but acquiesced.

As soon as Dad stepped through the door, the room took on a glow even Mom and I hadn't seen. The window curtains stretched across the Deco desk like welcoming arms, and Dad walked right into them.

Mom and I went out and softly closed the door behind us. We didn't ask what went on in there, but when Dad came out, he looked ten years younger.

"Let's see the rest of the place, Squirt," he exclaimed jovially.

No questions, no hint of disbelief, just the second-most, well, maybe, the third-most, joyous acceptance of the unbelievable that I had seen. Why had I had such difficulty?

Maybe it was because they had all known and loved Uncle James, and I had not. Or maybe because they had not grown up in the "Age of Irony," the way I had. Whatever it was, it had been a source of extraordinary comfort for them. It was just more of extraordinary discomfort for me, until the reality, I use that term loosely, sank in.

Mom and I exchanged smiling looks, again; and I took Dad's hand to lead him on the tour. When Dad saw the library, he went as still as I had. Although, I'm happy to say, he didn't burst into tears.

"You did yourself proud, you old coot," he muttered. Downstairs, I was sure the "old coot" was beaming.

BY THE BY, Uncle James instructed me to have Dad burn the letter. *It's nothing but bad luck, Jamie; no good can come of its publication.*

We made quite a ceremony of it.

While it was wonderful to have both parents on the same page, as well as having Dad and his beloved elder brother reconciled. Still, I could feel Uncle James's residual sadness. Hard as it was for me to understand it, since I knew more than I had let him know, he had loved Dennis's Dad as he did Mom.

Although he never came out and said so, he was in mourning for some time.

I never told him the entirety of what Armand had said, to Margo and me, on that last night. I particularly did not tell him my surmise about the blood. He knew it had to have been for some reason, but if he had heard it all, it would only have added to his pain. He already blamed himself bitterly for what he had not said, or more correctly, had refused to even think. Because his was a generous nature, he didn't recognize the jealousy, paranoia, and just plain insanity in someone he still cared for. I understood, because I had skirted around the idea of Dad being involved somehow, especially when I thought of my narrow escape.

When you think of it, it took a lot of intestinal fortitude for Uncle James to confront his old love, even from Beyond. He had paid me one of the greatest compliments of my life.

Uncle Zalman is actually doing pretty well, and, considering his years, hasn't lost his enthusiasm for life. However, it took a while for him to regain it, as well as his strength, because, like Uncle James, he blamed himself for not speaking up immediately. Unfortunately, he still regards my Dad with a more than a bit of suspicion, expecting homophobia to rear its ugly head any minute. Nonetheless, he is careful to keep it under wraps and is unfailingly polite.

Uncle James is over the moon to have regained his brother. Dad, for his part, would have been constantly at the house, unless Mom restrained him (bless her).

To our surprise, as well as secret delight, Uncle James is still stuck to the Deco desk. We don't know why, but that means he'll be around for a while. Selfishly, I'm the one over the moon.

And, oh yeah, the dress I mentioned—you know, the one Margo bought—well, it came home on her the other night along with a surprise companion. She had met another Wiccan (male) at a get-together of covens. They hit it off, and the "rest is history," as Uncle Zalman said. I think this just might be the "spell" she mentioned. The one that made her open up about Tim, that is, and then put it behind her. So far, it's going really well—"magickly," you might say.

Other things didn't go as well. Dennis retreated into a lawyerly formality that saddened me. But then, what do you say to the woman your father tried to murder? Moreover, what do you say when you find out Dad had offed Mom, to boot, or that he'd been intimate friends with the uncle of said woman? Miss Manners doesn't cover that.

How about the fact that he *wasn't* your father after all? My questions had sent Dennis down a new path. Oh yes, DNA tests proved Dennis's "father" was no relation. Dennis did some intensive sleuthing and turned up records that showed he was the product of a sperm donor—don't ask, I didn't—and his mother.

Thinking about Dennis's mother made me wonder. As far as we knew, she was the only odd man, er, woman, out. Graber and Bryson, since Armand had managed to leak the existence of the letter to them, were meant to join Tim Manning for another unholy trio. They didn't know how lucky they were. Were there others along the way? Once you've killed someone, adding to your score doesn't seem to be such a big deal. Maybe Armand's death sort of evened things.

All of the above made it impossible for Dennis to meet my eyes at our, now rare, encounters.

Even though I felt somewhat bereft, I have to admit some

relief, as well. On the other hand, that left Rundown, uh, Cole, to deal with.

So far, we've only managed to go on one "real" date. After all, our relationship has had almost as many awkward aspects about it as Dennis's and mine. The most awkward being that the murder victim is still looking over his shoulder. However, he feels we can break that unlucky Threes' Cycle that's been dogging me.

How do *I* feel about it? Time will tell, of course, but it's tough to resist a rumpled, Robert Mitchumy, homicide detective, who looks like he stepped out of 1942 with all the old-fashioned courtesies to go with it. So... I'll have to let you know.

FIN